THE SARCASTIC GHOST

Indigo Rose Publishing
118 Barnard St. #10662
Savannah, GA 31412

The Sarcastic Ghost

ISBN: 978-1-7326354-1-8

TABLE OF CONTENTS

THE SARCASTIC GHOST

CHAPTER 1

Theresa yawned with her arms extended as Saturday was drawing to a close. "Well, that's enough of that for tonight. If I keep this up, at this rate, I'll complete this season in the next six hours," she said to herself. Theresa rubbed her weary eyes while sitting in her bed. She picked up the remote next to her and turned the television off. It had been another one of those several-hour binge-fests, watching one of her favorite television mystery dramas.

Theresa had been in her room since eight that evening, watching back-to-back episodes while enjoying a honey chipotle rib dinner on a tray. She had prepared that meal along with buttered mashed potatoes and sweet corn, despite spending most of the day with her close friend, hanging out in town. It was getting late. She yawned again. Slowly, she got out of bed to place her dinner tray on a small mahogany table located in the corner, near the window.

Proceeding to the bathroom, she prepared herself for her night's rest. After going through the nightly ritual that ended with brushing her hair, she was finally ready to get a good night's sleep. She plopped back down on her bed, lying in the stillness of her darkened bedroom. She closed her eyes and reflected on the events of the day. But this moment of reflection was short-lived as her phone on the kitchen counter rang downstairs.

"There can be only one person calling me at this hour: Abigail Blume. You don't have anything to talk about this late other than trifles," she said aloud. *Abby, you are my friend, and I love you, dearly. But you can really be obnoxious and gossipy. I've had enough of your insights already. They'll last through the rest of the week,* she thought to herself as the ringing ceased.

As an experienced window-shopper, Theresa was a professional connoisseur of all things on sale, as well as what she thought *should* be on sale. While out and about earlier that day with Abby, she picked up a mint-green chiffon nightgown from a little boutique near Broughton Street that displayed a beautiful selection of intimate apparel and dresses.

When she got home with her prized acquisition, she immediately went upstairs to her bedroom and unwrapped the tissue paper packaging, placed it on a felt hanger, and hung it on a brass hook on the wall next to the window. When she'd first laid eyes on it, she'd loved it because the style and execution of the workmanship gave this new item a vintage quality. The attention to detail alone was worth more than its original asking price.

Theresa lay in bed for a few moments staring at her new nightgown and decided to put it on. "Well, what is the point of purchasing a new nightgown if I'm not going to wear it?"

She climbed out of bed and took off her oversized brown bed shirt, and exchanged it for the new nightgown. Stopping a moment to model it in front of her over-the-door mirror, Theresa got back into bed and lay down on top of the sheets, and stared at the ceiling. It was now a quarter past twelve, and she lay there for a few moments, quietly waiting for sleep to overtake her.

She was just about to fall asleep when she heard something faint and distant. "What the hell is that? Mice in the walls?" she whispered to herself.

The sound progressively grew louder as each moment passed. It would occasionally stop briefly before the cadence of the footsteps resumed. Theresa sat up in the bed as if to study the sound better. She then realized that the noise came from someone walking along the brick sidewalk below. *It must be a really silent night to hear someone's footsteps so clearly at this hour. He must be wearing some hard-bottomed shoes? Dress shoes, perhaps?* Theresa turned her head towards her bedroom window, gazing at the full moon partially hidden behind dark clouds.

As she listened to the steps growing closer and closer, her curiosity piqued, and she decided to see who was about to pass by her window. Theresa reached over towards her nightstand and turned off her light. She got out of bed and proceeded to walk to the window. Clandestinely, she pulled back the curtains and took a peek through the blinds. Peering in the vicinity of the gas streetlamp directly below her bedroom window, she saw nothing. The footsteps had stopped.

After her eyes adjusted to the change in light, Theresa noticed that there was the form of a man in the grey shadows standing outside her house. Curiously, he stood just outside the circle of the lamp's light. He took something out of his dinner jacket pocket. A shiny and metallic object flickering in the ambient light caught her attention. He then returned it to the security of the jacket, and within a few seconds, a red glow was emanating near his head.

"How annoying; he smokes. But at least he doesn't vape."

The stranger then stepped into the amber conical glow of light that was cast from the gas lamp, fully revealing himself. He was a well-built man in his twenties. Theresa admired how well he looked in his dinner suit and his glossy silk top hat. She was also taken in by the countenance created by the light and shadow of the lamp's flickering flame.

Oh well, I guess it's about time I said something instead of staring, she thought to herself as she admired the attention to detail of his dress. She moved to the other side of the blinds to change her view. *The black leather gloves are a nice touch. He could definitely impersonate Fred Astaire.*

Theresa was normally awkward when it came to speaking to new people on a personal level. She always felt that she was going to say the wrong thing. But this night—for whatever reason—she was feeling unusually bold. She decided to open her window and speak to the stranger under the gas lamp below before he walked away. And she decided to say the first thing that came to her mind before she chickened out. She pulled the blinds up slowly, unfastened the latched window, and slid it up. The earthy night air, crisp but pleasant against her skin, gave an extra boost to her confidence.

"Hey down there," she said. "You seem lost."

The stranger looked up and turned towards her in interest. He stared at her for a moment, with his youthful face full of curiosity that transformed into a pleasant smile. He then took off his top hat in a sweeping artistic gesture that was accentuated by the glimmer of the gas lamp's light on its silken surface. Within this same motion, he nodded his head in such a way as to form an elegant salutation before responding to Theresa's query.

"To the contrary, I'm right where I need to be," the dark-haired stranger said in a mellifluous tone as he returned his hat to the crown of his head.

Theresa waved back with her right hand eagerly before saying, "I really hope I did not startle you."

He rubbed his thumb and index finger on his chin in deep contemplation. "No madam, you did not startle me. I'm just slightly surprised that you can see through the veil."

"I guess I do have pretty good night eyes," Theresa said. "Like a hoot owl even on a moonless night like this." She placed a hand over her mouth to mask her smile.

"Indeed you have."

He has a British accent and it's the good kind—aristocratic and beautifully modulated. While Theresa thought to herself, she tried to maintain a straight face. Instead, she grinned.

"I can tell from your accent that you are from England," she said.

"That goes without saying. But please feel free to have another go at it."

"Okay, so given your demeanor, I think you are here on business."

"Hmm, I suppose some unfinished business of sorts." His face was placid. "There was a time I was occasionally sent here to check in on some of my father's business assets. But now, Savannah is just a nice city to operate out of for personal affairs."

"That's how it happens sometimes. I came to Savannah on business, too, and ended up settling down here." As she assessed his pedigree from her vantage point, she assumed he had to be from old money, and immersed in the family's business. "What type of business does your father have that had you traveling so much?"

"My father was an importer of commodities from British Honduras and British Guiana with a large storehouse located at the Seaboard Air Line terminals on

Hutchinson. He believed that having eyes in the field, from time to time, is a good way of observing who was worthy of their situation and who was not."

Theresa nodded. "Did you buy that"—she waved toward his attire—"at a local department store?"

The stranger scoffed. "Off the rack, certainly not! It was made to my specifications by the illustrious Henry Poole & Company, building number 15, Savile Row in London proper."

Theresa rolled her eyes. "Well, it's very nice that you could afford tailored clothes. Everyone I know shops off the rack."

"What a novel way of telling me the limitations of those that make up your social circle," he responded with an air of derision.

"I guess," Theresa said. "Anyway, are you going to meet someone, or do you live in this neighborhood?"

The stranger looked at her for a moment before taking another drag of his cigarette. "Really now, you're quite nosey you know."

Theresa was a little taken aback by that statement and her smile began to fade. "I'm not. Just so you know, I am a member of the Neighborhood Watch. That's why I ask, considering the time of night it is."

A smile appeared across the stranger's face. Looking quite amused, he tilted his head to the left as if he was analyzing Theresa before responding. "My dear, Foolish Wonder." He grinned, exposing his perfectly white teeth. "You are certainly not on the Neighborhood Watch. Furthermore, I highly doubt you know any of your neighbors, and most of your neighbors are too snooty to even associate with you on any level."

Theresa was dumbfounded by this accurate revelation, but did not want to incriminate herself. While she was thinking of a clever rebuttal, the stranger seemed to know what she was thinking by her hesitation.

He had paused for an instant. He was about to take another cigarette out of its silver case, but returned it to his coat pocket. "Madam, you are just prying," he said frankly. "What you want to know is for your own personal information and not for the benefit of the neighborhood's safety. So spare me your sophistry."

Theresa's smile was completely gone now. "You are a real piece of work."

"Pray, and why is that? What I told you is the truth, so there is no need to be vexed, woman." He looked up at her with amusement. "But I'll tell you what, some might think it's rude to stand in your window hiding behind the curtains with the lights off like some voyeur spying on pedestrians down on the streets below." He paused for an instant, squinting as if trying to read Theresa's expression in the poor light. "Of course, I do not trouble my concerns with the curious fancies of random people." He shrugged. "But some people are interested in peculiar folk."

Theresa, offended about being called out, began a finger-waving discourse on how the stranger did not know her well enough to judge her. She did this in an attempt to deflect unwanted attention from herself. But this seemed to only amuse the stranger further.

While Theresa was scolding the stranger down on the sidewalk, he casually reached into his pants pocket and removed a silver flask. He loosened the top with a quick twist and took a quaff. This action did not go unobserved by Theresa, who felt irritated as she abruptly stopped talking.

"Oh, do go on, dear, my saucy friend," said the stranger, "for I am quite fond of fiction. Shall I need paper and a pen to take notes?"

Theresa crossed her arms at this latest slight. "You weren't even listening to what I just said, and you're not funny. And it's illegal to consume alcohol outdoors in public."

"And so is solicitation, madam. If I did not know any better, I would have thought I was in the red-light district of Storyville, New Orleans." He examined his fingernails attentively in the glow of the lamp.

Thoroughly puzzled by this response, Theresa became quiet for a moment. She was curious as to what the stranger had meant. *But I am not selling anything? It's probably some flippant remark*, she thought to herself. She looked at him, standing there parallel with the gas lamp looking all self-confident and smug. He was not paying her any attention but was expecting her response. This annoyed her, but she took the bait. "And what do you mean by solicitation?" she finally asked. "What does that have to do with what I said to you?"

"Well, I figure since you were pointing out the legality of me refreshing myself with an adult beverage on a public street, I thought it would be prudent to remind you of the lawfulness of your trade."

"My trade? I am not trading anything. Man, stop speaking in riddles. What in the world are you talking about?"

"Madam, are you not trying to solicit yourself? And to think, all this time, I am here expecting a substantially discounted proposal to be proffered." With this, he broke into a broad grin.

"What? I can't believe you just said that to me!" Theresa thundered as her face flamed with anger.

"Calm down, woman. There is no need for you to throw a tantrum. You will give yourself apoplexy." He backed up a few steps and appeared to take in the breadth of stars. "Now, where was I, hmm? Oh yes, now I applaud your entrepreneurial spirit. That is quite clever of you to advertise the occupation of a courtesan with your exquisite negligee."

Theresa disappeared from her windowsill only to return seconds later, wearing a large shirt and holding an unopened water bottle. She was completely incensed.

The stranger looked up at her. "It is highly inappropriate to dismiss oneself unannounced in polite company."

"Polite company, my ass," Theresa muttered between her teeth as she flung the water bottle at the stranger. She overshot his head by a few inches, and it landed somewhere in the street.

To her surprise, she had missed him despite her precise aim at such a short distance. But as he still stood there with that smug grin on his face, she doubled down. She returned to the window sill with a small canister. Theresa then unleashed pepper spray in his direction and closed her window, laughing triumphantly. Behind the glass, a cloud of choking fog enveloped the stranger. Her laughter stopped when she realized that the pepper spray had no perceivable effect on him. He simply stood, unconcerned as if nothing had happened.

Theresa reopened her window. "What the hell is wrong with you?"

"Why nothing at all, woman. But please do carry on, for I find your antics mildly amusing."

"Whatever, I'm going to bed, and I hope you do not live in this neighborhood because I never want to see your face again." With finality, she reached up to close her window. "And just so you know, you could not afford me."

The stranger jingled the change in his right trouser pocket. "I beg to differ; there should be more than enough for you and refreshments." Once again, he took a swig from his stashed flask.

Before closing her window, Theresa made an obscene hand gesture before she closed her window and lowered the blinds.

"And goodnight to you too, for now, madam."

Theresa then peeked from behind her curtain to see if he was still there or walking away. But he was gone.

"Good, I am glad he's gone. I hope the police pick him up. It would serve him right." She walked back toward her bed. Although, she found it a strange thing that she did not hear him leave as she had heard him come earlier. Ten minutes later, she was still grumbling about the incident.

"I hope that bastard gets bitten on the ankles by a sick dog with crooked teeth on his way home tonight," she said aloud, rolling over to her left side. "And this is why I keep to myself, jerks just like that." She sighed.

CHAPTER 2

Theresa lay there in bed for some time awake, shifting about as time seemed to drag on. "I can't sleep, I wonder if Abby is still awake," she mumbled, not wanting to get out of bed again. *I should go down to the kitchen and get my phone. But then again, Abby likes to talk too much about herself when I need to talk about myself. And that's rude when I want attention too.* Theresa again closed her eyes and tried to fall asleep, but was unable to do so as the cathedral bell tolling the new hour crept through the silent streets and into her ears.

"Well, looks like I am not going to get any sleep," she said, sitting up in her bed again. Theresa noticed her new nightgown lying on the floor next to her dresser. She had left it there when she hastily changed into her shirt to address the stranger.

Reluctantly, she got out of bed and picked it up. As she withdrew her hands from hanging the delicate gown on its peg, she froze motionless for a moment.

Out of her peripheral vision of her right eye, she realized there was a great deal of pale light gathering in the corner of the room. She slowly turned her head, and it became apparent to her that the moon had finally crept from the clouds that had obscured it. "Okay, for a minute I thought that something otherworldly was about to go down," she said in a whisper that was followed with a nervous chuckle.

The moonlight beamed in the room out of the corners of the blinds. And since her curtains were white damask, it did little to abate this. The light of the moon rarely bothered Theresa, as its glow was always cast into the corner where a small wooden table and chair were situated. But something had been odd about it all that night. The dinner tray was in the same place, yet the whole area of the table seemed to be more illuminated than it had been in the moonlit nights in the past. As if it was producing its own light.

She went to the window and took a closer look. *Well, obviously, I need to get some rest. I am so tired that I don't even realize it. Let me take my behind to bed before I wig out further*, she thought as she turned away from examining the table.

She pulled back her flowered sheets and slid under them with her back towards her window. Theresa lay there for a little while staring at her pillow before she turned and sat up.

There is a nip in tonight's air. I think I'll need my extra blanket, she thought, as she reached to the foot of her bed to unfold the blanket. "I hope another cold front isn't moving in the area. This weather can really be bipolar," she murmured to herself beneath her cocoon of linen and wool. And within a matter of a few minutes, Theresa was fast asleep with her covers pulled over her head.

She awakened sometime later—half-asleep—to a dull metallic sound that she could not place, but was too sleepy to care about. She fell back asleep only to be reawakened again soon after. Theresa, now lying on her back, instantly sat up. The cause of sound was now evident to her; it was the sound of a coin spinning on a hard surface. But as soon as she came to that conclusion, the spinning ceased completely. There was no concluding clang of the coin coming to a halt as its gyroscopic momentum ended. There was nothing but a thick silence in the room. And she figured that the noise was in her room somewhere near the window. A wintry shiver of fear ran down her spine as the reality hit her. There was someone in her room.

She could see the glow of the moon's pale light through her woolen blanket. She pulled it off her face cautiously as if it had offered her some sort of protection and peered into the surroundings.

Theresa saw nothing but the same room she slept in every night. Then something puzzling caught her glance, for in the light of the moon there was a glint on her wooden table. Theresa stared at it for a moment before she reached over to turn on the nightstand's lamp. She threw her covers back, determined to investigate, but the sound of a male voice arrested her movement.

"Wonderful, you are finally awake," said the male voice that was not only vaguely familiar, but surprisingly close.

Now fully apprehensive, Theresa looked towards her TV first and then around the room again but saw nothing. She then moved over to the other side of the bed and cautiously looked off the edge, but again, saw nothing. She could see inside her closet as the double mashrabiya latticework doors were open as she always left them. Theresa got out of bed and inspected under it, but only saw her various shoe boxes. She walked over to the closet and felt through her clothes. Completing her search, she turned around and looked over the room again, still trying to figure out what was going on.

"Obviously, I am not asleep, and I have looked over the entire room," she whispered to herself. Next, she walked over to the bedroom door and was about to open it, but decided against it. She locked the door instead. Theresa was about to get back into bed when it dawned on her to check the window. *Right, I guess I didn't close the window all the way. That explains the nip in the air and that voice. I bet that pretentious English snot is drunk and came back to apologize to me*, she thought. But as she examined the window, she realized it was properly fastened. Out of curiosity, she opened the window, and her skin was met by the warm night air.

"Now, that is strange. How is it that my room is cooler than the outside air, and I don't even have the air conditioning on? I must be coming down with something." She shut the window abruptly. Theresa went back to bed after turning off the light. She pulled the covers up to her chest when she heard the voice again.

"You know, for a person that claims to have *owl eyes*, you are indeed as blind as a bat in the light of day."

Theresa, startled once more, again looked around the room and saw nothing. She placed the back of her hand on her forehead. *I must have a fever, even though I feel physically fine.*

"Woman, I do not have all night for you to doubt your senses. If you could see me earlier when I was at my leisure, then I am quite sure you can see me now."

Theresa turned her head towards the table, where the voice seemed to have originated. She saw nothing at first, but then the intruder's shape began to take a more semi-solid form. He stood near the table with his top hat in his gloved left hand and his right hand touching the table. From where he was standing, Theresa, for some reason, couldn't focus on his face. It seemed indiscernible to her in the pale moonlight that was cast about his facial features. His expression seemed both serious and relaxed at the same time.

Theresa hastily turned her light on again. The apparition smiled warmly before he bowed low like a well-bred gentleman of years long past.

"Madam, I do apologize for calling upon you at this late hour with all the sincerity I have to offer," the apparition said. "Especially after your apparent late-night feedings when digestive rest is especially important."

He tilted his head towards the dinner tray on the table. "But I owe you the formality of an introduction."

Theresa viewed the stranger, attentively assessing this phenomenon in her head.

"Here is my card, Ms. King."

As soon as he said the words, he was standing within arm's reach with his gloved hand extended, holding a small white printed card. Theresa took the card from his hand, and before she could study it, she noticed that he was back at the table, standing before the chair.

"Madam, may I sit down, please?"

Theresa only stared at him as she again felt her forehead with the back of her hand. Still stunned, she read the printed cursive words on the card: *Mr. Archibald Mallard Turner. 22b Eaton Square, Belgravia, London.* Theresa looked up at the apparition, who was now seated at the table again, then back at the card before she found her voice. "And do I owe this intrusion to a fever of my mind or the beginning stages of insanity, Mr. Turner?"

"Oh, my dear, it is nothing of the sort. And please, call me Archie," he said in a warm tone.

He was about to say something else, but Theresa interrupted before the apparition could continue. Theresa's facial expression altered as her ire rose. "So you mean to tell me that you are actually here and I am not dreaming? How in the hell did you get into my room, and how do you know my name?"

"Well, of course I'm here and you are not dreaming." He rested his right arm on the edge of the table and tapped his finger on the edge, but no sound came from the action. "You need to settle down a bit. Judging from your previous rascalities from this window earlier, that twitch in your eye tells me you are contemplating striking me. Now, as for your name, I got that off of your Mechanical Engineering degree from Clemson downstairs. But I do understand your obvious confusion over this highly irregular circumstance. All of this, coupled with your awkwardness about men and your apparent loneliness, my presence should have some effect on you."

Theresa was astonished. After staring at his pleasant but seemingly comfortable countenance, she walked over to take a closer look at him. She was about to approach him, but stopped when he asked her a question without moving his mouth.

"Why do you look like that?"

"Look like what?"

"You know, like you are constipated?"

"I am not constipated, and you are *not* funny," Theresa said. "You just can't help yourself from being rude, can you? And you have the audacity to say it to my face in my own home. What are you and why are you in my house, in *my* bedroom, and at this hour in the first place? I thought I told you clearly to take your ass home earlier. So how about you just do that for me right now, if you please? Reverse the magic trick, or whatever it was that you used to appear here, and go reappear somewhere else before I call the police on you."

Archie rubbed his chin in thought and placed his hat on the table. "I see no need for you to get so *warm* about such a trifle. Furthermore, once I have completed my purpose here tonight, then I will leave on my own accord. You may still call the police if you desire." He stood up abruptly and moved silently over the bare oak floors to the window, despite the dress oxfords on his feet. His back was turned towards Theresa, and he appeared to be looking at something down on the street below.

"I know you have an inkling of *exactly* what I am. And yet you are trying your best to tell yourself that it is not so, that it is impossible to see what you are seeing. Your reactions thus far make me ponder whether you have all your wits about you or whether you are really that courageous. However, I am not particularly inclined to believe the latter as, in my experience, foolhardiness is often mistaken for courage. Furthermore, just so you know, this is *my* home and it has been so for a lot longer than you could possibly imagine. And judging from your taste in clothes"—he gestured toward her closet— "what accounts for your imagination is not much. But that doesn't matter really. What matters is why I am here on this introductory visit, and it is simple enough."

Theresa sat back down on her bed as Archie walked back to the chair with his hand clasped behind his back. He sat, resuming his former formal posture.

"Well, whatever you are, I don't believe in ghosts."

"I don't believe in ghosts either, and yet here we are! Moreover, I do prefer the nomenclature of *specter*." He crossed his right leg over his left.

She gestured for him to hold his thoughts while she rummaged through the top drawer of her nightstand. She retrieved a small vial with a translucent liquid in it. Removing the cap, she flung the contents at him. The liquid passed through him, splashing upon the table and floor. Archibald raised an eyebrow.

"Do you mind telling me what that was about?"

"I'll tell you what it's about." Theresa tossed the vial into the waste bin. "That TV evangelist, Pastor Bryant, swindled me out of $19.95 with this bogus-ass holy water that obviously doesn't work."

The apparition closed his eyes and let out a deep sigh before speaking.

"Now, you should know that I have been here in *my* home for the past three weeks before I became completely displeased with you as my new guest. Though you are not as annoying to me as your fat friend, you are somewhat tolerable. But then again, younger spinsters usually are before they become embittered with life."

Theresa scoffed. "Look, I am not a *spinster*, and I am not annoying. I know you are trying to provoke me, but it is not going to work."

"Theresa, I am only stating the facts as they are. Therefore, there is nothing for you to be offended about." He then gestured towards Theresa's left hand. "You are unmarried and have never been. You also have no suitor of any type seeking you out, man nor woman. That seems to be the Oxford definition of a spinster to me. Plus, you have to be at least in your middle thirties."

Theresa closed her eyes and took a deep breath. "Look Casper, I am 26 years old. You know, like the number that comes after 25, but before 27?"

"Now that is an interesting surprise indeed. Perhaps you should invest in a wardrobe that accentuates your current age rather than adds years to it. You have a nice physique, but some exercise to tone things up and a bit healthier eating would not hurt you either."

She looked at him blankly before responding with words other than the ones she was thinking. "Thank you kindly for your advice."

"I am always glad to be of assistance to those in apparent need. Now back to what I was previously saying and my reason for being here tonight. Since I have been back, it seems the only respite I have received thus far from this most unfortunate situation is when you are at work or when you are off to market shopping for your meals. Outside of that, no sooner do I pass through the threshold of this house than I am immediately assailed with the loud cackling of frivolous gossip. That, of course, is due to you and that gravy-guzzling, waddling twit-friend of yours, Fat Abby. This annoyance is either in person or by you talking boisterously to her on your portable telephone. Either way, it is all the same to me: a dreadful bother. And to be frank with you, Madam, I'm tired of it all. What passes for your life bores me dreadfully. I can't take it anymore, and neither can the oak floors of this once peaceful place. One can almost hear the wooden planks beg for mercy when you bring that fat woman here tramping around like a prize heifer out to pasture. She has to be at least 21 stones."

Archie put his right hand to the bridge of his nose and let out a low sigh. "It is truly disgraceful that I cannot find peace within my own house."

Theresa was listening attentively, but could not hold her peace any longer. "First of all, you are really one mean-spirited spirit. Secondly, what do you mean *your* house and *your* guest? Man, you must be drunk or crazy. Maybe a little bit of both. But let's get something straight, I am not *your* guest. I bought this house with cash fair and square at a public auction. So I am certain you should have realized something so obvious with all your cleverness to know that I have the deed in my name. I am the lawful resident here, and you, on the other hand, are a dead man who, for whatever reason, is still hanging around this place. And don't give me that haughty look, you know good and goddamn well that I'm right. You should also know that I am not scared of you either. No ghost is going to give me sass about how I conduct myself in *my* house with *my* friends. So I'm not going anywhere, and you can kick rocks if you don't like it." Theresa paused and adjusted herself in her blanket before continuing.

"You are not even good at ghosting, do you know that? What ghost is only here a few weeks out of several months?" Theresa looked at Archie. He seemed unconcerned by the one-sided conversation. He rested his elbow on the edge of the table, and laid his chin in the palm of his right hand, supporting his head as he looked out the window. The moon was no longer visible, and yet he sat in a pool of light.

"Fine, don't answer me then. I guess you have decided to act as you actually are: dead. So you should be in your grave, where you belong, not roaming about spying on and harassing women at all times in the night. And besides that, you're an Englishman, not even a real American! So shouldn't you be in England at your sprawling country estate, dragging chains through the halls at night, *milord*?"

Theresa crossed her arms with a self-accomplished smirk. "And another thing, don't call my friend Fat Abby. She's sort of on a diet and sensitive about her weight, even though she is not serious about it."

Theresa's admonishment ended there. She grabbed a bottle of water off her nightstand and took a healthy sip.

Archie clapped his hands slowly and distinctly three times while Theresa was returning the cap to the bottle.

"You must forgive me, for I have always found it to be somewhat amusing when people think they have said something profound, when actually they have not." He stood up, removing his hat from the table and placing it firmly upon his head. "You know, you Americans have instinctively myopic views of very serious situations. And that false sense of bravado will not serve you well long-term, madam. But to be quite frank with you, Ms. King, you are an interloper on my post-life serenity. The legality of the papers you possess for this residence means absolutely nothing to me. You are not the first in this house, as you should already know, and I am quite sure you will not be the last."

Just then, a strong gust of wind blew over the house with a howling cry, and the building seemed to groan in agony.

"I am only here tonight because you were able to see me earlier on the pavement below, for some unknown reason, which is not normally the case for mortals. At any rate, I had originally wanted to discuss amicable terms with you, seeing that your life was already a casserole of nonsense. But you have mildly offended me by your impudent rash reproach. And for this, I will repay. You will see reason, or you will see nothing." He looked at his watch before returning it to the confines of his pocket. "What a pity, you have only been here for 5 months, a fortnight, 1 hour and 47 minutes to be exact. And now I must bid you adieu, madam. Rest very well."

He touched the brim of his hat and vanished into the darkness. She sat in her bed staring at the spot in which he sat, expecting to wake up from a dream. This state of mind was broken moments later when the cathedral in the distance unexpectedly began tolling the hour. Theresa turned on all the lights and locked her bedroom door before returning to bed with a baseball bat that she kept behind the door. Once in bed, she let out a deep sigh. "Yeah, he's definitely going to haunt me."

CHAPTER 3

At 10:43 p.m. on a Wednesday night, a relentless thunderstorm accompanied by strong winds prevailed over the city. Earlier, and because of a violent tempest, the power had been knocked out. The only light in Theresa's whole house emanated from two lavender-scented tea lights. Having only four in a pack, she rationed them. At best, they had a four-hour life expectancy. There was one tea light in Theresa's bedroom that sat upon the small mahogany table in the corner. The other tea light was situated on the counter of the second-floor bathroom. The rest of the house was devoured by a velvety black, lavender-perfumed darkness that encroached ever closer on the light of the candles. The gloom of it all gave the once inviting place a gothic, melancholic atmosphere.

Theresa had tried to sleep through the storm and blackout, but the incessant thunderclaps rumbled like the city was under a heavy blitz. Unable to sleep in peace, she put on her headphones and listened to an audiobook until the low battery alert came on. Removing her headphones, she rose from the bed and walked over to the candle's flickering radiance. She sat down at the table with a wooden-handled brush and a small bottle of peppermint oil. After she applied a few drops of oil to the bristles, she began brushing her hair in a preordained pattern.

Once that task was completed, she set her brush aside and sat there for some time motionless while the turbulence of the storm raged outside her bedroom window. She had her arms crossed on the table, and her head rested firmly upon them. Theresa listened to the sheets of water that cascaded down her windowpanes as she rested her eyes. As she sat there, random thoughts began to flood her mind. But even with her eyes closed, she could feel the varying glow and erratic movement of the candle's flame as if there was a breeze moving against it. This caused her to reopen her eyes immediately. Theresa was just about to get up to find something to write down her thoughts before she forgot them, but her eyes caught the rhythmic movement of the golden orb of light.

What a curious thing, she pondered. *This flame's fluctuations seem to be following a sequence, as if it was performing a dance. Surely there has to be some reasonable explanation for this?* As she studied the candle's small flickering light, she forgot everything else. Her attention was now completely engulfed in the unusual activity.

The flame quivered on its wick pedestal; the area immediately around the flame magnified. The grains in the illuminated mahogany seemed to be several times their normal size. This anomaly showed off the natural pattern in the rich, polished wood in a way that Theresa had not noticed before. The flame grew bigger and brighter. She felt like she was actually moving towards it, but she was not.

The more Theresa looked at this flame, the more it seemed to flourish in her presence. Theresa felt a sense of disproportion. It was as if she had become smaller and was staring up into the golden light without moving. And yet, even with this perceived change, the flame gave off no heat. And throughout this, Theresa did not move. She was not even afraid. The phenomenon intrigued her more than anything.

While she stared transfixed, an image began to take shape. It was indiscernible at first, but it continued to materialize until she was encompassed by it. Theresa shut her eyes as she realized that she was no longer sitting in her room, but rather in a strange and unfamiliar place. Her bare feet now felt the cool uneven surface of round pebbles as her nose was greeted with an earthy scent. As Theresa sat there, she could hear the low murmuring of a moving body of water.

"I must have fallen asleep without even realizing it. But strangely enough, I don't feel asleep," Theresa said aloud. She turned in all directions. The misty still air gave the area around her a more foreboding aspect. From the edge of the forest on the pebble bank, she stood to survey the area. She saw nothing but the forest in front of her. She couldn't see anything on the opposite side of the stream, other than white mist.

Theresa really did not want to venture into the forest, so she walked along the bank. After walking for some time along the shoreline in both directions, she came to the conclusion that she was on some type of large island. The water did not seem to be deep, nor was the current fast. But when Theresa placed her toe in the water to test the temperature, it went from lukewarm to freezing within a matter of seconds.

"Okay, I get it," Theresa said as she sat on the pebbles warming up her big toe that was still stinging from the cold with her fingers. "Stay out of the damn water." As she sat there, rubbing her toe, she noticed by chance that there was an obscured path. It was covered with ground moss, and led deep into the birch forest. She stood up, shook the pebbles from her shorts, and walked over to where the path began. Theresa looked down the meandering trail for a few moments before she decided to follow it.

"Well, it's not like I have a lot of options here," she mumbled.

When Theresa stepped into the forest, a soft breeze picked up behind her. The branches around her swayed, and it created a dance of light and shadow as she walked along the misty path. *Some of these trees are very old,* she thought as she crossed over the roots of two old birches. As she held to the side of one tree, feeling about the ground for secure footing, she heard a noise. It was a soft metallic sound that emanated from the woods.

It is like the melodies of various wind chimes, she thought as she wandered into a small clearing. There, she halted when she saw in the center of this place a moonlit altar. As she proceeded to the weather-worn stone monument, upon closer inspection, she realized that the surface was covered in illegible inscriptions. There were also three small empty niches fashioned into the side. As she moved around, examining the carvings, her foot landed on an uneven surface. Partially buried in the earth, there was something that had a glint to it. Working the object loose, Theresa picked up a smooth round stone of unusual color and radiance that seemed to shimmer in the moonlight. While analyzing her new find, out of the corner of her eye, Theresa realized that within the mist, something peculiar was taking place. She turned her head and saw a mass of flame-like lights flickered slowly, rising throughout the surrounding forest floor. The tiny flames were about the size of a thumb, emitting a soft, blue luminescence that did not permeate the darkness around it.

Theresa turned about several times, looking for the path she had come down earlier as the fog began to rise. Suddenly, she had the sensation that she was being watched. Not only that, but she also perceived that whatever was watching her was not alone. She found the path that led out of the clearing, but the orbs of light were on the path in front of her. She heard a multitude of indistinct voices; she tensed. Within an instant, there was an array of shadowy faces looking at her whose expressions ranged from curious to outright resentful.

But then she heard her name called from a faint voice drifting up from behind her, accompanied with the aroma of an ancient perfume.

She turned around quickly and saw a figure wrapped from head to toe in white winding-sheets standing still as a statue facing her. The outline of the facial features was eerily discernible through the cloth that covered it. The only color that this figure had was a wreath of flowers upon its head. Theresa's first instinct was to flee, but she lacked the ability to move her body. Then, a hoarse voice emanated from the corpse, at first as if it was a great effort to do so. But it soon softened, speaking briefly in a language that Theresa did not understand. But before she could respond, long vapors rose up from the misty luminescence like the smoke trails of burning incense. The vapors circled around her several times as a murmuring grew louder, making it difficult to hear. As it kept circling around Theresa, they merged into a thick billowing blanket, and encompassed her whole body. It was then that she felt herself drift into a slow descent with the whispers of many voices from unseen mouths as everything went black and silent.

When Theresa regained consciousness, she realized that she was no longer in the strange clearing in the forest, but was in a large wine cellar. This dimly lit place held a large inventory of different wines and liqueurs, varying in vintages that extended from the floor to the ceiling. She discovered a flight of stairs that took her up to the main floor.

Theresa roamed around in ambient light. She passed by several bedrooms arrayed in a Nipponese-style right down to the fusuma sliding doors and tatami mats. Theresa concluded that she was in an empty house.

On her way to what she perceived to be the front of the house, Theresa noticed there was an inner courtyard. The focal point in the courtyard was a small reflecting pool with shimmering waters as the moon sparkled on its surface. Drawn in by the beauty of this place, Theresa entered. And as she gazed into the reflecting pool, she could make out the inscription that said: *Everyone sees what you appear to be but few really know what you are.*

Theresa thought about the quote as she walked back into the house and was soon in the illuminated chic living room. This room was lit by recessed lights in the ceiling adjusted to showcase the decor. As Theresa moved around the living room, her attention was drawn to the light brown accent wall that stood out in the cream-painted room. On this wall, there were two large paintings of a man and woman resting in finely carved, gilded frames spaced apart to help highlight their prominence. Theresa presumed them to be the homeowner's ancestors while admiring the style of their dress.

He has very cold eyes, she thought as she surveyed the portrait of the young, dark-haired gentleman in his black frock coat. There had been a nameplate at the bottom of this portrait, bearing the gentleman's name, but the painted-over screw holes suggested that attachment had been long lost to the injuries of time.

Theresa turned her attention in the direction of the full-length portrait of the second subject. Here was a Creole woman with a radiant face that was made even more beautiful by her green eyes and luxuriant, wavy raven-colored hair that reached the middle of her back. She was in her late teens or early twenties, wearing the most beautiful white silk kimono tea gown with cherry blossoms scattered all over it. She was standing with her arms cradling a black toy poodle that had a satin bow on its head.

The name *Isadora de Coucy* was engraved on a brass nameplate at the bottom, and as Theresa examined the portrait of the woman, she couldn't help but feel that there was a familiarity about the woman's likeness in the 19th-century painting. When she turned around, a smartly dressed man standing next to her startled her to the point she almost fell.

"She is beautiful," he said, focusing on the painting.

Stumbling for words, Theresa attempted to explain the situation of how she ended up in the house. But to her surprise, he paid her no credence whatsoever. In fact, he wasn't even addressing her, but rather someone further back who was locking the front door.

There was a beautiful honey-skinned woman in a slinky black dress approaching the man who was still gazing at the painting. The man then seated himself on the sofa, and the woman returned, speaking to him as if they were the only two in the room. Theresa walked over to them in an attempt to get their attention. She gasped when she was closer to the newcomer.

The honey-skinned woman resembled the woman in the portrait. Then it dawned on Theresa that she knew this woman.

Theresa snapped her fingers. *I used to work with her years ago. That is Louisa Camille Du Pont*, she said to herself.

But why am I here? And why are they acting so oblivious to me being here?

Theresa reached out and touched her friend's arm. Louisa Camille jumped back, where she assumed a martial stance as her eyes focused in on Theresa's general direction. The man erupted in laughter. Louisa Camille's eyes shifted to his direction slyly as an unexpected kick brought her foot within an inch of his face. It was obvious to him, and Theresa, that she could have struck him if she'd wished to do so.

"So, Louisa was that wonderful performance attributed to jittery nerves or did you just want to show off your skills?"

"Neither, I just wanted to see your reaction." And she left the room to change her clothes. Theresa, meanwhile, examined the young man closely when, by chance, the mirror caught her attention. She saw his reflection in the mirror, but not her own, despite standing next to him.

It wasn't long before Louisa Camille rejoined her guests in the living room with a silver salver laden with refreshments. But it wasn't the refreshments that raised Theresa's eyebrow and made the young man sit up straight. Louisa Camille had put on a short silk robe that not only showed off her toned legs, but she'd failed to tie the sashes, leaving little to the imagination. She sat the salver on the coffee table and poured out two glasses of Hungarian Tokaji. With glasses in hand, she turned around and feigned surprise at the state of her robe. She then had her guest tie the sashes together before she took her place on the sofa.

As Theresa listened in on their conversation, she soon found out that the young man's name was Faraday and that he was a freshman at Gainesville. She also learned that Louisa Camille intended to get him into politics, much to his and Theresa's surprise.

It's strange how she seems so different. The last I remember of her, she was always shy, religious, and had a deep rural Southern accent. I understand people change, and living in the state of Florida makes people weird after a few years. But I don't ever remember her talking so eloquently, with that hint of a French accent, or being wealthy.

"Sweetie," Faraday said as he placed his glass on the coffee table. "I admire your hubris, but I am not even remotely the type of person to run for a public office. I am a struggling college student with limited resources to compete in any political arena." He was proceeding at length, reasoning on why he wasn't a good candidate when he noticed a change in his host's demeanor.

Louisa Camille placed her glass on the coffee table before staring at him for a moment with her dark, piercing eyes. She sighed and spoke frankly to him in a sharp New York dialect.

"Look, Faraday, I'm going to cut to the chase here. Our meeting at the gala was not a chance event. I know everything about you I need to know already, from your living paycheck to paycheck to your lackluster applied mathematics grades. Hell, I even know about that flaky Jewish woman you had a thing for in Dothan that treated you with the same regard a redneck has for his spit cup. Yes, I know about that too. And don't look at me like that; I would be foolhardy, after all, not to research *my* investment. It is my job to know, since I am in the business of knowing."

He said nothing but only gazed at her sternly.

"Faraday, I'm the person who is offering you a golden ticket to better yourself and raise your social standing in such a way you would have to want for naught. You don't have to worry about struggling to get your degree when it is guaranteed that you would get it."

"Tell me, why would a woman—who apparently can change her accent and dialect at a whim—decide that one day, out of the goodness of her heart, she wanted to elevate a struggling freshman? You know, after that amazing invasion-of-privacy thing."

"Oh my, you can be snarky and hilarious. Well, I guess I'll tell you a little about myself," Louisa Camille told him as she reverted to her alluring voice, which she used to assuage his anger. Theresa also picked up on the subtle way she was seducing him with the movements of her body as she spoke. She told him a bit about herself, information which Theresa found to be very interesting as she did not know her friend was from the Red Hook neighborhood of the Brooklyn borough. When she had finished, Theresa realized that she knew nothing of her friend.

"I didn't realize you had such an interesting background, Louisa Camille. All that traveling around the world, speaking seven languages fluently. It's all very impressive. And considering your ability to pry into the business of others as you wish, altering your personality as needed, I am almost inclined to believe that you are involved in a lot of shady schemes."

Louisa Camille looked at him with a blank expression, but Theresa knew that she was assessing his words carefully.

"Nevertheless," he continued with a large grin on his face, "I am inclined to take you up on your offer. *Senator Faraday* does have a nice ring to it. I guess I have plenty of time to think about this since there are three more years until the next election."

"Don't overthink it, you have less than three months before you will be selected to office. And 'selected' is the correct word to use as I plan to put you there by an act of a state legislator. You are to finish out an individual's term. All you have to do is show up occasionally, smile, shake hands, and don't make a scene."

So she has enough political clout to raise someone to power? I wonder what her real motive is behind this? Theresa wondered as it began to rain.

"So, which senator will retire so early into their term for this vacancy?"

Louisa Camille said nothing, but Theresa could see a slight smile on her face. The lights flickered as the sound of rolling thunder reverberated overhead. This was immediately followed by a loud crash of a lightning strike nearby that left them in darkness. Theresa turned her attention from the window back to see her friend in the dim light, unfazed by the storm, straddling Faraday.

"Well, she sure didn't lose any time finalizing that deal," Theresa said as the room receded within an instant. She felt herself pulled up and out of the room with great rapidity into the black of the stormy night's sky.

CHAPTER 4

When Theresa came to a standstill, everything was in utter darkness. For a moment, nothing was perceptible until she became aware of her new surroundings. It was not by sight that she realized that something had changed, but rather by sound. She could hear waves lapping against the shore intermingled with the rustling of foliage moving in a light breeze. The air carried the distinctive salty fragrance of the open sea.

As her eyes adjusted to the darkness, a hazy, grey image began to appear. The first thing she noticed was a marshland covered in fog as far as her eyes could see. She wasn't standing in the marsh, but rather upon an embankment as the moon revealed itself from behind a cloud. To her left side, the embankment stretched along the horizon until it disappeared into the dense fog completely.

There was a ten-foot wall on one side of the embankment, and calm ripples lapped against the granite stones. These stones were placed there to serve as protective riprap for saving the earthen structure from the erosive actions of the sea.

Theresa turned around in the other direction. She could only see about a hundred yards in front of her, as far as the weather conditions would permit. But Theresa was able to make out a large, dark shadowy mass further down. It was almost obscured by the greyish sheets of fog. She stared at it for a moment, deciding what she should do. And eventually, she headed towards the dark shadowy mass, seeing that she had no alternative but to head in one direction or the other.

"Well, at least I know that there is something in this direction," Theresa said to herself as she trotted noisily along the dreary footpath that was partially covered with vegetation.

This looks like it used to be some type of road at some point, but it has been long neglected. It's wide enough for a car to travel, although it would have to do so with a lot of caution.

As Theresa got closer, the dark shape's form began to reveal itself as nothing more than two trees growing out of either side of the embankment, parallel to one another. Their branches were so close that they almost intermingled over the footpath. One tree was dead, and yet the other was full of foliage. The dead tree was on the marshy side of the path and the other on the seaside. Theresa walked underneath their twisted branches. *Yeah, this is a little bit on the sketchy side. Looks almost like a gateway of some sort.*

When she had passed between them, she stopped to examine both trees. "This seems to be an odd place for someone to plant trees. Someone must have planted them, because there aren't any other trees—even far in the distance."

Theresa turned around and noticed that there was a shadowy figure within the fog that seemed to be standing on water. Theresa advanced along the partially overgrown footpath, and could see that there was a jetty. It extended about 30 feet from the side of the embankment into the water. Surrounded with the foggy vapor, and at the end of the jetty, was a figure. Curious as to what it could be, Theresa advanced onto the jetty to see what was shrouded in the grey air. As she closed the distance, a man came into focus. He stood at the end of the jetty. He was looking down into the swirling black waters a few feet below, occasionally splashing up against the rocks. This man wore a black overcoat, and the tail fluttered in the winds. He stood there as rigid as a piece of steel with his arms crossed behind his back. In his right hand, he was holding a black lacquer cane with a silver knob for a top, and a bottom capped off with silver.

Theresa stared. The man's statuesque figure added much to the impressive scene. Curious, she moved stealthily to his left side, attempting to get a good look at his face. It was then when she noticed a large light from a lighthouse far out in the distance. The beam made one revolution before it pointed in the northward direction, away from where he stood.

She then turned her head to the right and realized from the profile, to her dismay, who it was. "You've got to be kidding me, it's *this* asshole, Archibald," she muttered. *I should bust him in his head with one of these big rocks and be done with him. But since he's already dead that might make him vengeful and really annoying.* Theresa sat there on the edge in her thoughts.

I don't think I've ever had a dream this cognizant before. I think I should remember this all in detail when I wake up. It should make for a good story to add to my journal. Archie suddenly tapped the bottom of his cane on a stone on the jetty. It sent out three resounding echoes in the night air.

"It's about time you got here," Archie said.

Theresa was curious to know who he had addressed as she was looking in the same direction and saw nothing. Her attention was drawn to the absolute silence as the breeze had stopped and the sea became unusually still. Theresa crept forward on the side of the embankment and noticed something odd with the water. There was something white fluttering just under the surface, similar in motion to the fins of a butterfly koi. It seemed to shimmer like mercury.

Theresa slowly backed up to her previous location. She was just situating herself when a woman in a hooded wolf's pelt rose majestically and noiselessly from the water. She suspended in the air several feet over the water before moving to his level on the jetty. Her flowing white dress was blowing easterly in a breeze that seemed only to affect her. Her eyes were obscured under the wolf's head, Theresa could see her red tresses. She leaned her head back with her arms outstretched as if she had awoken from a deep sleep. She glided forward, towards Archibald with a confident listlessness.

Theresa looked at her in awe and admiration, wondering who or what this new apparition was.

The woman slowly raised her head. "Whatever, I am not late for anything. The fact that I am here tonight is not even a favor to you. It's charity. So what is it that you want, charity case?"

Archie sighed and raised his left hand to his forehead. "I am not sure if I detect a capricious tinge of saltiness, or is that just what passes for charm? No matter, though, they are one and the same to me, including making me wait just so you could make your theatrical appearance."

The other spirit smiled. "Stop talking like you have someplace to be. We're dead, and time stopped for us long ago. Besides, I had a prior engagement to haunt tonight and you knew that."

Archie scoffed. "It is not aggravation, but rather contemplation of the merits of your statement, but I am going to humor myself and play along."

She moved closer, within a foot's distance. He stood there with his walking stick in his right hand, tapping it against his leg in a repetitive motion. Theresa wondered if that meant he was aggravated by the other spirit or if he was studying her, since she could neither see his face nor read his body language.

Archie placed his right hand on her shoulder as he rested his left hand on the top of his cane. His head lowered as if in prayer. "I have a favor to ask of you, a task that has some urgency—"

A rumble of thunder in the distance thwarted Theresa's eavesdropping. It prevented her from hearing the nature of his request and the ensuing conversation clearly. She concluded from the smile on the other apparition's face and more relaxed posture that a favorable deal had been struck.

This image, for Theresa, was immediately interrupted by a curtain of silvery light. Theresa opened her eyes and was back in her own room, hearing a rumble of thunder fading off in the distance. She had her head resting on her folded arms, back at her wooden table. She sat upright, and wiped the drool off of her arm. The tea light had just burnt out, and a trail of winding smoke danced its way up to the ceiling. Theresa stretched her arms and peeked out of her window. The storm had subsided, and the sun was already rising on a new day.

CHAPTER 5

I t was early Saturday morning, and the sun was just cresting over the horizon. As with most dreams, Theresa had forgotten about her unusual adventure in its entirety upon her awakening that Thursday morning. The days following since Wednesday's storm had passed uneventfully. This morning, Theresa rose at daybreak to start on her week's wash and her couponing. By a quarter past seven, she was already back upstairs in the kitchen after loading the dryer.

After about ten minutes of couponing at the kitchen table, Theresa had a nice neat pile cut out for her weekend bargain hunt. She placed her coupons in a customized zip-up folder of her own design that categorized her coupons for quick access. She was just zipping her folder shut when she hesitated. A dull knocking sound came from the basement. *I guess I didn't clean out all of my pockets. I must have left some change in there.* She headed back down to the basement, dumping her clipping in the trashcan along the way. Within seconds, she had the dryer door open and began removing the hot damp clothes, placing them in an empty laundry basket that sat on top of the dryer. She had removed most of her clothes before she felt something hot, rounded, and hard at the bottom of the dryer drum.

She withdrew her hand and observed the object with marked curiosity. To her surprise, it was a small stone of a deep, luxuriant red color. As she moved it along her fingers, it sparkled in the light, which magnified its allure even more. She stood there for several minutes looking at the stone, wondering where she got it from when the spring-tension dryer door slammed shut. She jumped. Remembering that her undried laundry in the clothes' basket needed her attention, Theresa placed the stone in her pajama shorts pocket and began reloading the dryer. Since the washer had completed its cycle during this time, she began loading in her whites.

In the process, she knelt down to pick the errant shirt off the floor. Holding the shirt up, she remembered that she had worn that particular shirt to bed the night of the thunderstorm. As she squatted there by the dryer, the peculiar stone fell out of her shallow pocket onto the tile floor. The stone rolled against the dryer right under the shirt she was holding. She picked the stone up and held it next to the shirt. Immediately her head flooded with recollections of that stormy night's experiences.

It can't be possible; those places and that island of chimes were just a fanciful dream, most likely brought on by anxiety or something. Theresa doubted the circumstances as she ran her fingers through her hair. Reasoning with herself, she came to the conclusion that she had found it on the property at some point and had simply forgotten about it. Placing the stone back in her pocket and starting the dryer, she headed back upstairs to get dressed for her morning shopping.

Shortly thereafter, as Theresa walked down the stairs to her car in deep thought, her phone began ringing. Watching the phone ring, she thought, *Who else but Abby? I think I will pass on a conversation with her right now. It is much too early for me to digest whatever it is she has to tell me.*

Theresa returned her phone to her purse and retrieved her car keys when the phone alerted her that she had received a text message. Taking out the phone again, Theresa read the text message: "I can see you. Answer your phone!"

Theresa immediately looked around and saw her friend Abigail. She stood down the sidewalk, only a block over, waving both of her arms fanatically in the air to get her attention. Abigail called Theresa's phone again, but this time the call was answered.

"Hey, I am so glad I caught you," Abigail said, sounding out of breath. "Could you please give me a ride home?"

"Come on. I'll be waiting right here by my car." Theresa was somewhat amused to see Abigail make a half-hearted attempt to hustle down the sidewalk to get to her.

When Abigail crossed the street, Theresa realized that she didn't have any shoes on her feet, just socks with soiled soles. Abigail made it to Theresa, huffing and puffing. Abigail was so tired she had to bend over; she rested her hands on her kneecaps to catch her breath. Theresa looked Abigail up and down, disapprovingly, and folded her arms.

"Where are your shoes, and what are you doing in this part of town so early in the morning?"

Abby tried to straighten herself up, and was going to say something, but Theresa stepped forward, sniffing the air.

"Good grief, you smell like ashtrays and beer. Plus, you're covered in sweat, your clothes look filthy, and your hair is completely mussed."

"Geez, Mom, let me sit down first. I'm dying over here." She walked towards Theresa's stairs and sat down, exposing the grimy soles of her socks when she stretched her legs out.

Theresa rolled her eyes as she casually stepped over Abigail's sprawled-out body while she made her way back into her house. She returned almost immediately with a hand towel and a red plastic tumbler full of iced tea. Abigail gulped it down in haste. Once she had refreshed herself, she wiped her face down and began to speak in a more normalized tone.

"Actually Theresa, I found your street by accident, considering that I was looking for you. I got chased by two German Shepherds several blocks over. Conniving dogs at that, too; one of them broke off the chase only to take a shortcut to come around in front of me. I had to run across the street to avoid being attacked from both sides. Then, I almost got murdered by a doughnut delivery van. I don't think I've ever ran so hard in my life, and I would not recommend it to anyone. My poor feet are sore too."

"But why are you shoeless in this part of town at 9:30 a.m., Abby?"

"Well, you see, I was smoking last night for medicinal purposes. You know, to prevent glaucoma"—Abigail pointed towards her own eyes— "when I got the hankering for some ice cream and cookies while lounging on my couch laughing about something. I was watching reruns of that annoying old redhead who solves murder mysteries and then capitalizes on it by writing books for money. You know who I am talking about, right? She always gives guff to the suspect once they are in custody to get them all riled up again."

Theresa nodded. "I do know who you are talking about. But please, get to the point."

"Don't rush me, Theresa. So anyway, I decided to walk to the gas station at the corner of Tibet Avenue and Abercorn after I realized I had no such snacks in my kitchen. Well, to make a long story short, I met a man there at the gas station. He had a hot pizza in his car that he just picked up and I went home with him. Everything went great until his wife came home around 5 a.m. yelling as if she could not see two people who are trying to sleep. And then, I found myself ejected out of the back door rudely. Seriously, the nerve of that woman, considering I was an invited guest to her house. Anyway, I made my way down some dark back alley till I came to a small street by a cemetery, located across the street from a park with a playground. By the way, I just realized that I had my cell phone on me about 10 minutes ago when I called you." Abigail then picked up her tumbler and took another healthy gulp.

Theresa had been listening with a disapproving smile. "So, what exactly have you been doing these last few hours since you were turned out into the streets?" Theresa rubbed her temples.

"Well, I walked into the park and went to sleep on a bench for about an hour or so. I was still tired and hungover. I know I slept there for well over an hour until some nosey jogger woke me up, asking if I was dead, as if that was any of his business. The sun was up and since I was fully awake, I tried to figure out what part of town I was in. Once I figured I was in the downtown area, I decided to walk in the general direction of your house."

While Abigail was talking, Theresa was pouring generous amounts of hand sanitizer on her hands and her forearms from a small bottle she had retrieved from her purse. "Well, you should be proud of yourself, Abby. All of that walking and running around should make you feel like some sort of famous pedestrian. Now come along with me," Theresa said as she helped Abby up with her wet hands. "I am going to take you home. But not until after we wash off all of this skankiness, grime, and shame that you have accumulated."

"What is this *shame* you speak of?"

"Oh, it's something that I do not have enough soap in the entire house for anyway. And leave those socks on the doormat, please."

A half an hour later, the two were in Theresa's bedroom conversing. Abby was sitting on Theresa's bed in a borrowed robe. Theresa came into the bedroom from the basement.

"Here you go, Abby; I think these house shoes should fit your feet just nicely. Plus, they're lined with fleece. They are brand new, by the way. I just forgot what box I had them in down there." She handed the house shoes to Abigail.

Abigail held the shoes up with a smirk on her face before turning towards Theresa.

"So, why do you have shoes shaped like bear paws? I didn't know you were into wildlife like that, Theresa. I always figured that you were too prissy for animals."

"What are you talking about? I love animals, just preferably at a distance. Besides, I got them at a discount when I was ordering online a few months back. They were on a closeout sale for $3 or so, and I needed to reach my $50 limit to get free shipping. Furthermore, I never order enough to warrant paying the yearly club fees to get *free* shipping." This was said as she made the gesture of quotation marks with her fingers.

"Oh, I know exactly what you mean. Paying a subscription for free shipping negates the point of free shipping." Abigail inserted her feet into the house shoes. "But anyway, these are really comfortable."

"Your clothes should be dry in a little bit. I also threw your socks away. There was no point in washing them. The soles look like a pair of used brake pads. I got a new pair for you in my dresser."

"That's fine. I have plenty of socks at home. Besides, this fleece feels really good on my bare feet."

Theresa sat down on the bed next to Abigail. "So, how do you feel now that you have freshened up? Do you still have your hangover?"

"Actually, I lost my hangover when I got chased by those crazy dogs. That type of nonsense will clear your mind and body pretty quickly. And, by the way, I remember now. I didn't wear any shoes last night because I couldn't find them." Abigail rubbed her stomach. "But I am really hungry, though, and your house lacks the smell of food. Nope, nothing tasty at all in the air besides that faint masculine scent when we walked into the house."

"What do you mean, Abigail?"

"Why are you acting like that? You know you didn't cook anything this morning, and breakfast is a serious matter. Especially when one is starving like myself; it affects my emotions, and I am getting very emotional." Abigail pouted for Theresa's benefit.

"No, I was referring to the manly scent that you detected." Theresa stopped talking abruptly. She looked toward her room's open door before resuming her dialogue. "But no, that is not important right now. Your clothes should be dry and toasty for you. Come along, you can get dressed, and I'll start on your pancakes."

Abigail jumped to her feet with her hands over her head. "Hell yeah, pancakes!" She was out the door before Theresa had even stood up from the bed.

Theresa sat there musing as she heard Abigail thunder down the stairs. *That ghost Archibald is skulking around.* Theresa sighed, got off the bed, and made her way to the kitchen to cook breakfast.

Soon, the two were eating breakfast at Theresa's table, discussing miscellaneous topics. Abigail did the majority of the talking, despite doing most of the eating too. She explained to Theresa the merits of using milk rather than water during baking when she stopped this discourse abruptly. She had finally noticed that Theresa had stopped eating after a few bites and that she had drifted off into her own thoughts, staring off into the distance.

"You're not even paying any attention to me," Abigail said. "It's all over your face, too, so don't deny it. I'm not even sure what you're doing. Your arm has been on the table for the last five minutes, and I can tell from the movement in your shoulder that you're doing something under the table. And if you're doing what I think you're doing, I am not going to tell you to stop because this is your house." Abigail pointed her fork at Theresa, before taking a huge bite. "But I am not leaving this table until I finish eating my pancakes. These are good pancakes, by the way. I love how buttery and crispy these edges are. You are a damn good cook, Theresa."

Theresa only glared at Abigail for a moment before retrieving her right arm from under the table. She laid the stone on the center of the table for Abigail to see. Abigail picked up the stone to observe it better, holding it up to the hanging Tiffany pendant light over the table.

"What are you doing with a piece of porphyry? Are you thinking about getting some tile like this?"

"What did you call it again?" Theresa asked.

"This stone is called *porphyry*, which is derived from Greek or Latin. It basically means "purple," I think. But this particular variety is known as *Imperial Porphyry* and is only found in Egypt. It was a favorite royal building material of the Romans, the Byzantines, the Papacy, and yada yada. Just the other day, I came across a 1" x 1" x 1/2" cut tile of Imperial Porphyry that was for sale at an auction. The starting price was $160. That's why I'm asking if you are getting tile like this."

Theresa stared at Abigail.

"You seem surprised that I knew that. I know some stuff too, though it is not usually useful for my own benefit. Besides, my brother had a rock tumbler that came with a membership to get different stones every week to tumble. That stone was one of them that came in the packet. Though, it probably was about a quarter of the size of this one here. And it didn't have these quartz crystals in it." Abigail handed the stone back to Theresa, who looked at it thoughtfully as she spoke.

"To answer your question, I found this stone in my dryer this morning. I believe it was in my shirt pocket, but I am not at all sure how it came into my possession."

Abigail reached across the table. "I am taking your plate. You weren't hungry at all."

After cleaning the plates off, Abigail began washing them while Theresa was still looking at the stone, holding it up to the light.

"It's not that serious, Theresa. Maybe you found that stone somewhere in this old house and forgot about it. Oh, you know what? I found something that belongs to you."

Theresa turned towards Abigail, who was drying her hands off on a terry cloth towel.

"Like what?"

"Like this really cool-looking coin, I found it in your room." She advanced towards Theresa, placing the coin in the palm of her hand.

Theresa looked curiously at the coin. "Where did you find this coin?"

"It was on the floor near the leg of the table, near the window. I noticed it as I was waiting for you, sitting on the side of your bed. I picked it up, but I soon realized that it was a real coin and not a tinfoil wrapper concealing delicious milk chocolate, so I put it in your robe pocket. I forgot to tell you about it when you came into the room. My attention is easily sidetracked at times, especially when I am hungry. But I did remember to put it into the pocket of my track shorts while changing in your basement. Do you think it is some sort of token?"

"Unless someone made tokens out of gold, I should think not. Now, this is something I cannot explain at all."

"I don't see how you have these interesting items in your possession and can't explain them. And there is that scent again," Abigail said, as she turned around, following the aroma.

Theresa placed the coin and the stone in her pocket. She scanned the kitchen but saw nothing out of the ordinary.

Abigail leaned towards Theresa. "You have a man in the house, and you didn't want to tell me? Look at you, being all sneaky," she chuckled.

"Ok, it is time for you to leave the house, Abby. It's almost noon, and we need to hit the stores before it gets busy." Theresa got up from the table and grabbed Abigail by the arm. They hurried out of the house.

Before Abigail knew it, she was outside on the sidewalk as the front door slammed shut. She looked around for Theresa, but saw no one anywhere on the sidewalk, until Theresa called her name from the open window of the passenger side of her car.

Theresa hastily leaned over the passenger seat, opening the car door for Abigail. She saw the specter standing on the porch of the house, gazing at her with a surly expression. Without hesitating, she yanked her dawdling friend into the car and sped away.

CHAPTER 6

Theresa was sleeping soundly at her office desk when she was jarred out of her rest. "Goodness gracious, aren't you one sales engineer dedicated to your job?" she heard a voice say, gazing up at the cleaning trolley that was rolled into the side of the desk—and then, at the culprit—with her tired eyes. "What a surprise to see you here," continued the gold-toothed cleaning lady standing at her office door with a large grin.

"The real surprise is the fact that you're still alive, old Margaret."

"Yeah, I'm still alive and very spry. But bless your heart for trying me with the sass talk. Now mop that drool off your forearm and cheek." Margaret said as she tossed Theresa one of the folded terry cloth towels from her supplies.

Theresa turned her head to give herself some privacy. After Theresa finished wiping her face, she yawned and stretched out her arms. "What time is it, Mrs. Margaret?"

"Why I reckon it's almost 5:30 a.m. Saturday morning, Theresa. Don't tell me you've been working to the point that you had to spend the night here?"

The old woman rested her arms on her cleaning trolley as she scrutinized Theresa. "You're even in your pajamas and not in the natty clothes that you usually wear. I understand working late and falling asleep. As well as falling asleep at work, period. But this here is something new under the sun. You *actually* put on pajamas at work! If I didn't know any better, I would swear you were camping out here. And probably with enough frequency to be bold enough to change into bed clothes." The old woman laughed.

Theresa looked down at her desk. She rubbed the back of the neck, and tried to gather her thoughts to justify her awkward situation.

"Well, you see, I wanted to get caught up on some work." Theresa stood up. "There is a personal project I've occasionally dabbled in for some time now, so I needed the use of these ballistic charts to verify my equations."

Theresa began collecting the scattered books and charts into a neat stack on the left side of her desk. She rolled up technical drawings into a brown portfolio and placed them into the desk drawer. An engineer's scale, a pair of compasses, a French curve, and a set of technical pens also went into this drawer. Then, it was closed and locked. Theresa made sure that it was locked by pulling on the handle to check its security.

"I'm actually surprised you are here, Mrs. Margaret. I was under the impression that you had retired . . . or something more permanent."

The old lady smiled at Theresa as she sat down in a nearby chair. "And whatever gave you that notion, dear?"

"For starters, just the small fact that you haven't emptied my trashcan, dusted, or vacuumed in here in a very long time. And even when you did clean my office in the past, it was sporadic."

Margaret turned her head about, surveying Theresa's office. "This office looks very clean to me."

"I know because *I* am the one who cleans it."

"Are you having a hissy fit, Theresa? It is not like your office wasn't being cleaned at all."

Theresa folded her arms and rolled her eyes, but Margaret paid no attention to this.

"I'm retired already, and I have been so for many years now from Brewster-Jennings & Associates. Which explains my faithful inconsistency in cleaning these offices as I really don't care. This is just an odd job that I occasionally do to occupy my spare time with cleaning up after you grown folks. It's nothing more than a little extra cash for my gambling funds and free office supplies. But I did go on an extended stay with my sister in Warner Robins. Not that it made any difference here." Margaret laughed as Theresa wondered how the old woman still had a job. "So Theresa, what is the real deal with you being here tonight?"

"It is just as I told you previously, Mrs. Margaret."

"You're only speaking half of the truth. And half of the truth is a lie by omission. You are intentionally spending the night," Margaret said, pointing to Theresa's pajamas. "The purple gym bag sitting over there in the corner most likely has your clothes and toiletries in it. It's basically your overnight bag, but you are using it at work. This is odd because I heard you have that nice townhouse in the historic district." Margaret promptly took some gum out of her cardigan pocket and placed it in her mouth. "This situation is very strange indeed, and I like mysteries. Hmm, let's see here. You have a home, and yet you chose to be here. You do not strike me as the type of person to be out in the street at all hours; you seem too reserved. Plus, you seem to be an *extra single* woman."

Theresa's eyebrows rose. "Now, wait a minute, Margaret. Now what exactly do you mean by 'extra single?'"

"Well, I meant no offense. It is just the fact that you seem very goal-oriented, and that dedication naturally sets you out of the social realm of many people. Besides, you've never brought your significant other out to any company social functions or the Christmas parties. That is, if you do show up at all. But I digress. Furthermore, most people have some sort of mementos as a testament to their particular interest in another person. It is the same with people who have children; it is not something that is kept secret. And you have neither, not even a rub pet."

"And what exactly is a 'rub pet,' Margaret?"

"It is an animal that you can actually rub, of course. Anyway, Theresa, there's no need to remonstrate. Now let's have it all out. Why you are really here?"

After a few more half-hearted attempts at evasion, Theresa eventually told Margaret the reason why she had been spending nights at work for the past two weeks, since Abigail had visited. Margaret stared with earnest eyes as she listened to Theresa's recount of the events.

Once Theresa concluded her story, Margaret sat there for a few moments with her head down, muttering something to herself that Theresa assumed to be a prayer. She then reached down the side of her cleaning trolley and pulled out a brown purse. Margaret reached inside and withdrew a small white business card. Then, she began to write something on the back of it that piqued Theresa's curiosity.

"I suppose you probably think I have completely lost my mind. What is the name of the psychiatrist?" Theresa asked.

Margaret ceased writing and returned her pen to her purse. "Seriously now, Theresa? If I even remotely suspected that you were out of your wits, I wouldn't even be in this room with you any longer. Locked in my car is where I would be reporting you and your whereabouts to the proper authorities. What I just wrote down is someone I think might help your situation in getting that *hant* out of your house. He is quite well versed with the supernatural issues you are dealing with, and calling on his service is a cheaper alternative than moving."

Margaret leaned over and slid the business card across the desk. Theresa picked it up, unintentionally viewing the printed side first. It was the name of a local eyewear merchant located on Stephenson and Abercorn St. She quickly flipped the card over and saw what Margaret had written.

LOGAN

Ask for Wingfoot Botanical Supply
Yemassee, South Carolina

"And where exactly is this place in Yemassee?" Theresa asked.

"It is in Downtown Yemassee, or rather what passes for Downtown Yemassee, which really is nothing more than a railroad junction. There are a few sparse businesses located on either side of the road. You can't miss it because there is nothing to miss, really. It is a brick two-story building with a painted white façade in that classic turn of the 20th-century small-town design." The old woman hesitated and looked thoughtful. "Now that I think about it, the building sits catty-cornered from the train station. There is a vacant lot next to it, and on the other side of the building, near the second story is a barely legible advertisement for Cheerwine. But, there is no signage on the building signifying what it is, that's why when you knock on the door you must ask for 'Wingfoot Botanical Supply.'"

"What does this Logan look like?"

"Logan is a man of Muskogean descent with dark hair and eyes. He's probably about six feet tall, athletic, and an avid marathon runner, in fact"—she looked at her watch— "he should be on his morning run through the forest paths and down country roads as we speak."

"Well, how much will he charge me for his services? Is it one flat rate or by the hour?"

Margaret stood up, supporting herself with the handle of her cleaning trolley and turned it around towards Theresa's office door. She placed her handbag on the lower tier before turning around to Theresa saying, "That is something for you to find out for yourself. In any case, I am going on a cruise leaving from Tampa to the Western Caribbean today. I am really looking forward to seeing Mahogany Bay. You, on the other hand, need to skedaddle over yonder to Yemassee this morning to take care of your business. You have worked too hard for your own place to be sleeping *at* work. C'mon, get your gear together and let's get out of this place."

"But you didn't even clean my office," Theresa said.

"Theresa, your office is already clean. We had this discussion earlier, did we not? Besides, I am only here to mall-walk and collect some office supplies. Quit your whining. You have a *hant* in your house, but you're worried about getting your office cleaned. I swear, you youngins these days."

Margaret had just pushed her cleaning trolley out of the office door when she stopped and turned with a light blue spray bottle in her hand. "Step aside, Theresa. Now, you cannot say I did not do anything." She misted the office with air freshener. "There. Your office smells better already."

The two made their way out of the building after Theresa made a stop at the restroom to freshen up.

They parted ways in the parking lot after she thanked her. Theresa sat in her car watching Margaret's sedan pull out of the driveway in a silver streak as the orange glow of the morning sun began to show itself.

That lazy old woman sure has one hell of a lead foot. I could totally see her getting to Tampa in under four hours. Well, Yemassee is not that far away, so I should be back before noon, she thought to herself as she sat in her idling car. *I think I'll go by Abby's house this morning and drag her along with me. She could use a good airing out, considering what she does or doesn't do all week. I'll tell her that I am going to pick up some herbal tea or vitamins. Plus, if anything bad happens, I won't be alone.*

CHAPTER 7

It was a quarter to nine when the two friends arrived in downtown Yemassee. Abigail, who had been awake when Theresa arrived at her house, had willfully consented to go with her. There was a small caveat; her presence was predicated on the condition that they stop at some point along the journey so she could obtain fireworks for her own amusement. It wasn't long before Abigail eagerly acquired these items during a fuel stop in Hardeeville. While Theresa was getting gas at the filling station, Abigail sauntered off. Before Theresa had even finished screwing the gas cap back on, Abigail had already returned from the adjacent building with a large brown paper bag laden with an array of fireworks. From there, they took the on-ramp to I-95 and arrived at their destination 25 minutes later.

Having arrived, Theresa recognized the building from Margaret's description. Theresa rolled through the town's sleepy streets and parked parallel next to the building. Theresa then turned her attention to her friend, who was still preoccupied with the contents of her purchase. "Well, Abby, we are here, but apparently no one else is. This whole place is completely empty."

Abigail looked at Theresa, and then out the window to the storefront before returning her attention to the inside of her bag.

"You had your face in that bag the whole time. Why do you need so many fireworks anyway?"

Abigail clutched her bag with a degree of seriousness. "So the fun will last a lot longer, duh. What's the point of going to South Carolina and only picking up a handful of fireworks? Never mind, don't answer that. Hey, do you have a lighter or matches?"

"No, I don't."

"I wasn't asking you, Theresa; I was asking that guy standing at your window."

Theresa turned around, and sure enough, there was a young man standing there with a pleasant look on his face. Theresa locked her car door and rolled her window down slightly.

"Morning there, strangers. I didn't mean to alarm you, but you are parked in a handicap zone. Could you just move up one space, if you would please?"

"Oh, sure. I'm sorry. I wasn't paying attention," Theresa said.

"The only person who was alarmed was Theresa. And she is startled by everything," Abigail said.

Before Theresa could even put the car in gear, the young man, who was just standing on the driver's side, was already standing at Abigail's window. Gazing down at her, he had a cheerful look on his face. "Oh, by the way, I almost forgot, stranger, here is that lighter you asked for." The young man smiled, but put a lot of emphasis on "stranger" as he held his arm outstretched.

Once Abigail had the lighter in her hand, she turned and addressed Theresa, while she pointed at the guy. "This little dude here, this snide apple-knocker, apparently got jokes. And why are you still standing there looking all sketchy in those snug sweaty shorts and shirt?"

His smile subsided a bit, and he was about to reply, but Abigail cut him off before he could even get a word out edgewise.

"What did you do this morning to be so sweaty? Did you just finish up a marathon of jumping jacks in the hopes that your testicles would finally drop?" She then reached out of her window and felt about his arms and chest. "You're softer than the toilet paper I wipe my ass with."

"Abby, what is wrong with you? There's no need to get all ugly with him," Theresa said.

"Ugly? Far from it. I'm just letting this little boy know that I'm a lot better at being saucy than he is."

"All right then, and here is where I stop listening so I can avoid catching the dumb," Theresa said, sighing as the young man laughed.

"I don't mind Abby's antics at all, as I honestly find her to be quite interesting. And that is a plus, considering that she is attractive. Especially when she is all riled up," said the young man standing on the sidewalk.

Abigail blushed, then tried to hide the fact by turning her head towards Theresa.

Theresa, on the other hand, paid no heed to her friend. Instead, she got out of the car and walked to the sidewalk where the young man was standing.

She noticed his high cheekbones and his fine black hair in a single ponytail. Suddenly, she needed to ask, "Are you Logan?"

He looked at Theresa with questioning eyes as he tilted his head slightly to the side. "Yes, I *am* Logan, and who might you be?"

"Good morning. My name is Theresa. This is my friend, Abigail. We actually traveled from Savannah to see you. Well, actually, *I* traveled from Savannah to see you. Abby just rode along to get some fireworks."

"Well, nevertheless, I am here with you, aren't I?" Abigail asked.

Logan smiled at Abigail. "Abby, don't just sit there," he said. "Get out of the car. It's hard for me to size you up if you're sitting down with a bag in your lap."

Abigail set the bag down on the floorboard and got out of the car.

"Goddammit," said Logan. He snapped his fingers in disappointment.

"What's the matter?" Both Theresa and Abigail asked in unison.

"I just realized that you're here for my father, Logan the Elder, and not me, Logan the Younger."

"But, I'm not," Abigail said, and the side of Logan's lips began to curl upwards as he glanced at Abigail.

He looked at the two women as his cheerful expression began to fade. He held his head down slightly. Then, he spoke in a sullen voice to Theresa. "I hate to tell you this, Theresa, but I just realized that you came all this way to see my father, and my father is long gone."

"I'm very sorry for your loss, Logan," said Theresa, and Abigail followed with a similar sentiment.

Logan turned towards Abigail, reaching out both of his arms, gesturing with his fingers for her to embrace him. And completely moved by his pouting face, she promptly complied with his sad request. Theresa did her part in consoling Logan by rubbing her hand across his shoulders and upper back. After some moments of silence, as he was resting his head against Abigail's shoulder, still holding her firmly, Theresa asked Logan a question.

"When did it happen, Logan?"

"He left about two weeks ago on a Sunday afternoon. I was about to blaze up—some smudging—when my father called me to his side. He had been resting all day, lying under a quilt that my nana made. He coughed and told me to make him some tea of sarsaparilla. But when I returned to his side with the drink, he told me that he was leaving. That he was going on a spiritual journey with stops at Carowinds, Callaway Gardens, and other interesting vacation destinations along the way. He just went to the Gathering of Nations Pow Wow this past April and did not take me along on that trip either. But, you are probably wondering when he'll be back, and that is some time during the middle of next month. It's on the calendar inside if you want me to check?"

Theresa looked at Logan with a blank stare before bringing the palm of her hand swiftly across the back of his head. Logan quickly let go of his extended embrace of Abigail to rub the back of his head.

Abigail burst into laughter. "And that's what you get for messing with people, you dork. You're lucky you were still holding me, or you probably would have gotten kicked in your nickel sack."

By the end of Abigail's statement, Theresa was already opening her driver's side door. "Come on, Abby, we wasted enough time in Yemassee with this county character."

"Wait, please, Theresa. I apologize for the misunderstanding. Besides, you haven't even been in the botanical shop yet, and I know you don't want to go home empty-handed. I made a pitcher of lemonade this morning before my night run and sweetened it with the right amount of diabetus."

Abigail, who was now back in her seat, turned to her friend. "Theresa, let's go in the store. You came all this way to get vitamins or that special medicine you wanted. Did that rash come back?"

"Abby, stop, please," Theresa said in a hushed voice.

"Well, whatever, I am getting out, and you're coming along too. Logan, hold my bag since you like holding onto things." Abigail handed her bag of fireworks to him, and the three of them went inside the store.

Inside, the white curtains in the bay windows obscured the public's view. As Theresa walked into one of the double glass doors, she noticed that in the bay windows was a large quantity of beautifully polished flint arrowheads.

Abigail did not stay long in the store after she had her lemonade. She had learned from Logan that she could set off her fireworks in a clearing in the woods a few yards from the building on an old railroad embankment. Logan showed her the way, carrying her bag and a gallon of water in the event of a fire. This departure of her friend gave Theresa an unexpected opportunity of privacy to explain to Logan the peculiarities of her situation when he returned.

During the consultation, Logan was very attentive to Theresa's situation. He wrote down certain details in his notepad. When she finished relaying the events to him, he walked over to a bookshelf and made inquiries consulting several large, old leather-bound books. He was completely studious the whole time, despite the whirling and crackling of assorted small pyrotechnic explosions. This was followed by the occasional deep thud launch of mortars and subsequent explosions, which shook the windowpanes.

He then put some incense he had made from a variety of herbs grounded with a mortar and pestle into an oyster shell and carefully ignited it with his lighter. He made several passes around Theresa while reciting a chant under his breath and then concluded the ritual. Theresa was very impressed with Logan's knowledge on the matter, even though much of it went over her head. The counsel he gave put her at ease and made her feel quite confident in addressing the situation.

Theresa arrived in Savannah shortly before 12 o'clock with a small paper bag that contained two obsidian arrowheads, in addition to a jar of botanical hair cream made with coconut oil, tea tree oil, and shea butter. These small purchases were the least she could do considering Logan's generosity in charging her nothing for her visit, which in hindsight, most likely had more to do with Abigail staying up there with him to go sightseeing.

When Theresa got back home, the place was the same as she had left it. She went to the kitchen and set down a few groceries she had picked up at the quick-stop market on the granite countertop. She headed upstairs to shower and change her clothes. After finishing her shower, Theresa sat on the edge of the bed, thinking about what Logan had told her as she applied moisturizer to her face.

Logan had told her that the ghost did not seem to be a major concern, besides, of course, the basic inconvenience of having a ghost in the house. And Logan said it appeared that her ghost could be reasoned with since he did try to reach out to her with terms. Logan instructed her that she should host a dinner as a gesture of goodwill to hopefully discuss an amicable agreement. Logan's confidence in the matter gave Theresa confidence. Logan also told her that he would call the next day before noon to check on her progress. In addition, he'd relay any new information from his studies.

She walked down the hall to a sparsely decorated bedroom, which also served occasionally as an office. Theresa sat down at the desk. She opened a drawer, and pulled out a small black velvet box and opened it. From this box, she retrieved a glass jar of ink and a silver fountain pen. She placed them on the top of the desk. She then practiced what she wished to write.

After a few minutes of this, Theresa opened another drawer and retrieved a floral printed folder that had a selection of fine writing paper. She perused the contents of the folder for a few moments before finally settling on a single sheet of cream-colored semi-translucent vellum. She folded the sheet of paper into two even halves prior to running the flat side of a ruler along the crease to give it firm definition. She took her scissors from her pen holder after she had made some faint lines in the paper with a drafting pencil and began cutting carefully along them. When she had finished, she had created a perfect 5-by-6-inch notecard.

At this point, she wrote on the front cover as well as in the inside. Then, she stood the notecard on its side, slightly open, so the ink could dry without smearing. While the ink was drying, Theresa had taken out a silver glittery gel pen and was scribbling a large blotch of ink on a piece of scrap paper the size of a quarter. She then rubbed the piece of scrap paper with the blotch all over the note card, transferring some of the reflective material onto the card. This gave the notecard a faint, but noticeable shimmer in the light depending upon how you held it. This effect was made even more pronounced by the card's semitranslucent design.

On her way downstairs, Theresa stopped by her room to add a bit of elegance to her notecard, christening it with a hint of jasmine blossom–scented perfume. She put the card down on the foyer table. Theresa smiled at the success of her effort. She picked up the gleaming card again, reading the beautiful copperplate calligraphy in the light of the sun coming in through the textured glass that bordered the front door.

To Mr. Archibald Mallard Turner,

I graciously invite you to join me here this evening for dinner at 7 p.m.

Theresa returned the card to the table before venturing into her kitchen where she made preparations for her dinner guest. After spending almost an hour in the kitchen cooking the meal for later that evening, she walked into the dining room to set her table.

She headed upstairs to her bedroom to find something suitable to wear for the evening. Laying a large black garment bag from the back of her closet onto the bed, she unzipped it, revealing a beautiful light-champagne gown. It was the dress that she had won at a Charleston fashion show raffle two years previously. Made of chiffon, it featured a plunging neckline, a flowing silhouette, natural waist, crochet lace detailing, and bishop sleeves. Theresa had never worn this dress before because she never had an opportunity to justify wearing something so elegant. The dress was imported from Ravenna, Italy and crafted out of fine Italian chiffon. It even had *Fatto in Italia* attached to the inseam.

In front of the mirror, Theresa held the dress against her body. After she had finished amusing herself, she picked out a pair of strappy stilettos and simple tear-drop moonstone earrings to complement the dress. Theresa laid all of these items aside and sat down on her bed. With every preparation out of the way, she set her alarm and slipped under her blankets for a much-deserved nap.

CHAPTER 8

Theresa was pacing back and forth in her dining room at her end of the long rectangle table. *It's almost 10 minutes after 7 and I did all of this work. Where is he?* she wondered. "I know that I am not crazy and I have plenty of proof to verify the opposite," she said aloud to counter any self-doubt. And as she was just about to sit down at her chair near the dining room entrance—the chair slid under her, moving on its own accord, bringing Theresa to within a few inches of the table's edge. A shiver ran down her spine as her heart pounded against the walls of her chest. Theresa tensed up, clenching the sides of her seat cushion with her head tucked between her shoulders in a hunched posture with her eyes sealed shut. It was the only thing she could do to keep herself from fleeing out of the house. She slowly opened her eyelids to a surprisingly cheerful voice that drifted from across the other side of the table.

"How wonderful this is; not only am I invited to a lovely dinner, but I am immediately entertained with a game of charades by the hostess who is in rare form tonight," the specter said as his white-gloved hand stroked his chin. He looked at Theresa with a grin. "Well, let's see what you are getting at over there," he said, staring at Theresa and studying how she was sitting.

Theresa only stared back at him in complete silence, still frozen in the same hunched-over position except now her eyes were open. After musing on Theresa for a short spell, Archibald then snapped his fingers at her in satisfaction. "By Jove, I've got it!" he exclaimed, pointing at Theresa. "You are one of those quaint city park lunatics that stare at people who walk by."

Theresa straightened, and her eyes narrowed.

Archibald gave this action no credence and continued to speak. "You must know I am surprised that you actually invited me here to dine with you, given our last encounter. But here I am, albeit a few minutes late. I actually got home later than I anticipated due to unforeseen circumstances. So, I did not notice your lovely invitation until shortly after seven when I passed into the vestibule. But nevertheless, I apologize for my slight tardiness." He rubbed his hands together. "Now what is for dinner? The aroma seeping from under those lids is absolutely delightful."

Theresa stood up, pointing to the display of food at the center of the table and responded in a whisper. "I prepared broiled pork fillets cooked in apple butter and covered with razor-thin slices of almonds. In this covered serving tray, there is steamed saffron rice. Over here to the left of you are sweet rolls. This is a peach and granny smith apple cobbler sitting on this folding snack table to my right. And the wine bottle"—she threw her hands animatedly toward the bottle packed in crushed ice— "is Beaujolais Nouveau. Oh, and the silver pitcher next to it is just iced water."

Archibald beamed. "Well, Theresa, dinner sounds and smells scrumptious. May we begin eating, or is this display just like you—for looks, rather than for consumption?"

"Of course, *I* can eat," Theresa said slowly, as she looked at Archibald. "But how can *you* eat if you are a ghost?"

"I will eat if I desire to do so, though it is not necessary for my existence. And as of right now, I desire to indulge myself in some of this delicious dinner that you've invited *me* to enjoy." Archibald picked up his fork and pointed to his empty plate, indicating that she should put food on it.

Theresa gave him a sharp look, but nevertheless, she filled his plate with what he desired. After Theresa finished half of the wine in her glass, she felt more relaxed in the ghost's company. And this was accentuated by Archibald's compliments on her culinary skills.

"Theresa, this meal was absolutely divine. The wine was a perfect touch to the combined flavor of sweet and salty, an excellent selection for the meal too. You have surprised me very much."

"Why, thank you, Archie! I am not a wine expert, but the man at the market recommended it. I wasn't sure

if you liked wine or wanted some tea, considering—"
She let her voice linger there. She'd thought that maybe,
being an Englishman, he'd appreciate tea instead.

Archibald laughed. "I'm a faithful consumer of
adult beverages, my dear. If it doesn't have alcohol in
it already, I don't have any problem with adding some
to it. So really, it didn't matter what you served as a
beverage because I always could rectify it if I didn't like
it." He tapped his hand on a lower section of his jacket,
emitting a muffled metallic sound.

"Let me guess, you're carrying vodka." She raised the
wine glass to her lips pointing at his concealed flask
with her pinky finger.

"That is a very good guess, Theresa. It is the beloved
child of vodka: gin."

"What do you mean by that?"

"Gin is nothing more than vodka with juniper ber-
ries added during the distillation process."

Archibald stood up and walked over to the antique
mirror that was situated on the wall over a buffet, parallel to the dining room table. He stood and studied it.
Theresa eyed him from the table. He seemed so real in
her eyes as if he were actually alive.

"Theresa, come here, would you please?"

She finished off her wine glass and walked cautiously
to join him.

Archibald noticed how she stood in the reflection of
the mirror, and turned towards her. "It is quite obvious
that you do not drink often or at all for such a mild
wine to have such an effect on you after just one glass."

"I'm fine. I just don't normally drink wine. And I am not a lush. I just got up too fast without giving things time to settle." And she turned around back towards the dinner table, leaned over, and topped her glass off. While in this position, Theresa took a sip from her glass, spilling a small amount of wine on the white linen.

Archibald, who was watching her, added, "You are more of a lush than you know."

"Ah, we have a wonderful double entendre from Mr. Turner. Yeah, I bet you didn't think I would catch that." She turned towards him, wine glass in hand and right eyebrow raised.

"How can there be a bet when there is no wager, Theresa?"

Theresa rolled her eyes. "It was just a figure of speech, and you are clever enough to know that. You really like being contrary, don't you?"

Archibald shrugged his shoulders. "Not really," he said, returning his attention to the mirror. "Since I first encountered you, I have noticed that the quality and taste of the furnishings that you have been purchasing of late have improved tremendously. Also, I see you have developed an eye for antiques—all of this is also commendable—which brings me to this looking glass here in particular. Do you mind me asking where you acquired it and how much you paid for it?"

"I acquired this particular item from a small antique shop not far from Lafayette Square nestled away on a side street for just shy of $300. It is a little expensive for my taste, but I really liked it because it is so unique. The carved walnut frame is exceptional. It's a very well-made piece of Victorian craftsmanship." Theresa rubbed her fingers around the edge of her now empty wine glass. "And may I ask why you are so interested?"

"Just curious about how you came across this Flemish looking glass of the late baroque period. Even the glass is in remarkable shape, which is somewhat rare for a looking glass this old. And before you ask, *How do you know this?* I will tell you I have spent a great deal of time studying various subjects of aesthetics. I can even point out to you where the cleverly hidden artist's signature monogram, 'M' and 'A,' intermingles together with the year 1716. You may want to get an appraisal at some point as the value far exceeds what you paid for it."

"Now that is a very pleasant surprise. So you have been doing something useful with yourself! So tell me, can you give me a ballpark figure of its worth?" Theresa asked him as she touched the woodwork of the frame.

"Yes, Theresa, I could. But I have decided not to. If I told you, this piece of artistry may no longer be here for my viewing pleasure. And it has been so long since nice things have been in this place."

She placed her empty glass on the buffet table, then looked up at him. Her hand rose like it had a mind of its own. Her fingers spread, reaching out toward his face, until she caught herself, and walked away.

Theresa lay on the crushed velvet chaise lounge that was against the back wall of the dining room. She stacked the pillows up and then rested herself on her side. "I drank too much to calm my nerves this evening. So, I need to lie down."

"Dutch courage was wholly unnecessary, Theresa. In any case, I know you have something more to say other than polite conversation and basking in my boyish good looks. So let's have it all out. No one entreats another to such a fine repast out of the goodness of one's heart. There is always an ulterior motive underlining one's generosity, especially for a *meat person* to be bold enough to summon someone like myself to dine with them."

Theresa said nothing but watched him as he walked to the end of the table. He turned his chair around to face her in her reclined position and took out his silver cigarette case before he sat down.

"Would you like a Sobranie, Theresa?" he asked.

"You know that I don't smoke."

"You don't drink either, nevertheless, here you are sprawled out like some pickled Irishman on a park bench. I just figured I would ask in case you needed something else to go with your courage-in-a-bottle."

"I only drank because I'm the one talking to a ghost who's been mean to me and haunting me to the point that I can't even spend the night in my own house. You should be ashamed of yourself, harassing women." She shook her finger at him. "And don't give me that confused look. You know that you are a very mean-spirited spirit. And I didn't like your threats."

"Theresa, my dear, apparently you do not realize this, but threats are not supposed to be liked. After all, they are *threats*. But I did not threaten you directly. I only insinuated something ominous, and that is not the same thing. You see, with an insinuation, I leave it up to your own mind to do the psychological work. Now, if I made a direct threat, I would always have the inclination to follow up on it. You only got an innuendo, so you really have to stop living in the past. I mean really now, Theresa, that was weeks ago, and you're still griping about a general misunderstanding. You really need better hobbies to occupy your time. Now being the magnanimous being that I am, I long forgave you for your temerarious and petty behavior. Tonight is what you should be concerned with, my recumbent friend. I have paid you nothing but compliments, which you, as a spinster, should greatly appreciate. Life is far too short to be concerned with unfounded bitterness."

"Unfounded?" Theresa sat up quickly.

"Yes, unfounded, as in not based on facts."

"Bullshit, mister. You were in the house a few days back when I had my friend over. And don't you lie either because I smelled that cologne of yours in the air."

"Yes, I was, and what about it, Theresa? Are you really surprised that I would be home while you are here? I am here most of the time when you are. I just avoid you for your peace of mind since you can see me, and are unnecessarily excitable."

Theresa was quiet for a moment as she thought about it. "Okay, so why did you give me that salty look as I was leaving, like you were going to do something to me if I came back? Yeah, I think you were even pointing at the door too."

"Theresa, you left the door unlocked. Furthermore, it wasn't a salty look, just a look of surprise to see someone who is usually not neglectful. I only came to the door to see what was going on because I heard a commotion. You two were running out of the house. I stopped by the kitchen to see if there was a fire and then headed to the front door only to see you and your friend in the car. I was only pointing to get your attention to the door being unlocked. You should really be more careful, you know, as this city is full of guttersnipes." He returned the silver cigarette case to his breast pocket.

Theresa thought over what he said as he sat there amusing himself with his pocket watch, nonchalantly dangling the gold piece from its chain.

Dammit, I think he might actually be right, but I do not feel like conceding that to him. I'll just change the subject.

Theresa stretched her legs out, and using her feet, she knocked off her shoes. "So anyway, what exactly is a guttersnipe?"

"Guttersnipes are these bands of feral children that always roam the streets of Savannah, at all hours, regardless of the weather. But surprisingly enough on cue, if something unfortunately predictable were to happen to one of these unsupervised children, someone always steps up to claim ownership. At any rate, these miscreants are always looking for an opportunity to indulge themselves. And an unlocked door is just an open invitation for them to entertain themselves at another person's expense."

"Well, thank you for locking the door, Archibald. Though, I have a feeling that you wouldn't let anything happen to this house that you didn't want to happen. You seem to be too on point for that."

Archibald seemed amused by her. He turned his head and took another drag of his cigarette.

Theresa sat back up on the lounge. "I am hungry again. I think it's time for some cobbler."

"Oh, don't trouble yourself, dear. I will get that for you. After all, you have served me so graciously with your own hands this evening."

Theresa looked at him as he remained in his chair, continuing to smoke his cigarette in a methodical manner, filling the air with a faint and unusual aromatic scent.

I think this foolish wonder is having another go at me, Theresa thought to herself. She placed her hands on the edge of her seat about to get up when she noticed something about the table. Even though Archibald's body obstructed most of her view of the table, she could see a plate of some type move from one location to another. She saw nothing else because whatever was going on, the table was behind Archibald. She heard a ceramic lid removed and then replaced a moment later. A white satin serviette came fluttering across the room like a leaf in the breeze before resting in her lap. Before Theresa even raised her head, the fruit saucer was placed beside it.

Theresa looked up at Archibald, whose attention appeared to be elsewhere. He still held his cigarette out in his hand. She was amazed by the spectral activity, but curious about his silence as well.

"What are you thinking about?" she asked.

"My apologies, Theresa. I was just thinking that I may like you as a housemate, even if you are easily excitable. You have done small wonders with this old place, I must admit. Plus, you are easy on the eyes, front and back. But I am more fascinated about how you are able to see me without me willing it so."

Theresa squinted her eyes. "Thanks. I guess. But does this mean Abby can still come over?"

"Of course, she can. I have no issues with your now pleasantly plump friend. Abby, formally known as *Fat Abby*, has toned up very nicely since I first encountered her. Now, if I were her, I would have destroyed all the pictures that I had of myself that weren't headshots, so new people would think that my current situation is how I have always been."

"You are so freaking rude," she grumbled under her breath. "Anyway, she is on a softball team and rides with a mountain bike group on occasion. So the exercise she gets doesn't seem like exercise to her because she has other people with her to stay motivated." Theresa was about to get up and set her half-emptied fruit saucer on the table when Archibald personally took it from her hand. He was on her so fast that it startled her.

"I am not rude."

"Yes, you are, Archie, and you should have been raised with very good manners befitting a person of your social standing. Why you haven't even complimented me on my dress at all this evening? I know I look good, and you know it too."

"How one is raised and how one chooses to act are two different things. Just because I have not said anything about your wardrobe singularly does not mean I haven't taken note of it. The dress is beautiful indeed, but it is *you* wearing it that makes it spectacular.

"Wow, you really have a way with words when you want to be nice. Thank you very much, Archie."

"To be sure," he said.

There was an awkward silence that followed. Theresa looked at Archibald, but he paid her no mind as he was admiring his ungloved right hand.

Without looking up, he spoke. "Theresa, you are in friendly company, so if you have something to say, you might as well say it while you have the opportunity."

Theresa rested her chin in her left hand as she thought about a question. "Do you mind telling me a little about the history of this house? Like the people that lived here and your interactions with them, if any."

His eyes lit up. "Sure, I was expecting you to ask me one of those crying-for-the-moon questions worthy of those annoying parlour game boards with the alphabets and the numbers. But I shall tell you what you asked since it is a mere trifle of a question." He paused a moment, scratching behind his ear as if to ponder how he would begin.

"Before you moved into this house, this place was mostly vacant for about 7 years. It was inhabited by an elderly widow by the name of Mrs. Rosemary Rutledge, who resided here for 8 and 20 years until she crossed over." He got up and pushed his chair in before settling himself next to Theresa on the chaise lounge.

She stared as he reached in his dinner jacket for his flask. She wanted to hear more. "Well, go on, did she die in the house?"

"No, but she passed in an ignominious way, in some obscure nursing home in Port Wentworth. She was quite senile by then and had been advancing to that state for some time. Her faculties began to rapidly deteriorate during the last two years of her life, and she was confined to a nursing home the year before her passing."

"Did she know you were here and if so, did you also present her with a list of household demands like I had received?"

He sighed. "No matter how many millenniums pass, women will always exaggerate a situation to their benefit and detriment."

Theresa frowned.

"But to answer your question, Theresa, it is yes and no. And by that, I mean, she knew that she had an entity in the house by my actions. But she was unable to see me with the marked clarity that you do." He undid his flask top and poured off a shot that he quickly knocked back.

Theresa, eager to hear the rest of the story, gestured with her hand for him to carry on. "So what do you mean by actions, Archie?

"Such as, if she forgot to lock the door at night, I would lock it for her just like I did for you in your absentmindedness. Or if she left the stove on, I would turn it off, or if she fell asleep on a chilly night, I would cover her with a blanket. Minor affairs that became quite frequent with old age and while her mind decayed."

"Well, you surprise me certainly," she said with a smile. "That was a very sweet thing of you to do."

"I beg to differ, Theresa. Much to your dismay, I was only looking after my own interest, which is, primarily, this house. And that meant keeping the old woman healthy and alive as long as possible."

"I don't believe you, Archibald. Not even for one second."

"Well, that's the story I'm telling you. You can take it or leave it. It doesn't make any difference to me either way," he said as he raised his flask to his lips.

"That's a cute bluff, but I still don't believe you. You are not going to reside in a place that long without developing some type of affection for that person. Anyways, you said 'mostly vacant,' so what does that even mean? Were there squatters in the house at some point?"

"No, it wasn't that, just some college girls stayed here for three years. I believe they were members of a university soccer team. While Mrs. Rutledge was at the home for the aged and subsequently passed away, a man who was a friend of hers maintained the upkeep of the house. This gentleman had power of attorney over her property during her declining years. He was bequeathed this house in the will after her death, as she died without issue. And before Rosemary moved in here, there was a rustic half-witted gentleman from the bowels of Effingham named Lynwood Hall, who inhabited the place for two years in the early 1970s. He decided that he was going to be a DJ and called himself 'Disco Dollar' after burning his bridges at Union Bag plant."

"I take it that you did not like him," Theresa said, as she tried to read the expression on his face.

"To be sure, as he was a very obnoxious fellow and an asinine one at that. He was the type of person that wanted to be everyone but himself. He was an inadequate steward of this place, more concerned with blowing his savings on parties and turning the house into a stable. It got to the point that I decided to take an extreme measure to restore the tranquility."

Archibald then withdrew his pocket watch, opening the cover that protected the face before returning it to his vest pocket.

Meanwhile, Theresa wondered what he had meant. She moved further to the edge of the chaise lounge. "So, what did you mean by *extreme measure*, Archie?" Theresa asked, following up the statement with a nervous chuckle.

"What I meant was taking his obnoxious life from him. And if you haven't got the gist of that statement,

I mean to *kill* him." His statement ended in a loud thud as Theresa slid off of the lounge onto the wooden floor. She scurried across the floor, pushing herself along with her hands and feet into the corner of the dining room.

Archibald looked at her with a perplexed look on his face. "Theresa, I do not mind you making a fool out of yourself. But you should do that on your own time and not mine. I am not going to be here all night as I have other affairs to attend to."

"You killed a man for annoying you, and you expect me to sit next to you?"

"You really shouldn't be so judgmental, Theresa. It is very unbecoming. Besides, I did not kill him." He pointed to the spot where she had been sitting, and she returned to it cautiously with her eyes still glued upon him.

"Well, how was I supposed to know that you weren't a homicidal ghost?"

"If I were a homicidal ghost, this juncture would not exist, for I would have thrown you headlong over the banister long ago. You know, which would have made you one of those interesting, unexplained deaths the hoi polloi loves reading about. Yet, here we are." A faint smile appeared on his face. "But here is a novel idea, Theresa. You could have actually let me finish my story."

Theresa rolled her eyes. "Well, I do not appreciate those carping remarks about my relationship status. Especially coming from you, who are in the same boat as myself. Go ahead and tell the story, sir."

He looked at her with amusement before resuming. "So, in a nutshell, the opportunity never came for me to ease my sufferings. He took gravely ill with an especially virulent form of influenza. He went to the Old Candler Hospital a few blocks from here, and I followed him there, waiting for him to die."

"You actually waited for him to die in the hospital!"

"Calm yourself, Theresa. There is no need for you to throw another fit. If I already told you that I had plans for killing him, then waiting by his sick bed should not surprise you one bit. Besides, I wasn't going to harm an ill person. After all, that is unsportsmanlike behavior, as it would not allow one to feel any sensation of accomplishment. So, moving along, after spending a fortnight in the hospital, he was sent home to convalesce."

Theresa leaned toward him and said in a low voice, "I bet that pissed you off."

"On the contrary, he was in no position to resume his former activities, and that pleased me. He spent most of his time here, bedridden, as he was also dealing with a bout of pneumonia. Besides the frequent wheezing, which didn't bother me, the house was as quiet as a tomb."

"So, what happened then?"

"He got better and married someone well above his station—the nurse that was taking care of him on her home visits. They moved to the southern end of Florida, where they began their new life together. I actually liked her; she was a Degar woman who came here during your country's misadventure in Indochina. She had a ritual of going through every room in this house with fragrant incenses ritually reciting words in her native tongue. It was a prayer that connected the invisible world with this one."

Archibald stood up, looked at his pocket watch again, and turned towards Theresa. "I thank you for the wonderful meal this evening, but now it is time for me to retire. Goodnight to you." And then he vanished before Theresa could respond.

Yeah, goodnight to you too, you cocky, conceited ass. She sat there for a moment, looking at the spot where the ghost had been before lying back down.

"I am so tired." She yawned out loud, crossing her legs and muttering, "And I better not wake up molested."

CHAPTER 9

"Good morning, Theresa. Sorry to rouse you from your snoring slumber, but it is time for you to get up and head off to your profession. The alarm on your portable telephone upstairs was annoying me instead of yourself, hence the reason that I am here annoying you now. So ideally, you might desire to do something about that."

Theresa, who was half-awake with a blanket over her head, slowly pulled it down from her face. She placed her hand over her mouth and yawned into it as she turned her head towards the seat cushion. "I am not working. It's Sunday. And besides, I've taken the week off," she said in a sleepy voice before turning on her side with her back facing him.

"Oh, well that's wonderful because you probably would have been late anyway. Theresa, dear, are we sick?"

She quickly turned to face him and looked at him thoroughly. Her attention drifted to the left. The dress she wore the night before, lay neatly on the back of the chair. Her eyes shifted between Archibald and the dress before she lifted up the blanket and peered beneath it.

"In case you are wondering, it was I who placed the blanket over you. Furthermore, it was after you had already undressed yourself. And if it makes you feel any less awkward, the French knickers are a nice touch. Especially considering that you are somewhat of a prude."

She rolled her eyes at him. "Thank you kindly for covering me with a blanket."

"Not a problem at all. Considering that there was a chill in the air last night, perhaps you experienced one of those maladies of your sex, such as *hot flushes*?"

Theresa sat up on the lounge, holding the blanket against her chest. "Well, since you want to be funny about it, thank you for nothing." She stood up and was about to walk past him when she stopped abruptly. "And why in the hell are you wearing that Ebenezer nightgown?" She stared at his white nightgown and matching nightcap topped with a gold tassel.

"Theresa, you are a smart girl. It will come to you shortly as your brain starts to warm back up. Why would anyone wear nightclothes?"

Theresa circled around Archibald as she examined his clothing before she stopped directly in front of him. A large Cheshire grin spread across her face. "Now this is too rich, sir. Not only do you have your initials monogrammed on your nightgown, but you even sport them on your red velvet slippers sewn in gold thread, no less! Of course, I see it is only the best for you, m'lord." She curtsied and called him a *pretty boy* under her breath as she did so.

He tilted his head to the left slightly with a delighted expression. "You have very amusing caprices, Theresa. But it is almost time for me to start my day. I have reason to believe that I am to be commended at my social club as a deserving person. And I shan't be late for that, so good day to you."

The thought of him carousing with other ghosts made her shudder. In spite of that, Theresa reached out to grab his hand to prevent him from leaving, but her own hand passed through his. She pulled her arm back. Nevertheless, he noticed the action.

"Before you vanish off again," she said, "I just wanted to thank you for joining me for dinner last night." She noticed the table was cleared off. "And apparently, for cleaning off the table as well. I do not recall even hearing you do it."

"That is because you were sound asleep, and snoring like a big farm dog. But you are welcome, nonetheless. By the way, I had to move your boxed single person's meals to the bottom shelf to make room for the leftovers in your icebox. The dishes are in the sink awaiting your attention, whenever that may be."

"Oh, you couldn't wash them?" asked Theresa. She attempted to fold her arms in a serious manner but failed, trying to keep the blanket up.

"Heavens no, Theresa. That would be too much of servant's work. Seriously, it would be nice to have at least one servant back in the house. They can cook, clean, and be quite amusing at times." He snapped his fingers. "Why don't you hire a servant to clean up after yourself?"

Theresa walked past him, disregarding the question, and retrieved her dress from the back of the chair. She was at the other end of the table before she turned.

"Theresa, you obviously have something to say, so you might as well say it."

She sighed. "Look, if it is not too much to ask of you, I would appreciate it if you would enter a room that I am in like a normal person. You know, without those sudden manifestations that you seem to be so fond of. Oh, and speaking of fondness, you can really roll back on your male chauvinism. I understand that you're from a different time, and your mind is a little faulty. And just to be clear, I have nothing to offer in return, as this is not a tit-for-tat bargain. I ask this of you as a courtesy to me as you have the appearance of a gentleman. And even then, I use that word loosely."

Archibald rubbed his chin as he studied her. "Come now, Theresa, I do not believe that is all that you wanted to tell me."

"It doesn't matter. It is what I *told* you. Besides, I actually have things to do." And she walked out of the dining room without bothering to look back.

When she reached her bedroom, she carefully hung her dress back in a garment bag. She was placing it into the rear of her closet when her phone chimed, notifying her of a text message. She sat down on the edge of the bed when she realized that she had also missed multiple calls and text messages from Abigail. She read the last text message first, which said, *Theresa, if you are dead, press 1. If you are alive, press 2.*

Theresa replied with a 1 to her friend, and there was an almost instantaneous response that said, *Suicide?*

I can only imagine how her night went to be so animated this early, she thought. She began dialing Abigail, who picked up before the first ring even finished.

"Hey girl, it's about time you answered your phone! How are you doing and what have you been doing?" Abigail said in a chipper voice.

"I'm doing pretty good considering I might have been a little intoxicated last night on some French wine. You, on the other hand, seem to be in very good spirits. I take it that you enjoyed your time with young Logan?

"You better believe it, Theresa, which was a surprise considering he's an apple-knocker; he is quite entertaining and a bit of a mystic. And I'm still here out in the sticks. So, when did you start drinking?"

"I started yesterday evening to help calm my nerves."

"Cool beans, trying something new. I always said to myself that you would make one of those interesting functional alcoholics that conceals it very well."

"Well, thank you very much for making me aware of your fascinating expectations." Theresa's mind wandered back to the previous night's events. "Well, Abby, sometimes a change in your situation forces you to modify your activities. But enough about me, what did you get into?"

"After you left us, we went sightseeing down to the Old Sheldon Church ruins in the woods following the centuries-old *trail trees* paths to get there. The place was absolutely beautiful, surrounded by canopies of majestic live oaks draped in curtains of Spanish moss that shaded the antebellum tombs. It seemed like a nice quiet place that you would like to visit. We also took plenty of pictures and even had a picnic while we were out there. I can't wait to show you when I get back."

"That does sound very nice. When are you coming back?"

"Well, we are going fishing today, that's why I had spent the night. I'm probably going to come back home sometime before Wednesday. There is so much that Logan wants to show me here."

"I'm really happy for you, Abby, that you're having a good time. Especially considering the abrasive footing you began with him yesterday. But I forgot to tell you, don't rush into bed with him yet."

"Theresa, really now, I can't believe you just said that! I would expect something like that from my mom or most of my family, but not you."

"I don't know why, since I *know* you, Abby."

"Hmm, touché. But your advice is late. And it's not really my fault; it just kind of happened. Hmm, now how did it happen?"

Theresa laughed. "Abby, you really don't need to go into details. By the way, is Logan still asleep? I want to ask him a question about something he's supposed to be working on for me."

"Logan got up around two hours ago. He left the house after we warmed up to do some spiritual Indian stuff before the sun crested over the horizon. He should return shortly. Do you want me to tell him to call you, or are you going to call back?"

Theresa paused for a moment before responding, "No, it can wait. Besides, he was supposed to call me. I am just getting a little ahead of myself, and I shouldn't be."

"Are you going into work today, or are you there now?"

"No, and I took the week off. I had enough of the Byrks and their ceaseless meddling. It's really unnerving having to deal with such jackleg individuals who are all over you. It is really adding to my stress level. I need this time to unwind and recalibrate my focus."

"Well, I am glad you're finally using some of that vacation time you accrued, you workaholic. So what are you going to do with your time off?"

"Nothing much, just get caught up on some home projects that I want to do but keep putting off. I may paint some walls downstairs or move some furniture around. Whatever I feel like doing after I go through these home decor books I got from the library. But right now, I'm going down to the kitchen and fixing myself something to eat."

"Okay, Theresa. Have fun. I will talk to you later."

Theresa hung up and got dressed, ate breakfast, and then headed out of the house on a few errands that had her home a few hours later. One of those stops was to her office where she picked up some files. When she got back into the house, she set her files and book on the kitchen table, and turned her attention to the dishes in the sink. Once finished with that, she sat down at the kitchen table.

"Servants, my ass. He was going to say woman's work." She opened her book and began to read for a while. It was still early in the afternoon when she finally got up for a drink. When she closed the door of the refrigerator, she noticed Archibald standing in the main entrance of the kitchen with a casual air about him. He was wearing a cream-colored Panama suit with a matching Panama hat. Brown leather gloves paired with the brown leather shoes complemented his outfit. Both blended well with the maroon grosgrain bowtie.

Hmph, from his demeanor, I guess he wasn't lying about getting a commendation.

"Look at you standing there without a care in the world and doing nothing useful in it either," she said.

"And you are correct," Archibald responded as he approached the table. "Good afternoon, Theresa. May I sit down?"

"Do as you please, sir."

And Archibald did just that; he sat down and began talking to Theresa in such a pleasant way that she forgot any ill feelings towards him. In fact, she was very pleased that he was such a good listener and so very perceptive. At some point, the conversation turned to her week off from work. She told him some of the situations that were going on at her place of work to gauge his perspective on the matter.

"Theresa, you have high expectations of change from people who you know do not appreciate the meritorious conduct of the individual. People such as the Byrks cannot appreciate the hard work of others, for that is not how they rose to prominence. Their fortunes are based on chance and not strength of character. And because of this, they can only appreciate merits that they can pass off as their own. Anything else is just a reminder of how precarious their situation is."

"How do you know all this from what little I told you?"

"I have a tendency to pay more attention to that which is not said, rather than to what is. Reading between the lines, as it is called. But don't take my word for it; just observe their interactions among themselves and with others. Working there for as long as you have been there, the rampant nepotism, cronyism, and other assorted nonsense surely has taken a toll on you. But that is in the past. What is important is what you have learned from it. What are you going to do now?"

She was thinking about what she just heard. Theresa wondered whether he was trying to charm her by being attentive to what she had to say or if he was really sincere. *Maybe he's doing both. I think I will keep my guard up, just in case.*

"So what are you doing over there, work-related tasks on your week off? Tsk tsk tsk, apparently you don't know how to take time for yourself."

"I am taking time for myself. This is not work-related; this is a personal project I have been dabbling in off and on for a while."

"Well then, what is it?" Archibald leaned forward over the table to examine.

"It is personal!" said Theresa. "Besides, I don't even know you."

"You don't know me, but you know me well enough to get pickled-up in front of me, fall asleep, and then when I come back to check on you—being the wonderful magnanimous person that I am—you were naked on the couch with your derriere tooted up in the air. Not to mention, you had one hand hanging off with your fingers gripped around the neck of the bottle."

"Stop exaggerating, I wasn't naked!"

"Calm down, Theresa. There's no need to raise your voice. The neighbors may hear and will never look at you the same way again. Besides, I am the one telling the story from my sober first-person account. And if I decide to embellish a little bit for dramatic effect, well, that's really not my fault but rather yours."

"How in the hell is it my fault?"

"Simple. You give me substance to embellish."

Theresa stood up hastily and pointed her pencil at him. "I know exactly what you are doing, Archibald. You are trying to screw with my head, you ass. And you started off like you wanted to be nice."

Archibald, who seemed to be amused, only looked up at her.

Theresa then gathered up all her work from the kitchen table. She was about to leave when she paused right by Archibald. Then, she turned and whispered in his ear in a sweet sing-song voice, "I do not like you."

He turned around in his seat as she walked away. "Well, that's fine, Theresa. I guess I'll just go home then."

"You just do that." And she passed out of the kitchen. A moment later, Theresa's voice came thundering back to the kitchen from another part of the house. "Shut the hell up."

CHAPTER 10

As the days slowly progressed into weeks, Archibald and Theresa occasionally fell into the habit of spending a few evenings together. Saturday evenings, in particular, they spent watching movies or occasionally talking about various topics in the parlour of the house if she was up late when Archibald got home.

This old reception room was a spacious thirteen-foot wide by sixteen-foot-long room whose walls were recently painted in a flat Prussian blue above the semi-gloss white wainscoting. The nine-foot walls were topped off and complemented by white crown molding. There was a two-foot stripe of ceiling that followed the outline of the room before the ceiling recessed four inches further. This separation between elevations was marked by molding that was also painted in Prussian blue to contrast the white ceiling. In the front of this room, there were two large windows. White damask curtains with gold embroidered fleur-de-lys covered the windows. A white marble fireplace was centered to the left and engraved with a frieze that read, "A man should be upright, not kept upright."

Above the fireplace was a large flat-screen TV mounted to the wall. The fireplace was flanked by two corn plants, each four feet high, sitting in fire-glazed blue ceramic flowerpots. These were, in turn, flanked by padded teal and white Moroccan upholstery chairs. The hardwood floors were of oak and situated in a herringbone pattern, stained in a dark color that made them look almost black and yet still revealed the grain. A large white and grey Persian rug contrasted greatly with the floor. Upon this rug sat a big, handcrafted teak coffee table from Burma. A matching velvet blue couch and loveseat sat on the right side of the wall. The loveseat was bordered on the right by an end table crafted of driftwood by skillful hands.

On this night, in particular, Archibald was dressed in a red velvet smoking jacket with his initials embroidered in gold over the left breast pocket. The jacket was complemented with black satin slacks and styled Turkish slippers of a burgundy hue. Archie had several smoking jackets of various artistic motifs. He also had a seemingly endless array of vintage clothes that represented the upper end of society, and he wore them according to his whims. In addition to these, Archie always wore them with a red, velvet smoking cap whose silver tassel was similar to that of a Fez. Theresa noticed over the course of their time together that it was not uncommon for Archie to change clothes several times throughout the course of the day, according to the social habits of his era.

As they watched the television in silence, Theresa took note of his cool reticence throughout the program, despite what was going on. And after the program ended, she became thoughtful.

"Theresa, is there any particular reason why you have been gazing at me for an extended period of time?" Archibald asked, inadvertently interrupting her thoughts without even bothering to cast his eyes in her direction. "Understandably, I can be quite mesmerizing to your eyes. But is there anything else that meets your fancy?"

"Yes, I was captivated by your looks. Perhaps I should take a picture to savor the moment."

"You can try, but you will capture nothing, my dear."

"I was being sarcastic."

"Oh yes, that I realized, Theresa, and it is greatly appreciated." He clapped softly, mockingly. "That brings me to something I was thinking about earlier. Since you will not tell me what you were thinking about, I will communicate the interesting thought that came across my mind just now. I was just thinking how uncanny it is that I have more of a social life as a Shade than you do with a beating pulse. Now you take a few moments to marinate on that, my dear." Archie stared at Theresa with a smirk on his face.

"What is there to marinate on when it is just another one of your trifling jibes? But let me humor you because you must be bored now that the movie, *The*

Uninvited, is over." She folded her arms and sat back in her seat. "You really must take me for some type of a loser in your dead eyes, eh?"

"To the contrary, my dear," said Archie. "In order for you to be a *loser*, you have to actually make an attempt at winning something and then subsequently fail at that. And you, on the other hand, are not doing that. You are simply reveling in your mundane complacency. You are living in the moment as if it is going to last forever. I hate to be the one that points out the obvious, but time is not on your side, and I am proof of that account." He adjusted his legs in his seat. "Not that I whiled away my precious time like a committed spinster, of course."

"I know what you are doing, and it is not going to work." She glared at Archibald's face before shoveling another scoop of Belgian chocolate ice cream into her mouth. This was followed by a bite of her chicken tenders from the plate on the coffee table.

He only gave her a slight smile before he returned his attention to the cigarette that was now in his hand. He observed her enjoying her meal as he spoke. "You have a very peculiar appetite at times, Theresa. It is akin to a hungry hostage, grabbing whatever she can consume."

Theresa only continued eating as if she had not heard him. A few moments of silence passed, and Archie was humming a soft tune, amusing himself as usual. Theresa muted the remote as she listened to him with interest.

"What is that pleasing tune that you are humming over there?"

"It is the melody of a song called 'The Girl I Left behind Me.' It has some folkish verses that go along with it that are best left to the Irish tenors."

"You should still sing some of it so I can at least know how the song goes. I am quite sure that you have a pleasant singing voice that can carry a tune."

Archie sighed. "But alas, I do not. Despite being endowed with many gifts in addition to other numerous fine and refined dispositions, I do not have the gift of song."

"My, how modest you are, Archibald." Theresa cut her eyes.

"Ah, I see that your discerning observation is at work again, my dear."

Theresa swallowed the scoop of ice cream in her mouth and pointed at him with her empty spoon. "Umm-hmm, I know. Why don't you tell me something interesting about yourself?"

"Theresa, talking about myself is just so boring as I already know the story from beginning to end." He continued to smoke in a casual manner.

Theresa, who was slightly annoyed by his nonchalant response, looked at him curiously for a moment. "What in this world and the next are you talking about when you are always talking about yourself? Hell, yesterday you even narrated your whole day speaking in third person like a goddamn fool."

Archibald turned his head towards her as he rubbed his chin. "Hmm, I suppose you are correct on that account," he responded as he thought about the statement. "But unfortunately for you, I don't feel motivated at the moment. Besides, considering that there is some validity in your statement, you should motivate me so that I will be more inclined to tell you what you want to hear."

Theresa crossed her legs and folded her arms, not knowing the intention of his statement. "And how *exactly* am I to motivate you?"

"You can start by telling me something about yourself that I do not know already. Something that is interesting, mind you. Particularly, like why it is that a reasonably attractive woman who is as accomplished as you is single. I have noticed that of all the pictures you have sprinkled around this place, not a single one shows you with a person that could be perceived as a 'significant other.' And I find that to be quite curious as you are not suffering from that self-imposed retardation that seems to be so popular with women nowadays in your age bracket."

"You are kind of losing me, could you be more specific?"

He closed his eyes momentarily and placed his hands together. "Yes. I have noticed that lost look on your face again. I was speaking in regards to the assorted humbuggery that many of your sex engage in, such as professing to desire a particular type of gentleman, yet entertaining themselves with the complete opposite of the gentleman they publicly profess to be the object of their desire. And this trait is usually exacerbated by the endless parade of public self-affirmations that are supposed to boost their self-esteem while mitigating all of their shortcomings. But when that is sufficient enough, they typically blame men for all the ills of their situation, most of which, is usually created in their heads." He paused for a moment to look at his watch.

"Those dodgy 'New Woman' attributes that repel respectable men instinctively. This situation is further concatenated in your community in recent years by the matriarchal aspect. You have no such issues that I can make out so far. Nor do you appear to be embittered. You do not engage your time in the customary fiddle-faddle, but rather, you are here studiously working on the house, or in that secretive study of yours, or trying to pick my head, so you can figure me out. But please indulge me as to the reason that you are in this solitary predicament? And please be quick about it, for I wish to watch the news tonight."

"I didn't know you were *so* interested in my personal life as to go to great lengths to snoop."

He rubbed his hand across the brow of his head and sighed. "You make your life sound interesting, and it is not. Besides, I only made an observation based on the obvious."

Theresa's eyes squinted as she muttered to herself under her breath that he was stonewalling.

"Righto, I think it is only fair that I should know a little bit more about you considering that you are always violating *my* privacy."

"What are you even talking about now? I don't follow you anywhere, and I don't know where you keep your stuff in the house. Besides, it's impossible for me to follow you if I wanted to. You know, you being a ghost and all. That cigarette you're smoking must be laced with something."

He held the cigarette up to his face, studying it. "Oh, how I wish, Theresa."

"What?"

"As I was saying, you have been violating my privacy since I got back to the house. You have been doing it all the time, and you're doing it right now."

"I'm doing what? I'm just talking to you!"

He stretched out one hand to calm her down. "Settle down, Theresa, there is no need for you to engage in hysterics in polite company. And besides, I am talking about the ability you have to see me at your leisure. Now, even you must admit that this is not a natural condition. No, it is not normal at all for the average meat person in this age."

"Well, it's not my fault! It's not like I asked for it."

"Nevertheless, you are the beneficiary of this type of voyeurism. So instead of me minding my own business in peace and quiet without you noticing my presence as a normal person should, you constantly harass me and gawk at me. And this is even more exacerbating, considering you have no other intimate relationships with men. Therefore, I feel it is only proper that I should know a little bit more about you. After all, one can never be too sure about the company one keeps these days, and I would be remiss not to ask."

Theresa set her empty ice cream container down. She then rested her elbow on her knee and put her head in the palm of her hand, staring at him before she gave her response.

"Look, it's no great mystery, Archibald. The fact of the matter is I am somewhat shy. Socially awkward, as some would call it." Archie simply stared. Theresa squirmed in her seat. She couldn't take the silence. "Well, Archie, you do understand what I'm saying, right?"

"Of course I do, Theresa. It was as clear as the proverbial crystal. You have a mousy disposition. But what I want to know is that part of your life that is not so translucent." He then gestured with his hand for her to continue. "You may proceed with your story, if you please."

"Well, I normally do not chase men like some women do as if serial dating is a career or hobby. I have enough that occupies my time. But it may please you to know that I do not have an issue talking to people that I am actually interested in. The words may not come out right like I've thought them through in my head, but I do make proactive attempts, and preferably, the conversation is one-on-one or with certain people that I know around me. Those are usually my terms with little deviation. But I don't like talking to people in groups where others can hear what I am talking about. It makes me nervous, and I do not like other people to know what I am up to. But just the other day, I saw someone that looked interesting working the front desk at a hotel where I met a client for lunch. We conducted our business in the lobby, and from my position, I could occasionally look over in that direction to check him out as he went about his task. When my business was concluded, I went over to speak to him about nothing in particular, just to feel his personality out. I was interrupted by some irritatingly, boisterous snowbirds checking in. So I went about my business elsewhere."

"That must have been very disappointing for you, being so close to your objective and yet thwarted in your efforts."

"At the moment, it was an annoying inconvenience. But I did notice what type of car he drove when he had stepped out earlier, so I took note of the make, model, and that it had a Florida license plate. On my way home the other night, when I brought groceries, I drove past that hotel and noticed his car there. So, I pulled in the parking lot and walked into the lobby. He was right at the front desk. I told him that I forgot my planner as a pretext for my presence. From that point, I engaged him in a friendly conversation that lasted about twenty minutes or so until his shift was over. We went out for a quick bite to eat, and that was that. I verified that he was from Florida, a town around the Lakeland area. Plant City, I believe. Overall, he seemed nice enough with a good disposition. Though I realized he was not as tall as I would have preferred, it is something that can be over-looked with strength of character. Then, I came home to my haunted house to reflect on my evening."

"Yeah, you are going to *friend-zone* him over your height requirement, plus some other convenient excuse,

Theresa. But your level of craftiness is highly commendable. And to think, all this time, I thought you were taking those long, scalding showers to make up for the warmth you lack socially. Now, tell me about the relationships you have been in so I can better gauge you."

"Stop trying to figure me out, nosey ghost! Besides, I am only *friend-zoning* him because he eats with his mouth open like a goat and has the table manners of one."

Archibald only smiled, running his fingertip across his eyebrow as she continued.

"I'm going to give you the CliffNotes version of the two serious relationships I've been in. Both of these relationships ended on amicable terms. This was due to different career paths that led them to seek their fortunes in other parts of the country. One is in a domestic partnership and the other is working on his fourth or fifth child with that Fertile Myrtle he's involved with. His first three were triplets: Alexis, Andrea, and Alexander. On occasion, we reach out to each other, usually around the holidays."

"Tsk tsk, Theresa. Your love life is as boring to me as it should be to yourself. You really should do something about that to liven things up a bit."

"What the hell are you complaining about now? You should be happy that I don't have any crazy issues."

He produced a crooked grin as he gave her two thumbs up.

"Umm, okay. So Archie, do tell—why is such a man of your special social standing at home on Saturday nights repeatedly? What happened to your Saturday evening card games? Did we have a falling-out with some of our deceased card buddies at your social club, Mr. Social Butterfly?"

"Oh, it is quite simple, really, as I decided to take a break from gambling to catch up on reading."

"You no-pulse liar, I haven't seen you remotely read anything. And reading other people's mail does not count either."

He sighed. "Well, I am currently forbidden from participating for eight weeks because of a vile accusation levied against my good name of cheating at the gaming table."

Theresa feigned an expression of indignation. "Oh, poor Archie, I cannot imagine why someone would say anything negative about you. Whatever led them to that assumption about you?"

Archie folded his arms. "An anonymous tip, I was told. Besides, no one likes to be accused of something that one is going to do before one actually does it. That is quite rude and discouraging."

"Anyways, with the procrastination aside, Archie, tell me how you died, please? Besides, with the 24-hour news cycles, the news is going to beat the same topic into the ground, so you're not going to miss anything."

But he only stared at her with an indiscernible mannequin-like expression without responding.

She continued pressing the point to no avail as he reclined, pretending as if he was asleep. "Oh, I see now. You must be ashamed to tell me the details of how you were murdered. I'm guessing that you were either stabbed or shot to death. Hmm, or maybe even poisoned, now that I think about it?"

No sooner had she finished her statement, than Theresa's empty ice cream container flew off the coffee table and smacked her right in the center of her forehead. It didn't hurt; nevertheless, she was still indignant as little drops of melted ice cream spattered her forehead and her hair. She stood up and wiped her face with the white terry cloth towel that she'd brought to the couch with her meal. She then patted her hair while glaring at Archie, who was still positioned as he was earlier with his back towards her. She walked over to him, and knelt down. She said calmly into his ear, "You little chickenshit ghost, you can stop playing like you're asleep, as we both know you don't need to sleep."

He did not make a sound, but she could discern a snigger as she returned to where she had previously been on the couch. "You know there is nothing funny about an assault with a pint of ice cream splatted in your face."

"Come now, Theresa, let's stop acting like it was a full pint and that something more than your feelings were actually hurt. All of that surliness you are displaying is wholly unnecessary. Furthermore, I'm sure that was not the first time that you have had your face spattered."

Theresa gave him a cold look followed by a colorful adjective.

"Oh my, it has been a long time since I have been called that."

Theresa stood up, saying, "Well, I have had enough of this for this evening. I am going to bed."

"I guess you are going to knuckle under and settle again, eh, Theresa?"

"Yes, I am going to bed, Mr. Archibald Mallard Turner. I am not particularly tired, just really bored at the present moment." She picked up the remote and the bare plate, and turned the television off.

The smile quickly left from Archibald's face, and he sat up in his seat. "There is no need to be so tart, sweetheart."

"I am *not* your sweetheart," retorted Theresa sharply.

"You are not anybody's sweetheart, sweetheart. But that doesn't change the fact that it is a term of endearment for someone whom I hold in such high esteem. Besides, what makes you think I was murdered by anyone, considering how charming and refreshing I am?" He gestured for her to have a seat, and she sat down again.

Theresa scoffed as she turned around to face him, "Oh, stop inflating your ego, you little dead man. After all, it is the same *charm* that threatens me about my occupation in this house. That same charm that makes you say anything you feel like, or as recently as tonight, makes you hit me in my head with an ice cream cup."

"My sincerest apologies, dear." Archibald stretched out his arms and yawned.

"Sincerity, my ass, but you *can* start with answering my question."

He sighed and looked at the fireplace as the wood had begun to smolder then burst into flames. "My death was not the end result of a malefactor, nor did I pass out of physical existence in this house, but rather in the Near East while traveling. I was summoned out of my flesh in bed while in the ancient city of Heliopolis, Khedivate of Egypt, on the 4th day in June 1906 Anno Domini at 3:34 a.m."

"Do you know what you died of?" Theresa asked as he solemnly watched the flames dance on the logs.

"The coroner's inquest conducted on orders of the British Consulate could turn up nothing. Apparently, because it pleased God to do so while I was amusing myself on holiday."

"I'm sorry to hear that. You must have been severely inconvenienced by the unfairness of it all."

"Quite so, Theresa. I was dreadfully inconvenienced. It was truly an annoying affair as I was unjustly deprived of my old age. You should know that I had always desired to be unrealistically hypocritical while also espousing piety in my declining years," he said, now standing facing the window of the parlour into the black of night.

"Why were you in Egypt in the first place, and were you alone?"

"Egypt was one of the more interesting stops on the Mediterranean tour. In fact, it was near the midpoint of our itinerary. From there, my party was to travel overland via the Roman Road to Jerusalem. Then, from that most coveted city, we would travel up the Levant, making our way to the port of Latakia where we were to set sail on a commissioned steamer that would have taken us around the Anatolian peninsula to Constanti-nople. The Sublime Porte would have been our last destination, at which we were to board the Orient Express to begin our journey back to the island. And as for the second part of your question, my personal secretary was in the room when I expired, despite being sent out earlier. She had a tendency to be headstrong, you should know. We had discussed plans previously to go down on the noon train to el-Faiyum for our party to view some of the Faiyum mummy portraits, which would have completed our Egyptian tour. Egypt was the final leg of the trip that started three months earlier when we left from Marseille."

"It must have been very nice to have money for that kind of travel," Theresa said, putting her derision aside as she jotted down notes. "I always wanted to travel out of the country, but I either lacked the funds or have been too afraid of traveling alone in strange places. You, at least, had the companionship of your personal secretary with you to share your experiences with."

He smiled as he was thoughtful of old memories. "I had more than one traveling companion, as there were five of us in all. In addition to Paelaysia Zavoyko, my personal secretary, there was also hoary old Abraham Pendleton. A son of David, he was a short-statured man who was by trade a skilled clockmaker in the city of Bath. Eudokia Nicephorus was my dragoman of Greek extraction. He was also a eunuch who was familiar with the customs of the Mohammedans. And lastly, there was Ojo Kanu, who was a highly skilled artisan originally from the Aro Confederacy, but had made his way to Midsomer Norton in '84 as a youth."

Theresa felt for the first time a degree of pity when she saw how he looked, reflecting on the memories of his friends.

"But honestly, Theresa, there was nothing unusual that day preceding the hour of my death. I had a collection of Oriental oddities and rugs that I had purchased, crated to be shipped home that morning. I then went for a walk around the old city where I purchased some postcards that I mailed later that afternoon after tea with my companions. A visit to the Turkish baths, dinner, and a friendly game of whist concluded my day. Besides my late-night conversation with Paelaysia, I felt fine as I prepared myself for my night's rest."

"When it happened, I did not know that I was no longer part of the physical world. I thought I was in a state of pleasant dreaming. I knew that it was a pleasant dream because I remembered looking at myself lying there in the bed saying in my thoughts, 'Look at you, you handsome rascal.' My body lay there in the bed so tranquil and still facing the ornate nightstand. There was a warm golden glow from the lamp illuminating my face. And as wonderful as this scene was, it seemed to drag on. I must admit it did become a bit tedious. After all, one can stand in the mirror to admire oneself for only so long. Then, I perceived that someone was undoing the lock of the room door. The door opened noiselessly, and immediately closed. A shadowy, gowned figure moved silently into the room and paused. I heard the figure let out a sigh distantly before moving noisily across the floor towards my bed. I could not make out who it was, as I was now standing a short distance from the bed. But as the figure passed in front of the lamp, it became apparent that the being was feminine. She went over to the opposite side of the bed and slid between the sheets with the gracefulness of a cat. She moved next to my reclined body in the light that illuminated her face. To my surprise, it was Paelaysia, my secretary. For some reason, I did not recognize her with the mix of light and shadow. She placed a hand on my shoulder as she spoke to me in a whisper."

"Eventually, she realized that my chest wasn't moving, and she became somewhat frantic. She tried to wake me after holding a small hand mirror under my nose to see if there was any condensation on it. She made two more attempts that involved singeing one of my fingers with a match and a slap across my unresponsive face. Seeing that all was lost, Paelaysia then got on her knees and quietly sobbed with her disheveled hair lying across my face. She muttered a prayer in the Muscovite language. She then crawled back into bed and wrapped her arms around me after kissing and caressing my motionless face first. At length, I realized this was no dream, but rather an unfortunate conclusion to a life that had been so promising."

He paused, reflecting on the matter.

"Before I knew it, I was in the room lying on a granite slab, with my corpse being cleansed by individuals who appeared to belong to a religious order. They rubbed me down with a thick, brownish-red liquid that, by the scent of it, contained frankincense and myrrh. They also had an interesting way of getting camphor oil into the body, but I will omit those details. So, after being wrapped up in a burial shroud, my body was sent back to the English Isles, where I was entombed under the floor of the family chapel. There are some nice words on my very ornate ledger stone from my parents, none of which I wish to remember at the moment."

Theresa, who had been writing previously—jotting down details that she thought were important—was now tapping the tip of her pen against the piece of paper. She had one eyebrow raised as she studied him. Archibald, who had been peering out of the curtains, was arrested in his movement when he saw Theresa's face.

"I see you are giving me that look of yours again. So, tell me, what did I do now?"

"That is precisely what I'm trying to figure out," she answered, still examining him.

"Theresa, you have a particular way of contorting your face when you want to know something. It is a look similar to a cat stalking its prey. And to be quite frank, it is unladylike, and I do not approve of it."

Theresa only stared at him momentarily. She then gesticulated with her forefinger for him to come nearer. She did this while she patted the seat cushion next to her. He sighed and made his way around the coffee table before settling down on the far end of the couch.

"So please, tell me what Paelaysia said to you, or rather your corpse? You seemed to omit that detail, and I am naturally curious."

"Oh, I figured that it was not pertinent since I was supposed to be talking about myself. Paelaysia was just talking some claptrap about how she loved me and other Venus-related nonsense. She had been at this particular hobby for about a year. Sometimes, she would steal into my bedchamber when she thought I was firmly asleep trying to shape a romantic feeling for herself by whispering into my ear. She did not stay the night, but always left well before daybreak as if she were never there.

"In the time that I concluded to be the start of her nighttime forays, I began to develop an affinity for her. The first clue in this mystery came after I held a social event at Belgravia in which the wine flowed freely. Paelaysia, who was trying to be a social drinker, had to retire to her quarters earlier in the evening. That morning, I awoke to her pressing her body against one of London's most prominent erections. She was still in a degree of slumber before I whispered, 'Good morning, Paelaysia.' She opened her eyes, seeing the first rays of day entering through the curtains, and recognized my sleeping quarters. She sat up in the bed. After peering under the linen, she blushed and hurried herself out of my bedchamber as bare as the day of her nativity. With the conclusion of that peculiar event, I dressed myself. Affairs required me at Bishopsgate, after which I went down to Whitehall. My cab brought me home late that evening, and when I inquired about Paelaysia, the housekeeper informed me that Paelaysia would be indisposed all day. Once I got settled, under the guise of concern, I went to her room to satiate my curiosity. Eventually, she told me that she was a somnambulist and that it was a malady for which I could not judge her because it was beyond her control. This was followed by other shaming tactics that were wholly unnecessary, but mildly amusing to see so poorly executed."

Theresa looked at him disapprovingly as she shook her head. "And you wondered why I thought your death was a result of a crime. Anyways, though I do not approve of her methods, I could understand how frustrating it must be trying to court your attention. Especially from a person that is too much in love with himself to notice her feelings. Paelaysia's love fell on deaf ears—both figuratively and literally. That seems to be the only real tragedy of the story. After all, by your own admission, you were only *inconvenienced* by your death. And it obviously did nothing to remove that chip on your shoulder." Theresa muffled her mouth as she yawned. It was very late for her, and she was tired.

Archibald looked at her with a sense of surprise before walking over to the mirror to examine his shoulders. "Theresa, I beg to differ, for I am still bereft. In fact, you should commiserate with me as a good friend should. Furthermore, one must love *oneself* first in order to love others. It is a good trait to possess for a variety of reasons. It allows one to realize self-worth, and how it factors in relationship to others." He looked at his watch before he headed back to his seat. "I am also not responsible for the romantic inclinations that another may have for me. Besides, Paelaysia was an excellent secretary and a romantic interest would only allow for distractions from her work." He paused as he realized that Theresa had left the room on her way to bed with the remote just as the news anchor began speaking.

In other news tonight, a Savannah local remembers Florida senator Thomas Fairfax who passed away in his sleep earlier this week near Calloway Gardens. But first, it's time for sports...

CHAPTER 11

The following Monday morning, Theresa was upstairs in the second-floor bathroom. She was styling her hair in the bathroom mirror when she dropped her silver hairpin. It bounced along the polished marble floor. *Great, I hope that I didn't break it.* She got down on her knees and began feeling about in the space between the sink and the toilet. It was not long before she felt the metallic object at the rear of the toilet base, just out of view. Theresa was backing out from the space when she heard a voice behind her.

"So, what has you on all fours this early in the morning, Theresa?"

Theresa turned and sat up on her haunches. Archibald stood in the doorway in his night clothes. She hesitated. He walked over, and extended his hand to help her up.

"Good morning, Theresa, you look quite vibrant. And might I add that floral hair grip is very beautiful." He took her hand in his and examined the hairpin that was in it. "Hmm, it is undoubtedly in the Art Nouveau style. Sterling silver set with sapphire blooms."

Theresa, who had been sidetracked by how to interpret his initial statement, was now very impressed by his observation of the hairpin. She even felt a new sense of pride in its ownership.

"You have very good eyes. Not many people can distinguish real sapphires from costume jewelry."

"How did you acquire such a unique piece, if you do not mind me asking?"

"Old Margaret—a semi-retired woman who sporadically works as a half-ass cleaning lady—gave these to me as a birthday present last year."

Archibald then engaged Theresa in a pleasant conversation that lasted about ten minutes in which he skillfully levied compliments. He even placed the hairpin into her curly tresses. Moreover, he massaged her shoulders as she attended to her affairs at the sink.

From the intensity of his attentiveness, Theresa perceived that he wanted something.

I think he is trying to butter me up this morning, but for what? It's not like he can actually borrow money, so what could he possibly want with me?

She glanced at him out of the corner of her eye as he sat on the edge of the bathtub. *But I guess I will soon find out.*

"Theresa, I am temporarily bored."

"Oh, really?" Theresa pretended to be surprised. "I did not think you could ever get bored looking at yourself in the mirror all the time."

"Do not be silly, Theresa, for I do not think I could ever get bored of that. But I do need a slight change of pace, like allowing me to accompany you to your place of work. It's not like anybody can see me and I wouldn't get in the way of anything."

"Umm, I don't know about that," Theresa said, cautiously. "That would be kind of weird."

"To the contrary, it would be no weirder than it is right now. Besides, asking to come with you is just a pleasant formality. I plan on accompanying you anyway."

She sighed. *He is so arrogant. Even his name is arrogant.* She leaned toward her mirror as she applied her eyeliner. "I disinvite you to what you have invited yourself to, sir. So you cannot ride with me. And don't try to be clever and think you can follow me to work because I drive really fast. Besides, my job is located many miles from here, and you don't know the address."

Archibald only looked at her with an unchanged expression. "Theresa, you look so cute when you are trying to gloat. Now much to your chagrin, I know exactly where you work."

"So, you were stalking me at work like some creeper?"

He chuckled as if he was greatly amused. "Theresa, there you go with that inflated sense of self-importance. It is quite pretentious and unladylike. Now, I only went looking for you when you went missing for several consecutive nights out of concern for my vested interest. Knowing that you did not have a significant or even an insignificant other, my first thought was that you were moonlighting as a stripper or something else along those lines."

Theresa stopped what she was doing and turned towards him. "A *stripper*? I am shocked that you would say that."

"I am not and nor should you be considering what has left my lips up to the present moment. Besides, at the time, I figured that with your humdrum life that you found an occupation to moonlight to release your tension. After all, on the surface, you live a seemingly unadulterated life, and in my experience, no one is that untainted in all aspects of their life. Everyone has to vent somewhere to indulge a natural inclination. I noticed, prior to your nighttime disappearances, that there was a large amount of varied literature pertaining to ammunition in your home office down the hall. Furthermore, I noticed a collection of ammunition of different calibers sitting in the bottom of the bronze, mesh pen-holder on your desk with other precision measuring instruments conveniently sitting next to it. I also noticed the draughtsman's drawings in the rubbish with detailed notes in your fine penmanship. Therefore, I took into consideration since you did not own firearms of any caliber, and that you seem to be doing a lot of research on ammunition itself, that you are employed at a munitions plant. The way you dressed told me that you were not employed in something that requires a lot of manual labor, but rather something such as research and development or sales."

This ghost is talking to me like he's Lieutenant Columbo and I'm guilty of something.

"At any rate, Theresa, I found your whereabouts with due diligence. It was on a Saturday at the hour of the wolf, I finally found you in your office, behind your desk. You were on the floor sleeping on a red beach towel. Your head rested on a roll of clothes as you mumbled something to yourself while rubbing your own bottom. I figured that someone from your imagination took you on a date that went well."

Theresa looked both embarrassed and annoyed.

"But satisfied with finding you, I went back home."

"Why, you crafty bastard," uttered Theresa.

"And now I am going downstairs to wait in the car," he said as he stood in the doorway. "And when we get to your place of employment, make sure you point that fellow out for whom you were preening."

"I don't know what man you are talking about. In fact, you are always talking about something I do not know about. Besides, there is nothing wrong with a person looking nice for themselves." She glanced at him in the mirror as she applied her eyeliner.

"That form-fitting trouser suit that you are wearing to accentuate your attributes says otherwise. For example, the unusual amount of attention to detail that you have placed into your hair this morning. Not to mention the special-occasion fragrant shampoo that you sparingly use, which you obviously applied quite liberally. Apparently, you are trying to attract someone's attention." With that, Archibald turned on his heel and left Theresa in the bathroom alone.

Shortly thereafter, the two arrived at Theresa's place of employment: Seaboard Metallic Cartridge. Theresa had stopped at a coffee shop along the way and was consuming her Cuban sandwich as Archibald looked towards the trees at the edge of the property.

Theresa had not spoken to Archibald since they had left the house. It was not because she was really cross with him, but rather, she did not know how this situation with him accompanying her to work was going to play out. Nevertheless, Archibald was unfazed by her silence, and had done the talking for the both of them.

He fell silent upon their arrival. His attention became fixated on something else. In the meantime, as they sat in the parking lot, she ate a quarter of her sandwich before wrapping it up to save for lunch. She took another swallow of her green tea when she noticed that Archibald was still staring out of his passenger side window.

"So, what is it over there in those woods that has your attention?" Theresa asked. "Oh, never mind that question. It isn't important. Just so you know, I do have some apprehension about you forcing me to bring you here."

He turned his face toward hers. "Theresa, *forcing* is such an exaggeration; I am not forcing you to do anything. I am just coming along to fulfill my need for entertainment. And considering I am with you, I look forward to being thoroughly entertained today."

He smiled and returned his attention to his passenger window.

"Whatever. But don't try me today with your shenanigans or else." She held her hand up near the back of his head gesturing as if she intended to slap him.

"Oh, really; tell me more."

"Exorcism tonight, that's what. And straight to hell you go. Yeah, I said it." Theresa quickly retracted her arm when she perceived Archibald was turning back. She held her head down as she pretended to be brushing crumbs off of her lap.

"That is so cute, Theresa. I guess it is never too early for some braggadocio, eh?"

He reached over to her as she was carrying on, and touched her softly under her chin. She looked at him.

"But obviously, you are used to talking to little people and, apparently, trying to intimidate them," he added.

"Oh, that's right." Theresa snapped her finger. "I have to pick up Tater Tot from Waldorf today after work."

"Pray tell, who is this *Tater Tot*?"

"Tater Tot is my sister Traci's child; my niece. That's just a nickname we call her because she used to love to fling tater tots at people with incredible accuracy. Her birth name is Frederica-Sabina Campeggio. I'll tell you more about her when you get to my office."

"And all along I was under the illusion that you were an only child. Well then, Theresa, make sure you carry your headphones with you. That way, you can talk to me without anyone getting suspicious about your sanity." He paused and seemed very thoughtful. "Now that

I think about it, considering your normal antics, those suppositions may already be confirmed. But let us go in, I am just dying to see who it is that has you *in heat.*"

She rolled her eyes and reached into the back seat to retrieve her laptop briefcase. When she turned around, Archibald was standing in front of her car, waving his cane in the air.

"Come now, Theresa, there is no need to dillydally in the car all morning."

Theresa sighed, and got out of her car.

"So Theresa, tell me the itinerary of your work-day," Archibald requested after he returned from his self-guided tour of the premises and took a seat near her desk.

Theresa, who was sitting at her desk reading a letter with a smirk on her face, folded it back up and placed it in her desk drawer.

"I was just about to check on that right now. I responded to all of my emails while you were out on your stroll. That is something I do first when I get to my desk." She leaned over to the side in her chair and retrieved her planner out of her briefcase. "Let's see what I've got scheduled for today." She sighed softly. "How can I forget this guy here? He is a retired Colonel of the United States Marine Corps named Elias J. Barnaby. I have spoken to him several times over the phone, and he is kind of boisterous. I always have to turn my volume down when I speak to him. That aside, in all honesty, he does seem like a nice person. But I have been trying to set up an appointment with him to finalize his paperwork for the last two months, since he lives in Kentucky, but his businesses are in South Carolina. He owns a chain of stores called Wade Hampton Sporting Goods and Hampton Tactical Firearms Training scattered throughout the low country. But something keeps happening; the last four times our appointments never came to fruition. I know I can get him a better deal as an ammunition supplier, but he can't find out if he never comes in. I don't like protracted potential business transactions. He could have at least sent a surrogate in his place. It seems that a number of these ex-military people these days are trying to cash in on their experiences, real or mostly imagined."

She closed her planner and just happened to look down the hall through the open blinds. "I guess that is him finally coming down the hall, and 20 minutes early!"

"If that is the case, the receptionist would be quite remiss, or is that type of slackness the norm here, Theresa?"

"It's the norm. She is one of the owner's relations here temporarily to receive a mollycoddled impression of the workforce." She stood up from her desk and made her way towards her door.

"Hmm, that makes sense. But are you certain it's your client?"

"It's him alright, plus he's far too happy in his stride to be working here at all. Okay, it's time to put on my game face. Now you behave, please."

Theresa greeted the gentleman at the door with great civility as if she'd known him all her life. She escorted him to one of the two chairs situated in front of her desk. He was just as boisterous as Theresa had said minutes earlier. Archibald paid careful attention to him as Theresa made small talk before settling into business.

"Excuse me for a moment, but I have your paperwork tucked away in the file cabinet over here." She got up and walked over to the cabinet directly behind her desk. "Let's see *Wade*; it is on the bottom shelf." She squatted down to open the bottom drawer to retrieve the folder.

The retired Colonel was almost leaning out of his seat to take a look at Theresa. He muttered, *smother my face*. Archibald heard the bawdy utterance, but it was indistinguishable to Theresa.

Theresa stood up and turned around with his folder in her hand, smiling. "I found it. I'm sorry, but did you say something?"

Mr. Barnaby's cheeks turned rosy as he began speaking. "Oh, I was thinking out loud, about how ammunition was *a lot better than mace*."

"Oh," said Theresa. "Well, you would be correct, sir. As you probably already know, we manufacture some of the finest quality ammunition on the eastern seaboard. We also have contracts with agencies within the Department of Defense, and we are the providers of premium ammunition for over 20 state agencies and municipalities."

During this time, Archibald tapped his cane against the floor as he chuckled from his seat in the empty chair, set against the wall. Theresa glanced in his direction as the chair was situated between two areca palms near the side of her desk. Theresa found herself distracted by looking over at Archibald's curiously smiling face, so she decided to walk around her desk and address Mr. Barnaby. She did this so her client might not notice these peculiarities on her part. With her back to Archibald, she went over the ins and outs of the contracts. She heard Archibald distinctly say, "And now he is getting a front dose."

She put her hand behind her back and made a gesture with one finger extended before retracting it.

"Theresa, I have some questions"—Mr. Barnaby pointed to the papers— "that I wish to highlight when I go on my tour of the facilities with the plant foreman."

Theresa was very attentive to this, handing him her pen, but Archibald was even more attentive when he said, "Theresa, do pay attention to the fingers on the hand he is writing with. There is something abnormal about this that is a lot more interesting than your current conversation."

She tried not to pay attention to what Archibald had said, but curiosity soon got the better of her. Theresa, who sat so close to him, did not wish to be obvious. So she purposely slid her moleskin notepad on to the floor, allowing it to fall towards Barnaby's direction. Instinctively, the older gentleman reached down and handed it back to her.

"I noticed you looking at my hand. Those goddamn VC gooks cut my fingers off at the joints, and I will always hate them." He held his hand out, so Theresa could clearly see what was left of his maimed appendages. The stubs had healed burn tissue as they obviously had been cauterized to stop the bleeding. Theresa shuddered as she turned her face away from the sight with her eyes shut.

"Oh, I'm so sorry, Theresa. I certainly wasn't trying to offend you," he said.

"No, you are fine. It is nothing really. I just got an unpleasant visual of the act when you extended your hand. How long were you a prisoner of war?"

"About a week until I made my daring escape to safety with my severed fingers in my pocket. I caught my host slipping after a night of partying on rice wine."

"Okay, wow," Theresa said nervously as Archibald laughed behind her. She stood up, adjusted her fitted waistcoat. "Well, it is about time that I took you to see our efficient production line. Charles Monmouth, our plant foreman, will be more than happy to address your technical questions." She escorted Mr. Barnaby out of her office to another part of the complex, and Archibald stayed behind.

Theresa returned to her office a short time later. After she shut her office door and closed the blinds facing the hall, she inquired into what Archibald had spoken about earlier. He told her as she placed her laptop on her desk.

After he relayed the facts to her, Theresa laughed in disbelief. "I think you are totally wrong about him. He is a very nice old man, even if he is a bit of a roughneck with a pinch of salt. And in fact, he has a daughter around my age. To be honest, I think you mistakenly heard what you were actually thinking. You know, like projecting one's thoughts onto others."

"Having a daughter around your age doesn't mean anything, Theresa. You are not *his* daughter, and that makes you up for the chase. Furthermore, if he were given the opportunity, he certainly would not pass up a chance to sweat on your back. Plus, he is a very spry individual if you had not noticed." He checked his pocket watch for the time before continuing on.

"You should also know, by now, that I have no qualms about telling you how I feel. So I certainly do not need a surrogate to express the feelings you may think I have."

"Sure, buddy," Theresa said, as she finished her work on her laptop and took Mr. Barnaby's folder back to the file cabinet. "Oh, are we projecting again?" She turned abruptly towards him, closing the bottom file cabinet drawer with her heel.

"I was not checking you out. I was just reminded for the third time today that you have on a raggedy thong with your new trouser suit. It was quite obvious when you tooted your bum out. I am sure the old Colonel, who has a daughter near your age, greatly appreciated it, nonetheless. Earlier this morning, as I sat upon the edge of the bathtub in my boredom, I noticed how the pinstripes on your trousers converged together at the seams forming chevrons. That did catch my attention. But since there was nothing else of any serious consideration to keep my attention, my mind quickly wandered back to a dream I had."

Drafting on some vellum, Theresa stopped and turned toward him. "Now this is really interesting. A ghost who not only sleeps, but actually has dreams also. It probably was full of kink too, knowing you with your projections."

"Au contraire, Theresa. It was a religious dream. I just dreamt that I was the thirteenth disciple at the Last Supper, sitting next to that exalted being, the Son of Man. He turned to me and said, *Archie, old boy, it is You that I love the best.* I then awoke to you trying your hand at singing in the shower and doing surprisingly well with a little help from my imagination."

"Well, okeydokey then," Theresa deadpanned. "So check this out. This morning when we got here, there was a letter in my mailbox from Linda Byrk, my boss. Apparently, she had something to say about my wardrobe, and what I wore last week."

"Oh really, and what was that, Theresa?"

"The note said my clothes might have been a little bit too revealing. Not that I was actually showing skin, but my dress was tastefully form-fitting. The Bordeaux diamond midi with the contrasting black waist that I treated myself to from the boutique."

He nodded his head in recollection.

"Well, she said it might cause unnecessary distractions in the workplace, which can lead to accidents or loss of production. Those words are actually written in the letter." And she placed the letter at the edge of her desk for him to view it.

"That is indeed very interesting, considering the subject matter. Did you check the cover of the envelope to make sure that it was not addressed to someone else, and given to you by mistake?"

"Yeah, I'm not even sure if you are trying to be funny right now, but I'm moving along with the story. So, I went down to that woman's office to tell her how I felt about that on my way back from taking Mr. Barnaby to manufacturing, but she was on the phone. I gave her a salty look, though. So it won't be long now before she drags her long, lanky ass down here to see what is going on."

Theresa picked up her pen and tried to continue her drafting, but soon placed it back down on the table. She had worked herself up and was somewhat irritated.

"Are you having fun with this?" she asked Archibald.

"Not at all, but I am not bored either. I was not ignoring you this time. I am just in my own thoughts at the moment, while you are trying to rile yourself up unnecessarily. But on that account, bear with me for a moment, Theresa. It seems to me that this letter stems from personal misgivings, rather than the actual dress code. That information would normally have been included or referenced in such an important letter. And this, I do not say off the cuff. I say this because, in my self-guided tour of the premises, I found out that those who have the benefit of corporate nepotism dress in styles that range from vagabonds to Parisian harlots. And judging by the commonality, I perceive that today is not some rare or special occasion for these employees. So it would behoove you to save this signature letter as proof of workplace harassment—like how about hiding it along with those special drawings of yours that you are working on right now?"

"You have a knack for acute observation, Archie."

"I find it prudent to pay attention to people in order to ascertain their true character. Like who they actually are, rather than what they pretend to be."

Something caught Archibald's attention before he divulged his thoughts any further. He turned his head towards her office door. "Oh, you have a guest coming."

"What guest are you talking about?"

"It is your coworker in the office next door," he said, pointing his silver knob–handled cane towards the wall. "He has been pacing outside your door for a few minutes now, and I guess he decided to make up his mind. When you left earlier with the Colonel, I noticed that he spied on you as you passed his office."

"That's just Marcus, the office shitbird. Do you think he heard our conversation?" she asked in a hushed voice.

"I doubt it, and I would not care if he did. It is not like you never used your phone for communications with people outside your office. Besides, why don't you sashay over to the door and see why he is dilly-dallying around?"

Theresa walked over to the door and opened the door on her coworker. "Why are you hanging out near my door, and what do you want, creeper?"

"Perhaps he also realized that you are in heat and wishes to broach the topic?"

Marcus looked dumbfounded, but he finally spoke to her in a low stuttering voice. "Theresa, may I come in?"

Theresa stood aside.

As she walked past Archibald on her way to her seat, he spoke to her. "This Colonel Methuselah may not like this."

She paid Archibald no mind outside of a quick glance. "So, what is it that you want, Marcus, that has you pacing back and forth outside of my office? You act as if you are in some type of trouble."

"Umm, well, *trouble* is such a heavy word," Marcus said nervously as he ran his fingers along the back of the chair. "I like to think of it as a situation that you might help me with." He paused there for a moment, looking down at the seat cushion.

"Look, Marcus," Theresa said curtly, "I do not have all day to waste waiting on you to speak. I have other matters that need my attention. So say what you've got to say or show yourself out.

Archibald narrowed his eyes as he looked at Theresa. "I detect a tinge of animosity towards that young man." He uttered those words to himself just as Marcus started to confess to Theresa.

Marcus told her that he was in an unfavorable situation with his girlfriend, who *correctly* suspected him of infidelity after going through his phone. He admitted that he was able to cover his tracks in all places but one. He went on to further explain in detail when Theresa stopped him, holding her hands up in the air.

"I really do not need to know all these lurid details of your escapades. And for the life of me, I don't know why you would cheat on a woman who is a body builder, one that has a temper. You are far dumber than I originally took you for, and I say that without any enmity."

"Yes, I know this already, Theresa," he said with pleading eyes. "That is why I need you to help me with a white lie about my whereabouts Thursday night of last week. Nyané is in Orlando at the moment, at a tournament, but I am expecting her to surprise me here at work sometime soon. She is sneaky like that and will find some pretext to check in on me. You know how you women just do not know how to let a matter die peacefully."

Theresa frowned, and Archibald nodded his head with an air of approbation.

Theresa placed her elbows on the desk and brought the palms of her hands together as she gazed at Marcus. "I am not going to lie for you, Marcus. You made the choice to gamble, so you knew the risk that you were running in your relationship. But if she kills you during your beating, and by chance I happen to be interviewed by the media or police, I will say nothing negative about your deceased character."

Marcus held his face in his hands as he rocked himself in the chair.

Archibald, who had been listening attentively, spoke up. "Very good, Theresa. You did the right thing. If a lie is to be told, it should be respectable and told for the benefit of oneself rather than charity for others. Besides, this lecherous fool has given up valuable information that has placed him within your power."

Marcus, who was now sitting up, asked Theresa why she was staring at that empty chair so attentively.

"Because it's obviously a really nice chair that does wonders for the atmosphere of this room. Now, as for yourself, you need to go back to work and do whatever it is you do over there besides looking at anime."

Marcus sighed, but got up from his seat and walked over to the office door. He placed his hand on the door handle when Theresa spoke to him.

"Nyané will not be back until Sunday, so do not look downcast— it's a dead giveaway to all that something is wrong. Besides, you still have some days left above ground. I may be inclined to help you if you can help me once I've thought your situation over."

Marcus's face brightened up, and he was about to say something to her when she told him to please go. Theresa then turned to Archibald.

"Now you've got me thinking of how to scheme just like you." She realized that he was lost in his thoughts again, and was about to return to her project when he addressed her.

"You give the word such an unsavory aspect when a scheme that is properly executed can be a good thing. If your absurd colleague on the other side of the wall actually put some real thought into his schemes, he could have avoided this temporary inconvenience. But I digress. Besides, I only told you of your options."

"So what do you exactly mean by 'temporary incon-venience,' Archibald? You make it sound like he's not going to face any repercussions for his actions if he is caught in his lies."

"Theresa, the repercussions Marcus will face will not be of the nature that their relationship will be jeopardized. A person that witless with his philandering has been undoubtedly caught many times before. Hence, the reason his significant other is always checking up on him is that she already knows he is fickle. It is often that people tell lies to themselves to justify an unfavorable position. It is also a way for them to avoid or mitigate culpability for the failure of an *ideal* situation that they created in their own heads. Nevertheless, she puts up with it by continuing the relationship because she most likely does not want to be alone, or she feels she has invested too much time to quit now. It is similar to how people often find themselves in non-complementary careers, but they never leave because they are afraid of the risks they may run going off on a new venture. Having to start over is one of the main reasons many people will remain in their situations."

"Maybe she'll leave this time."

"I highly doubt it, Theresa. She went through his phone and still allowed him to explain his infidelity with trite explanations. Let that marinate for a moment."

This conversation was cut short when the office phone on Theresa's desk began ringing. Theresa knew from the display that it was an inside call from a coworker down the hall. Theresa considered her a "work-friend." Her office was over the main entrance. Theresa gestured to Archibald with her finger that she needed a moment, and then placed the phone on speaker.

"Hey, Leilani, what's up?

"Hey, Theresa, the roach coach just pulled into the parking lot in case you're hungry."

"Oh, no thanks. I have a sandwich I brought for breakfast that I'm going to finish."

"Sounds like a plan, Theresa, but I'm hungry, and I am going down there to find me a salad to drown in dressing. Oh, by the way, that new courier guy that you have a thing for just pulled up outside. I will send him up to your office since you're not coming down."

Theresa nervously glanced over at Archibald as she simultaneously snatched up the headset to the phone. But much to her chagrin, she only heard a dial tone as Leilani had already hung up.

"So Archibald," Theresa said, striking up a new conversation anxiously, "I was meaning to tell you that I was working on my own personal design for a new .22 long rifle caliber earlier. It will be a 45 grain .224 long rifle projectile with a semi-jacketed torpedo construction and a polymer sleeve to serve as a gliding jacket. With new improvements in powders, the bullet retains higher velocities and energy downrange starting out at 1,590 feet per second out of a 16.5-inch test barrel. A significant improvement over what is currently available on the market."

She unlocked her drawer and pulled out a technical drawing, along with prototypes of the proposed cartridge. She then pulled out a grey metal cylinder that was about ten inches in length, unscrewing the bottom to showcase a blued barrel of almost equal length that was perforated in a rotating spiral pattern.

"I have also designed this integrated silencer that an operator can turn on or off by a simple tactile quarter-inch twist to the right of the cylinder. This allows the operator to use either subsonic or sonic ammunition without any loss of pressure should the operator choose to use that."

Archibald examined her work with marked interest. "You are very industrious, as well as mechanically inclined, Theresa. You have ingenuity worthy of Sir Joseph Whitworth. It is very impressive, indeed. But I do have a question for you."

"I am listening, Archie."

"How do you plan to make these gems come to fruition?"

Theresa was caught off guard by the question, and it showed on her face. "Well, to be honest with you, I am not sure. I wanted to get my work patented, but the cost is prohibitive. Filing a patent with a patent lawyer is in the ballpark of 5 to 10 grand. This silencer alone may require five to six patents. So I see myself requiring about a hundred thousand, give or take, to finance this ideally. That is why I am thinking about bringing my design up at the next board meeting to see if the company would like to patent and produce my concepts in exchange for a percentage."

Archibald shook his head. "Theresa, when one is a sole proprietor of something great, one does not take on associates."

"And where am I going to get the money from then? From you, sir? Are ghosts lending out credit now?"

"That is dependent on your credit score, Theresa. But you should be prepared to receive the guest that you dolled yourself up for today. Tidy up your waistcoat and hopefully he will not notice your big head."

"Big head?"

"Yes, Theresa, you have a big head, as in the opposite of a small head."

"But my head is not big, it's normal sized," she said and placed her hands on both sides of her head.

"Of course, you would reconcile yourself with that conclusion, Theresa, since it is your own. Furthermore, I was not asking for your opinion, but rather giving my factual analysis on the size of your head."

Theresa was about to say something when Archibald raised his hand, holding his cane as he turned his face towards the office door.

"Perhaps this man, who has you in rare form, will silently notice the expanded circumference of your head also."

Archibald's remarks got Theresa's ire up, and she was about to deliver some choice words to him when the door opened.

"Hey, Theresa. What is with that mean mug murder face?" spoke a tall man as he stepped into her office. He had a whimsical facial expression with a light coat of perspiration on his forehead. He wiped it off as soon as he closed the door.

Theresa's face softened as she was caught off guard by the question.

"Oh no, I just accidentally bumped my knee against my desk as you were coming in, Palmer. I was just irritated at my clumsiness," she said while she rubbed her knee, glancing over at Archibald in the process.

"Well, that explains it," Palmer said as he approached her desk. "It almost looked as if you were pissed at someone. By the way, I don't have any packages for you today. Leilani said you had something to ask me, but she didn't know what it was."

"Oh, that's right," Theresa said. "I just wanted to know how long it would take to send a four-pound package to San Diego."

Palmer looked at Theresa curiously before responding to her. "It is from 3 to 5 business days, with the fifth day being at the extreme end of the standard shipping schedule. I must admit though, I'm quite surprised you asked that considering you must have been shipping packages for years from here, and you are tech-savvy."

"That is true," Theresa consented. "I only ask because I thought I overheard someone saying the other day that the shipping times had changed or were about to change with your company."

Palmer seemed satisfied with that answer and turned to leave. "Well, I'm on my way; I have to return back to the loading dock and make a second run since two of our guys are on vacation. You have a real nice office, by the way. It has a homey feel. Nice seeing you again."

"Okay, see you soon," she said in a quiet, somewhat disheartened voice.

Palmer began walking to the door as Theresa pretended to be examining some papers at her desk. She happened to notice that Archibald was not sitting in his chair. She turned towards Palmer and saw Archie holding the door handle, while a perplexed Palmer was trying to open it, to no avail.

"Theresa, is there a trick to opening your door? The handle seems like solid steel."

As she approached the door, Archibald whispered into her ear, "Repeat what I tell you, verbatim." He did all this even though he was several feet away, and his mouth was not moving.

Palmer stood aside, so Theresa could try her hand at the door. She placed her hand on the door handle and turned towards him. "The only trick is you have to turn the handle down." And she opened the door with ease, much to Palmer's amazement. Theresa looked at him and said, "You look surprised or embarrassed. I can't tell which, but you should not be either."

He looked at her and pushed the door closed again and then attempted once more in vain to open it. Palmer looked at the door again and then at Theresa with a very confused expression. But this softened as he looked at her admiringly. He was just about to speak when the door suddenly opened.

"Oh, excuse me," Marcus said. "I did not mean to interrupt." He entered her office. "I wanted to give you this case of dual fountain pens. I figured that you would get some use out of them." He placed the small box on Theresa's desk, and left just as quickly as he came, opening the door with ease and shutting it behind him.

"It is still your moment, Theresa. Do not let a minor distraction dissuade you," encouraged Archibald.

"Don't feel bad, Palmer. My grandmother used to have bouts of feebleness also. But now she takes those multivitamins, and she is just as spry as ever."

Palmer turned his attention to her after looking at the door. "I didn't know you were full of jokes, Theresa."

"By all means, Palmer, feebleness is not something to joke about. In fact, if there is any joke, then it's on me because I actually thought you were pretending to be feeble."

"And why would I do that?"

"I thought that you were using the guise to provide you with the perfect opportunity to ask me out to someplace nice."

Palmer smiled and without hesitation asked Theresa out. They concurred on some plans, and he left smiling. She then locked the office door and sat down at her desk, grinning from ear to ear, in addition to thanking Archibald for his assistance. He reminded her of the time, and she made preparations to leave.

CHAPTER 12

Within an hour, Archibald and Theresa were making their way across town to pick up Theresa's niece. While en route to their destination, Theresa finished her sandwich. As they waited at a traffic signal, she noticed Archibald slowly waving his right hand in a rhythmic beat. When he ceased his tempo, she said, "You know, I realized I really don't know much about you."

A slight smile appeared on his face before he responded. "Strange, for I have always told you what you need to know. But since I am not the type of person who just volunteers information about themselves unnecessarily, it may behoove you to actually ask me what you desire." He followed this with a wink.

"Thank you, sir. I will keep that in mind. So tell me, was your quest for entertainment satisfactory today?"

"Yes, it was, and I am so glad that you invited me to accompany you."

Theresa scoffed at that statement, but he paid no heed to it as he continued.

"I must say the owner of your company is a beastly woman. She is reminiscent of a tall Joseph Merrick, but a lot less attractive. You never told me that she was so gangly or facially challenged. I actually found myself inadvertently sizing her up as I gazed upon her. But tell me, how did she get those peculiar scars about her face?" He asked as he pointed to the side of his own face.

"A few years ago, Linda was attacked by unknown assailants on two different occasions. Well, the shooting also could count as one. So, I guess, she was attacked three times in all."

"Details, Theresa, details."

"I'm thinking; don't rush me. One morning, Linda was attacked on her way to work early one morning during the last Indian summer. While waiting at a red light, near the 1853 viaduct, she was snatched out of her driver's side window, and dropped on the ground."

"Hmm." Archibald rubbed his chin. "That is a pretty surprising feat. Such a tall woman pulled out of her auto like that. How many assailants were involved in the attack?"

"Linda told us that it was just one, a short, masked person dressed in black, and that she thought it was a woman. When Linda got up on her feet, she saw no one. Her car, which was still in drive, had rolled into a utility pole that prevented it from going into the Savannah–Ogeechee Canal. Then, her assailant stepped out of the shadows nearby and took a fighting stance. Enraged, Linda tried to rush the masked person that appeared to be waiting for her, but was met with a swift kick to her thigh which felled her. The assailant then quickly got on top of her and proceeded to deliver blows to Linda's face while sitting on her chest. The attack was halted when the headlights of a car turning off of West Broad onto Louisville Road caused the attacker to flee. Linda said the assailant quickly scaled the side of the wing-wall with the nimbleness of a cat and was out of sight. She managed to get herself up out of the road before she blacked out. She woke up in the hospital where she was laid up for about a month after that incident. That is how those marks originated on her face."

"A very peculiar incident."

"I agree. Within a period of ten months, Linda was literally driven off the road down into an embankment, and someone sent a bullet through her dining room window. The bullet passed less than an inch from her neck. After that incident, she took an extended vacation to the Adirondacks. I think it was somewhere near Mount Marcy. She was away for several months laying low."

"Who did they apprehend for these criminal activities?"

"Not a single person was brought in for questioning. Which I always thought was a bit odd. But I did remember that old Margaret told me privately that she found it peculiar that every time Linda would take her anger out on Louise Camille, something happened to her within a week's time. Linda has a bad habit of talking disrespectfully to people that work for her. This is more noticeable when she is caffeinated and has nothing productive to do with her time. From what I've been told, she has always had that unpleasant disposition. And because of it, she is really afraid to be alone, always thinking someone she did wrong is out to get her."

Archibald smiled and then chuckled under his breath. "It's nothing, Theresa. People usually get what they deserve, so I find Linda's situation refreshing. But besides that, and the multiple supervisory positions that are redundant, I noticed something very singular about your place of employment—"

"Oh, what was that?"

"In general, the rampant nationalism masquerading as patriotism all over the place. The slogans and whatnots mounted on the walls in picture frames, which at no time in this country's history had ever existed in practice. Though in all fairness, the *American Way* has always existed. That ability to be comfortably numb to the realities affecting all of one's countrymen is an American tradition. I suppose that is why in such a patriotic country, so many of the veterans are neglected, and state-sanctioned larceny against the citizens is prevalent. That is why these legends and illusions of Americana are necessary, as they instill a false sense of historical reality under a veneer of patriotism. Those who are particularly susceptible to this grand illusion are those who are not privy to their country's history outside of a cursory glance. And that is not only neglectful, but it is dangerous to the longevity of the democracy.

"As I passed through the grounds of the complex this morning, I noticed a picture of Paul Revere sitting prominently on the wall behind the receptionist's desk. It was the nighttime scene of Paul Revere's 1775 daring midnight ride, complete with the Old North Church fading away in the background. As I gazed upon it, I couldn't help but be reminded of Mark and Phillis. But specifically Mark, especially after what I saw in the clearing while we were in the parking lot."

Theresa, who just proceeded through an intersection, looked at Archibald out of the corner of her eye. "I know I shouldn't ask this, but who are Mark and Phillis, and how do they relate to the picture in the lobby? And what did you see *precisely* while we were in the parking lot this morning?" She muttered under her breath, "Probably more ghosts."

"Mark was enslaved, seeking to gain his freedom, just like Paul and friends. And considering his circumstance, and those of his compatriots, their attempts for liberation were even more just. But as fate would have it, that liberation would not happen. Both Mark and Phillis—his female associate—on September 18, 1755 in Cambridge, were executed for petty treason and murder of their owner—Captain John Codman of Charlestown—a swift and cruel man by means of arsenic. Phillis was chained to a stake, and her body was consumed by flames. But Mark was hanged by the neck, and his body was carted back to Charlestown where it was gibbeted. There was a desire by the civil authorities to make him a lasting example in the minds of the enslaved. He was clad in an iron cage, similar to the shape of his body, after being covered in tar to preserve his dead flesh. It was hung up in Charlestown where it became a well-known landmark, being suspended there for 20 years by the time Paul Revere passed by it on his fateful ride. In fact, Paul Revere had stated in a letter about his famous Midnight Ride of 1775, *After I had passed Charlestown Neck, and got nearly opposite where Mark was hung in chains, I saw two men on horseback under a tree.*"

Theresa, appalled, unintentionally turned her head towards him as he was looking outside of his passenger window.

"Mind the direction of your machine, or you will come to grief," he said, and she applied her brakes just in time not to go against the signal.

He then resumed speaking in that matter-of-fact way of his. "And what I witnessed this morning, you would have noticed too with your 'owl eyes' if you weren't wolfing down your food. It was a subtle manifestation of the old Ten Broeck Race Course, reliving a scene of past misery as today is the anniversary of those events."

Archibald stopped speaking abruptly as he turned his attention towards Theresa. "Hmm, speaking of misery, that looks like your friend, Abigail. She's taking a stroll over there across the street."

Theresa spied her as soon as he said it. "Well, if that is her, I wonder what she's doing at this time of day?" Theresa pulled over and hailed her friend from the car just as she was about to cross another street.

"Hey Abby, what are you up today?"

Abigail turned around with a surprised expression at hearing her name called. "Right now, I'm motivational-walking for health and wealth."

"So how is that working out for you?"

"Tired, still broke, and I think I'm lost?"

"Well, do you want to figure it out or do you want a ride?" Theresa didn't have to ask twice, as Abigail quickly got into the car.

During the ride, Theresa learned that Abigail had been in the downtown area eating breakfast with her brother, and that she had gotten into the habit of walking 15 miles per week, which was the reason she was out today.

As they pulled up to the Waldorf School, Abigail, who was sitting in the front passenger seat, got up to sit in the back, but Theresa stopped her. "You didn't have to move, Abby. Tater Tot always rides in the back seat."

"Oh, that makes a lot of sense," Abigail said. "But I could ride back there with her. Your niece is just so freaking cute."

"Anything to get in a back seat," said Archibald. He'd been sitting behind Theresa since Abigail got into the car.

Theresa glanced at him in her rearview mirror, but continued talking to Abby. "Are you going to stay here, or are you coming with me to sign Tater out?"

"Oh no, I'm getting out. They have those tasty Scotch oatmeal cookies," Abigail said. She checked her phone while she waited for Theresa on the sidewalk.

Archibald also informed Theresa, as she was retrieving her identification out of her purse, that he would wait in the vehicle.

Theresa and Abigail returned with the little girl walking in between them. She held onto both of their hands. When they got to the car, Theresa, who was carrying Tater Tot's backpack, placed it in the center of the rear seat. After she retrieved a booster seat from her trunk and secured her niece in firmly, they set off.

"I don't know how you get about with your backpack because it is pretty heavy for you. I'm surprised your parents let you go to school with that."

"It's heavy because we went to the library today, and I checked out cool books! But you should've pulled it by the handle like I always do, Auntie. It does have wheels."

"Well, how many books did you check out?" Theresa asked.

"I got a big book full of pretty pictures about animals, another one on how to draw cartoon characters, and an old children's book the library assistant recommended with a pretty cover called *The Lost Princess of Oz*. It's a sweet book so far, and not dumbed down like the newer children's books."

"Now that sounds interesting," said Abigail, wiping the crumbs from her mouth.

The little girl chuckled softly with her hand over her mouth. "Well, *I* think it's interesting you just *nom nom*

nom three large cookies like the Cookie Monster without even biting your fingers off."

Abigail turned to Theresa, speaking hurriedly in a hushed tone, "I think your niece is judging me."

She then turned towards Theresa's niece and said half-seriously, "Little girl, are you judging your elder?"

"Oh, Aunt Abby, no. I didn't judge you. I was only pointing out what I saw. And besides, you shouldn't use a word such as 'elder' to refer to yourself. That's what the old people call themselves, and you are in the flower of youth. And you have been working out, and it really shows." The little girl grinned.

Abigail turned towards Theresa laughing. "You see how your niece butters me up?" she said as she reached in her pocket and handed the little girl a dollar.

"I wouldn't use butter, Auntie, just margarine. I read somewhere that it is better for you."

Theresa could see that Archibald was amused by her precocious niece. "So, I take it you had a good day at school?" she asked.

"It was awesome, as always. The best part was going to the big library on Bull Street. The new librarian lady in charge removed the carpet in the area where the street people used to hang out. And now that area no longer smells like the pee-pee mattress in the alley that you told us not to bounce on last month. Miss Mandy made me her assistant today, and I learned her first name. The *F* in Miss Mandy's first name stands for *Felony*."

"What? I always thought your teacher's name was Mandy. I never would have figured that it was a surname and a very unusual one at that. Are you sure about that?" asked Theresa with a frown on her face. "Perhaps it's pronounced differently or something."

"Mandy is an old Scandinavian surname that has been Anglicized," Abby interjected.

"Yup, I saw her driver's license," Theresa's niece continued. "Miss Mandy told me a story about how her name came to be. Her mama named her that out of spite to her dad, who went to prison for stealing other people's stuff. I told her that she shouldn't be that honest about her family. I think pretty fibs are ok to tell people."

Theresa just shook her head at this as Archibald smirked. Meanwhile, Abigail found a sizable piece of cookie that was in between the folds of her shirt and promptly ate it.

They soon arrived at Theresa's sister's house, where Traci greeted them warmly. All entered the house with the exception of Archibald, whose presence was naturally unbeknownst to everyone, but Theresa. He remained near the car, smoking under a dogwood tree.

A few minutes later, Theresa, having completed her mission, headed toward the car when she heard Abigail hailing her from the front porch. Abigail had decided to stay for dinner with Theresa's sister after she learned that she was cooking lasagna. Theresa was hurriedly approached by Abigail, who held out to her a small velvet jewelry box.

"What is this?" Theresa asked. She extended her own hand to receive the small box.

"Theresa, why don't you open the lid and find out for yourself?" Her friend responded with a smile.

Theresa took the box and opened the lid hesitantly. "There'd better not be anything alive in here, Abby." She saw a ring, and a matching set of pearl-shaped earrings with gold flora backing shaped like the petals of a rose. Both were a deep, luxuriant color with a shimmering property. They were quite beautiful. Though the ring was the same color, it had more luster.

"What is this, Abby?" Theresa continued to gaze into the box with admiration.

"What else could it be, Theresa? It's the porphyry stone you found awhile back. My brother made it into jewelry for you. It took him longer than he expected, but look at the end product. Do you like it?"

"I love it, Abby, I really do. Especially the ring. It seems to have more of a shimmer to it. But how much do I owe your brother for this craftsmanship?"

"You don't owe him anything, Theresa. He said it was the least he could do since you've always helped him." Abigail paused for a moment. "Tolan will be back in town in a few weeks; you can thank him yourself in person."

While Abigail was talking, Theresa removed the ring from the box, admiring it in the sunlight. "It looks like the ring will fit my finger."

"It should," said Abigail. "All of the rings in your jewelry box fit my fingers just fine. So, that is the measurement my brother used. So stop gawking and try it on."

No sooner had Theresa placed the ring securely on her finger, then something caught Abigail's attention. "Now that is a face that I don't know. Theresa, there is a shirtless man sitting in the front seat of your car slumped forward like he's shitfaced. Did a drunk just get into your car?"

Theresa quickly turned around and saw Archibald just the way Abigail had described him. *He does look dead, but how can Abby see him?* Thinking fast, she decided to pretend she didn't see Archibald.

Theresa quickly took the ring off of her finger and returned it to the box when Abigail exclaimed, "Where the hell did he go? He was just there."

Theresa was thoughtful and turned towards her friend as she walked towards her car. "Abby, you are just tired and hungry. There is no one in my car. I'll talk to you later."

CHAPTER 13

After Theresa pulled off from her sister's house, she waited until she was well down the street before she addressed Archibald. "You should know, Abby saw you pretending to be dead."

"I *am* dead," he insisted. "I felt a queer sensation as if I was drawn swiftly up into the air by something I could not see. But thankfully, it has abated. Whatever strange events that have transpired today, I can be sure with all certainty that it had something to do with you."

Theresa scoffed.

"Theresa, there is no need for you to feel petty. Especially when such an important issue is affecting me."

Theresa pulled up to a stop sign and turned toward him with searching eyes.

"Theresa dear, now is not the time for those impromptu Oriental impersonations of yours. Even though I am quite fond of almond eyes, naturally occurring, of course, squinting like that is not good." Archibald snapped his fingers. "I have a question."

She signed heavily. "All right, what is your question?"

He surveyed her a moment before addressing her. "I was wondering, since you are free this afternoon, would you be so kind as to take me for a short excursion to South Carolina? It is not that far, perhaps an hour or so. Plus, I will fill your tank up with petrol."

Theresa thought about that. She even wondered how he was going to pay for her gas. After she thought about this, she just smiled and said, "No. I am going home to take a nap."

He grinned and turned his attention back to his passenger window.

"Stop looking devious," Theresa told him. "Are you that surprised I told you *no*?"

Archibald smiled at her. "No. I just found it humorous that you did not engage in your normal vacillating on the matter. And that you would conclude that you are actually going to get some sleep when we get home."

They rode down rural Highway 321. It took them through a scenic drive of the cypress swamps, farm fields, the quaint forgotten hamlets, and the thick forest of the South Carolina Low Country for nearly an hour. At Archibald's directions, Theresa turned off at a fork in the road, passing through the village of Garnett.

"We are not just going for a ride through the country; we are going someplace in particular, aren't we?" Theresa asked. She pulled off the side of the road near King's Branch, a lonesome Baptist church. It sat amidst a pine forest.

"You are correct; we are going to Paul Hill Cemetery, which is almost five miles from here, mostly down dirt roads used by farmers and hunters."

Theresa sighed as they left the church. They arrived at the old burial grounds after traveling through a meandering dirt road, deep into the viridescent forest, and walking the last 70 yards on foot due to a fallen tree.

Theresa noticed that the sounds of nature faded the closer they got to the old burial ground until there was nothing but a still silence. As they stood at the overgrown entrance, Theresa turned towards Archibald, pointing her finger at his chest. "If anything happens to me, you will never have peace in the house."

"Theresa, I don't have peace in the house now, as you are pretty nosy, chiding, and raucous for such a small woman. But you don't see *me* complaining about it."

Theresa frowned, her eyes glared.

"There's no need for you to get all warm about it. I do not know why you just did not stay in the car if you had apprehensions. But not only did you get out; you went to your trunk and changed into gym clothes."

Theresa sighed and turned her back toward him. "I am not getting *warm* about anything. I just did not want to be left in the car by myself in a forest possibly inhabited by banjo-plucking backcountry sodomites."

"You are right, Theresa. I think I see one now over yonder holding a stick of butter."

Theresa turned, looking around her, only to realize that Archibald had stepped off into the cemetery without her.

The cemetery was in a large clearing with weather-beaten scattered headstones and statuary that reached well into the forest over a rugged landscape. The foliage was so overgrown that it resembled a large, forgotten garden.

Theresa was walking, while trying to read the inscription on a crumbling tomb when Archibald's voice startled her.

"Theresa, it would behoove you to pay attention to where you are walking. You can easily twist your ankle on the uneven ground or fall into a sunken grave."

She walked closer to him as he navigated his way through the cemetery when she came to a stop. "Why is that in here?" Theresa asked as she indicated a miniature brick cottage that was about five feet high. It sat not far from the path on a small mound. She immediately went over and examined the structure without even waiting for Archibald to respond. The little house had a tin shingled roof, four curtained windows, a small door, and even a chimney stack topped off with a salt-glazed chimney pot.

"This curiosity before you is now one of those rare novelties of this country called a *dollhouse grave*," Archibald said to her, while still standing on the footpath. "Look inside the windows there, and you will see that it is filled with the toys that belonged to the little girl that sleeps beneath the house."

As she gazed into the small windows, they heard the rumble of a storm in the distance.

"There is also a rainstorm fast approaching, you will need to take shelter."

And he led her away to a partially obscured mausoleum. It was hidden behind a wall of blooming heirloom roses that completely encompassed the wrought iron fence around the structure.

Theresa entered the half-opened gate following Archibald's lead, and was careful not to prick herself on the thorns of the roses that had climbed up the gate like a trellis. She passed under the dogwood tree at the entrance of the mausoleum and read the name over the steps. *Montague*, she thought to herself as heavy drops of rain began to wet her hair. Theresa hastened to the steps, standing next to a column on the porch of the Greek Revival mausoleum, where she watched the sky open up. "Great," she said. "Not only am I in banjo country in the middle of nowhere, but I am also stuck in a cemetery during a downpour with your wily ass."

"Theresa, are we complaining again when there is no need for you to get so excited? After all, the rain will not last for long, and we can be on our way after it subsides. Besides, you've seemed to enjoy the journey up to now."

She heard a low groaning behind her. Theresa turned around and realized that the double lattice, patina-covered, bronze doors that had previously locked out the antechamber were now open. She slowly took a step back when there was another faint sound of something ponderous moving and then coming to a halt.

Archibald went inside, vanishing into the dark abyss, leaving her alone. He returned shortly. "Aren't you coming in, or do you prefer to dawdle?"

"You are out of your damned fool mind if you think I am going to follow you in there." She attempted to fold her arms to bolster her statement, but a sharp crack of lightning overhead sent Theresa flying into the structure.

She entered the dark sepulcher following Archibald's lead, but paused within the doorway, as she could not see any further. Something shifted under her shoes. She knelt down and realized she'd stepped onto a pile of coins. She came to the conclusion that someone had slid them under the chamber door at some point. Gathering a few coins in her hand, she noticed that two nickels had a Native American profile of a middle-aged man's head with a buffalo on the reverse. They were dated from 1909, 1916, and 1923. The third coin, a dime, showed a woman in a winged cap.

"What do you think all this loose change means?" she asked Archibald, who'd been paying attention to her, but was now staring off into the dark chamber. Theresa sniffed the air as she replaced the coins on the floor. "This place has a musty smell. It's kind of like old people, but with a hint of spices. Maybe anise and mint."

From out of the solitude of the still darkness, there came a distinct reply. "Humph. Smells like old people? Well, aren't you one uncouth so-and-so."

At this, Theresa began to back out of the doorway. She whispered to Archibald. "I just heard a woman's voice in here."

Archibald started to respond to Theresa when the voice in the darkness said, "Oh, I wasn't anticipating that she could hear me."

"Despite the *obvious* that this mortal can hear and see me," Archibald said bluntly.

A short conversation ensued as the voice engaged Archibald vehemently in a foreign language. Theresa thought that maybe it was Latin, but couldn't be sure. Archibald responded back to this unseen entity using this language in a calm, collected tone. Theresa, who was listening attentively, at first perceived the conversation to be about her, but then thought it was mostly about him. This thought was cemented when she heard herself mentioned directly.

There was another close flash of lightning, and it made Theresa flinch. When she looked up, she saw a faint vestige of a face peering out of the curtain of darkness as if listening half-heartedly to Archibald.

She looks annoyed with him, Theresa thought, debating her next move. *I should leave, but it's raining too hard, and I really don't know my way out of this place.*

The only response Archibald got was a few words in a new language that Theresa didn't recognize at all.

"If you are going to insult me, at least let it be in a language I understand, so that I can properly savor your insults. Not in this Koine Greek," he said to her in a tone that denoted he was amused by her actions.

The entity let out a short, profanity-laced commentary in English. But Archibald was unfazed by her curt retort. He only chuckled and vanished within an instant.

The entity's attention now rested on Theresa. In an exasperated voice it said, "He has stepped out for the moment, but he'll be back." There was a sigh, and this time she spoke in a softer tone. "Theresa, go out of that door and look to your right. You will find a wooden crate. Bring it in here. It has candles that we need to use for light, and then we can close the door."

Theresa did as she was told, and soon, the gloomy chamber was illuminated with an assortment of votive and seven-day candles placed along the wall every few feet. Theresa stood there staring intently at a dusty, ornate vase made of alabaster in the rear of the tomb, situated prominently on a marble altar. Mounted on the wall behind the altar was the remnant of an ancient Roman mosaic slab held in place with bronze claps. It depicted a Roman standard-bearer holding the standard of Legio XIII Gemina, while wearing a wolf's pelt that obscured most of his face.

Strange how that wolf's pelt on that soldier looks so familiar. That's right, in my dream of Archibald at the seaside, that female ghost he spoke to hid her face behind one of those.

This area of the tomb was stepped up in elevation, and there was a thick layer of dust on the top and around the floor more so than in any part of the chamber. Within this layer of dust, there were dried petals that had been scattered near the base of the pedestal. She placed two of the seven-day candles on the altar, one on each side of the alabaster vase. She then lit them with her keychain lighter.

It occurred to her that she had not seen the face of the voice since she came back in with the candles.

Theresa turned to see the door closed and a small female figure stood in front of it. That is, floating a few inches above the floor. This transformation surprised her as the entity was nothing more than a mere shadow a moment ago. Theresa stared, and her gaze was only returned with a confused look.

"Theresa, you don't have to stand there; you can put the lid back and sit on the crate."

Theresa was still holding the crate but sat it down near the altar, and headed toward the entrance where she left the lid earlier. A cobweb-kissed coffin, sitting parallel on the wall opposite of the one where she had set the candles, caught her attention. Theresa decided that on her return journey, she was going to walk near the casket. Seeing that the attention of her hostess turned towards the two flickering altar-candles, she proceeded within reaching distance of the casket. A large portion of the coffin lid was damaged and missing, exposing the remains of a woman, covered with a silk veil.

Theresa's eyes were first drawn to the fine gold chain with a cameo clasped to it, gathered around on the vertebrae of the decayed neck. The passage of years did not destroy the corpse's thick, burnished hair. Her wavy tresses were still neatly braided around on the sides in an intricate manner. The hair was kept in place by gold hairpins, and she was marveling at this artistry when her eyes caught something else. The deceased was embracing the remains of a small child whose crown was covered with the same wavy hair as her mother.

For the first time her curiosity transformed to something else—*pity*.

"There were 23 coffins here, at one time," spoke the soft feminine voice. "But only this casket remains here, as you can obviously see."

Feeling somewhat embarrassed about peering into someone's coffin and thinking it may be perceived as ill-mannered, Theresa held her tongue. She quickened her pace back to the crate by the altar. After replacing the lid in its proper place, she sat down, facing her hostess who was hovering at the edge of the altar with a nervous smile.

"So, why did they move all the coffins except this one?" But before the other could respond to her query, a thought came into Theresa's head. "I am very sorry for looking into your coffin. I guess my curiosity got the best of me."

"Your nosiness is no issue to me, Theresa," the entity said to her with a wink. "Besides, that is not my coffin, as I was never interred in one. It wasn't my family's custom at the time. That is the coffin of Regina Rainey and her child, Patrice. Both were victims of a worldwide pestilence that was known as *Spanish influenza*."

"So, what did happen to the other coffins?" Theresa asked, her interest piqued.

"They rest in a new mausoleum in Oklahoma. Hiram Montague, the grandson of the builder of this place, Sinjin Montague, thought it was an affront to the dignity of his family to have his father's tawny love child entombed here with the rest of their family. So, he had them moved there along with the rest of the living relations that were willing to pack up and go."

"Wait a minute. I understand that he was spiteful," Theresa said. "But how was he able to convince his relations to go with him to Oklahoma?"

"Hiram became very wealthy after marrying into the Osage tribe who lived on land that contained large reserves of black gold. He became a widow shortly thereafter and generously offered his relations the means to start over in Oklahoma. You should know that once the information got out that oil was found on the Osage reservation, the locals in nearby neighboring towns decided to transfer the Osage people's wealth to themselves through guile. They did this by marrying into the Osage communities and then systematically killed them off, thereby allowing the wealth to transfer into their hands and subsequently, their descendants by claiming Osage status. All the deaths were chalked up to natural causes. But to this day, I am not sure how he caught wind of a scheme in Oklahoma from a gambling house in Port Royal."

Listening attentively, Theresa pondered what she was just told and shook her head. She let out a long sigh. "I take it that you are not a member of the Montague family from the way you speak. Yet, why do you reside here, if you don't mind me asking?"

The entity turned around and pointed to the vase upon the altar with a small cream-colored hand. "This worn alabaster amphora here is my cremation urn. I came into the Montague family when the antiquarian,

Mr. Sinjin Montague, purchased my urn from a cobbler who had it in his possession while traveling through the Netherlands in Brielle on the day of Kalknacht in 1844."

The entity spoke highly of that man's erudite character to the point that it was apparent that she had an emotional interest in him.

"Having a crush would do that too," Theresa said as she noticed a softening to the entity's facial expressions in retelling her memories.

The entity's face blushed, and she held her head down smiling.

"Was he able to see you?"

"Yes, but it wasn't at first. I learned later that he gradually became aware of my presence. I stayed with him and accompanied him on his journeys for the next 17 years until his life came to its conclusion while at sea on a return trip from Siam with his son. His body was buried at sea minus a small memento." She then hopped off the edge of the altar, standing within an inch from the floor and pointed towards the corner on the opposite side of the altar.

Theresa stood up and saw a marble pillar about four feet high with a small box on it obscured by cobwebs and shadow.

"In that box over there is his heart, if you wish to see it."

After Theresa moved aside the cobwebs with a piece of wood she took from the crate, she leaned over and carefully retrieved it at her hostess's behest. She placed it at the center of the altar between the glow of two candles, and lifted the jade lid cover off the ossuary. She did this slowly after she had blown the thick layer of dust away. As she held the lid in her hand, she noticed that there was a motif of three hares chasing each other in a circle. "I wonder what that means," she murmured to herself as she carefully set the lid aside. After taking a deep breath, she peered into the opened ossuary. There was a faded velvet pillow with a dark brown object in the center of it. "It looks like a big raisin," Theresa said.

The entity, twisting her neck to look into the box, scrutinized the contents. "Hmm, it looks like a scrotum to me."

A few seconds passed as they looked at each other before they burst into laughter. They returned to their respective seats and continued their friendly conversation. It was at this point that it occurred to Theresa that she did not know her hostess's name and inquired about it.

"Oh, I am sorry for that oversight, Theresa. I am called *Charlotte of the Rose* or just *Charlotte* for short." Charlotte's demeanor then changed slightly as she continued. "Everyone that knows of me calls me that, except one individual who calls me *Gingersnaps* because he's a rude, arrogant, rash-face, dumbass." She said this last part with an air of contempt.

"You said you are *called* Charlotte, but what is your birth name? I saw some words that were barely legible across the top of the vase. But since I cannot read Latin,

I don't know what they mean. Do you think it could be a clue to your name?"

"It is because I had long forgotten my own name by the time I was brought back to this world. And the inscription on my urn was damaged by the passage of time, to the point that my name was no longer decipherable. The words you saw were just a part of a tribute to *Restitutor Orbis*, the Emperor Aurelian."

The Emperor Aurelian? Theresa wondered to herself as she looked at the ghost.

"How long has it been since you were alive?"

Charlotte began counting on her fingers at such a fast pace that Theresa couldn't keep up. "It has been 1,746 years since I was a mortal."

"Whoa, that is a really long time!" Theresa exclaimed as Charlotte shrugged her shoulders. "But I am curious to know how you came up with that particular name if you had forgotten your own?"

"An interesting woman that went by Yolande of Jumièges gave me my name six centuries or so ago."

"I take it that she was not of some relation to you?"

"No, she was not, Theresa. She was a house servant of a black-hearted necromancer named Phillips, who was in possession of my funeral urn. Seeing that it was made of valuable alabaster, she took my urn home as part of her payment after Phillips's curious and untimely death."

"What did she do with your urn once she got it home?" Theresa asked, examining the alabaster urn again, running her fingers along the centuries-old engravings. The beauty of the natural stone seemed to be more radiant than before.

"She set it on a cabinet on the opposite wall over the fireplace between two small windows. I suppose that she had initially intended to sell my urn, but she never did. When the spring came, she planted a white rose in my urn on what was left of my ashes without realizing what she was doing. This was before she knew that my spirit still resided within my urn. She did not have the outré ability to see me like you and the Necromancer had at will." Charlotte scrutinized Theresa as if she was pondering something. But she continued on with her story.

"It was the Necromancer, Phillips, that used his dark magic to bring me back to this world to serve him. Whenever he desired something of me, he would always say, '*Slave, come forth!*' to summon me or '*Slave, do this,*' and I was forced by his power to do as I was bid. That was my name for the beginning of my new existence back into this world of the living. I knew that a person of his ability must have known my true name. But when I asked my master, he said that the title of *slave* was all I needed to serve him, as I was just *his* property."

"Wow, he sounds like a real asshole."

"That is exactly what he was, with the shit still in it. I chided him about it on occasion, along with some unkind words about his fat neck and tart hygiene, but alas, it was all to no avail, as he was as obstinate as a rock. But anyway, Yolande gave me this name after conversing with me in her dreams, the name of her favorite cousin who was carried off by marauding troops as a child. This was after the rose she planted came into bloom, hence the name *Charlotte of the Rose.*"

Theresa stood up and moved a little closer to Charlotte and said warmly, "It is a good name for you. It is very pretty, just like you are."

Charlotte's cheeks turned rosy as she brought her hands to her face in an attempt to cover them.

Theresa was quiet for a moment as she watched her endearing freckled-face hostess try to compose herself. And then a thought came into her head. "Charlotte, I'm curious to know why the old coins are on the floor and a crate of candles sitting outside?" she said, pointing towards the door. "Oh, and how did you meet Archibald? The look of annoyance you gave him earlier was almost the same as the looks that I give him."

Charlotte smiled and laughed to herself. "Those coins over there are supposed to be my payment from a few locals in exchange for favors I would occasionally do from time to time. You know, because apparently I really have the need of mortal money and would work for such low wages." She scoffed as she rolled her eyes. "But I am glad that most of that nonsense stopped decades ago. Those candles, on the other hand, were brought here by a young man who lives down the road near the railroad tracks. And I honestly do appreciate them, especially the ones that smell like baked cinnamon apple pie and cookies."

Theresa laughed as Charlotte continued. "Now, I met that charming bastard Archibald in the summer of '26 at a party hosted by Raby Castle in County Durham, England. I ended up in England after coming across a travel brochure of the country in a house I was haunting. It piqued my interest, as it reminded me of the travels I took with Sinjin so many years earlier. I had been in the country for only two days roaming in the countryside after visiting Hadrian's Wall when I encountered a lonesome soldier of the Great War. He was finally making his way back home to New York to cross over with his dying mother, but informed me about the events from the direction he had come. So, I soon found the place late that evening and was graciously admitted to Raby Castle, wearing the finest stola I owned."

As she said this, her garment changed into a beautifully embroidered stola that was a light yellow with a red palla, embroidered in gold along the edges with geometric patterns. The scene was breathtaking to Theresa as she had never seen a garment of that style. It was quite beautiful. Charlotte's dress then reverted back to the simple white gown she had on previously. Theresa came to realize that Charlotte's features became more pronounced and more lifelike as their time together continued.

"After I was properly introduced to everyone, I was engaged in conversation by several of the previous Lords of Raby Castle. Through them, I was introduced to many of the various apparitions that had attended, which included a few Jacobites who were still carrying on like sore losers. In my socializing, I learned that there was a game of Whist going on in the kitchen. Being fond of card games myself, I decided to check it out. That was when I first saw Arch sitting at the card table with three other men. He was dressed in a priest's cassock, elbows on the table, and a cigarette in his hand. He had that nonchalant self-satisfied look then as he does now."

I'm not even going to ask why that conceited fool was dressed up like a priest, Theresa thought to herself.

"When a seat became available, I sat down and was cordially greeted by a Highwayman that had a bullet wound over his left eye, and a judge named Jeffreys whose large black eyebrows gave him a sinister countenance. Arch said nothing, but looked at me with a peculiar smirk on his face. He said something in Welsh, and from what I could gather, it was something rather vulgar. His off-colored comments made many in the room laugh, and some of the women blushed. That's when I told him that his winning streak had come to an end."

"Well, did you beat him?"

"Hell yeah, I beat him six times consecutively, and he was triggered for a long time too! I was gloating in his stupid face as he crumbled one of his cigarettes. I asked him why he was surprised that he lost so many times when I told him that I intended to win from the start? And this fool told me, in a matter-of-fact way, that it was a policy of his not to take flat-chested women seriously on any occasion."

Theresa held her head down as she tried to cover her laughter with her hand. She looked up when she heard Charlotte let out a sigh.

"Alright now, Theresa, that shit wasn't funny."

"Charlotte, forgive me if this question sounds odd or silly to you, but what makes ghosts linger on in this world?"

Charlotte paused as if she was taken off guard by the question. "One's reason for still being here in the realm of the living can vary greatly. Sometimes you don't know, and other times, it is very obvious. Such as a victim of a murder wanting justice, someone doing penance, unfinished affairs in this world, or even a broken heart can keep a soul on this side of the veil. Or as in the case of Arch and myself, they are held here by the bonds of necromancy."

Theresa nodded, satisfied with Charlotte's explanation. *So, Archibald has a spell on him. I wonder what else I can find out about him?*

Charlotte hopped off the edge of the altar and descended towards the floor without touching it. "The rain has stopped, Theresa. The storm is heading back out to sea."

Theresa, who had lost all sense of time and her whereabouts, was now paying attention to the weather outside, and could hear distinct rumbling in the distance and stood up.

CHAPTER 14

"You know," Theresa said thoughtfully to Charlotte of the Rose, "Archie doesn't tell me much about himself. And sometimes when I do ask, he has a clever way of speaking that is tantamount to evasion."

"Well, we can always find out for ourselves," said Charlotte enthusiastically.

Theresa looked at Charlotte perplexed, but rephrased her previous response. "I've been trying that to no avail. He always finds a clever way to dodge the questions. But hey, why are you smiling like that all of a sudden?"

"I don't know." Charlotte smiled curiously. She extended her hand forward to Theresa and implored her to grab hold of her hand.

Theresa reached out to meet Charlotte's, but retracted it. "Is there something weird about to happen?" Theresa asked as she sat on her hands.

"Of course, but no weirder than it has been so far. Besides, you may find the change of scenery interesting." And then Charlotte tapped Theresa on the center of her forehead while saying some sort of chant without her lips moving.

The next thing Theresa knew, Charlotte was whisking her along by the hand at a terrific speed through a sea of dark clouds before they were enveloped in a blinding light. Theresa had closed her eyes when she realized that they had alighted. Charlotte was trying to shake her hand free.

"You squeezed my hand pretty hard, Theresa."

Theresa's attentions were more absorbed in her new surroundings. She gazed around. They were in a large city whose rooftops extended into the horizon. There was not a single automobile in any direction, but a light traffic of horse carts of various shapes and sizes. Two women with pretty hats quickly navigated the street in a serpentine manner to avoid the piles of horse manure. There were also various street vendors with pushcarts moving up and down the streets, hawking goods from jellied eels to pea soup to coffee.

The fashion people wore were of late-nineteenth-century vintage that varied from wealth to rags. Theresa heard the sound of a man and woman conversing close by. She turned and hastily stepped out of the way as a smartly dressed officer in a bright red tunic and a pillbox hat escorted a woman who did not seem to be his equal. He walked directly where Theresa was standing, passing through her as he made his way down the sidewalk.

"They are nothing more than shadows in a distant mirror of things that have been," said Charlotte, who had been observing Theresa. "They cannot hurt you, nor can you interfere with them."

"What year is it exactly?"

"It is Tuesday, March 31, 1891 at 11:04 a.m. in London's fabled East End. We are just a few blocks from the real debauchery. But alas, that is not what we are here for."

Charlotte smiled and pointed towards a large three-story stone and brick Georgian building directly across the street from them. The building was well-kept; nothing was particularly out of the ordinary, with the exception of a penny-farthing parked by a short flight of stairs.

Theresa looked at Charlotte only to find her still staring towards the door across the street. She was just about to ask Charlotte something when the door opened.

A man in a brown tweed county suit appeared in the doorway. He paused there for a moment as if the light hurt his eyes. He rubbed them and strolled down the stairs as if he was in a dream. He retrieved a flat cap from his jacket pocket and placed it on his head before removing the penny-farthing from where it was parked. The way he walked, moving his large bicycle to the curve of the sidewalk, swaying slightly, made Theresa question Charlotte whether or not he was drunk.

"He's not a drunkard, been chasing the dragon since one this morning."

Theresa looked at Charlotte with confusion.

"He's high from opium, Theresa. That building he just left is actually an opium den and a brothel masquerading as a mix-use building to throw off Scotland."

Theresa scrutinized the building further. "But it looks so nice on the outside. It even has flowers hanging from the window boxes."

"There is a world of difference in how things appear to be and what they actually are. But never mind that, here is our bicyclist, heading our way."

The bicyclist was in the midst of a volte-face and passed right in front of them.

"That is Archibald!"

He didn't get that far before his bicycle collided into the side of a parked carriage. This sent him flying over the handlebars like a rag doll with his bike on top of him. Surprisingly, he got himself up relatively quickly, and recovered his penny-farthing.

A woman of considerable character from inside the carriage stepped out and began to address Archibald in no kind words for jarring her carriage. He appeared to be listening attentively as he stood up, brushing his clothes off. But when she had concluded her tirade, he made a vulgar gesture with his hand before returning his attention to his bicycle. The woman, who was in shock momentarily by this unexpected affront, reached into the carriage and pulled out her parasol. She began levying blows against Archibald's head, back, and shoulders while calling him an *impertinent street rascal* in the process.

Archibald seemed more annoyed than hurt, and with a sudden movement of his hand, he arrested her arm in mid-flight. While holding her, he leaned his bicycle against the carriage and then removed the parasol from her hand. He tossed it back into the carriage before turning his attention towards her. His rapidity caused her to flinch, but he only stared at her. He released her arm.

"Madam, I understand that you are apparently jealous of my bicycle, which unlike yourself—despite having a good saddle—is ridden hard, quite frequently to the point that one is always full of fond memories of it. But nevertheless, this is not about you, but rather it is about me having an accident. Yet, you did not realize that because you were too busy using my unfortunate situation to draw what little attention you could get yourself."

He lifted his finger and wagged it in her face with taunting disapproval. The woman who had recovered herself was about to say something when Archibald brought his finger to his lips and shook his head. He then helped her into her carriage, gave her his card, and closed the carriage door. Cordially, he tipped his hat to her before recovering his bicycle. Before mounting the penny-farthing, he turned to her. "I look forward to you calling upon me. You know, with a proper apology and all." He told her good day, and he rode away, turning down the next block.

Charlotte then took Theresa through several scenes of Archibald's mortal existence within the blink of an eye. They saw Archibald intentionally annoy people, which was of no surprise to her. But she also saw how he gave wonderful, passionate public speeches concerning women's suffrage, the merits of helping those less than fortunate, and railing against atrocities in the Congo Free State. And he followed up faithful to his words by making sizable donations to match his stance. She also saw the gambling at various clubs along Pall Mall, and the borderline criminal activity that he was involved in that allowed him to practice his eleemosynary preferences.

She also saw the woman from the carriage, making frequent apologetic visits to Archibald's home, incognito in the late hours of the evening. This activity was very much to the dismay of Archibald's personal secretary, Paelaysia, with whom, on occasion, he had a very personal relationship. She saw him sometimes eyeing the woman from the window of his house.

"We have just enough time to make one more stop," Charlotte said, standing outside of Archibald's Belgravia home.

"The place we are going is near the Danson House, a locality I wish to see. You will be left alone until the scene plays to its conclusion."

Theresa thought about it. "Some tour guide you are. What if an emergency should arise? I won't be able to contact you."

Charlotte pouted and stomped her foot on the slate pavement, but it didn't make a sound. "I am going to Danson House! But if you should have an emergency, the possibility of which I find to be highly unlikely, just say 'pickle pickle.' That's your safe word, and I will return in an instant."

"Huh. Pickle pickle?" Theresa muttered, only to realize she was by herself. She looked around and saw that her surroundings had changed. She was in some type of basement that had brick walls appearing to have been built upon the older walls that had elements of religious flush work and Cobblestone floors. It appeared to be night, and the place was dimly illuminated with several gas lamps that were placed at intervals along the wall.

Since the room looked ominous to her, she was about to walk in the direction of the stairway when she heard a familiar voice, speaking in a jovial manner.

"Which of these two do you like the best, sir?" Theresa immediately turned around and saw Archibald standing next to a burly man who was seated and bound hand and foot. He was sitting in front of a large open grate in the floor where the sounds of moving water emanated.

Archibald continued speaking to the man. "You can leave the environs of London completely, or you can remain with a ball of lead in your head. The choice is wholly yours, sir."

"You don't have the bollocks to do anything to me," retorted the other man in a gruff cockney accent.

Archibald only smiled and checked his pocket watch. "One minute you have to make up your mind. Starting now, sir," Archibald said to the other man as he stood holding the watch dangling in front of his face by its gold chain.

Theresa took several cautious steps toward Archibald when she saw that the bound man had been badly beaten across his face. His left side took the greater brunt of it.

She also noticed that there was a gentle slope in the floor to facilitate good drainage towards the opening in the floor where he was positioned. It was at this point she realized that the man's arms were fastened with a chain that ran through a wrought iron ring mounted on the floor, directly under the chair that connected with his ankles. This clever arrangement prevented any meaningful movement.

After surveying the whole scene, Theresa approached Archibald and asked him what he was doing several times, but her efforts were to no avail. He did not respond. She then tried to address the bound man, but he was just as oblivious to her presence as Archibald was. Then, she remembered what Charlotte had told her.

"Your time is up, sir." Archibald said abruptly. "Have you made your choice on the matter?"

The man spit blood out of his mouth. "You and that little bitch can go to hell."

Theresa took a few steps back when the thud of a blow landed across the bound man's head. She headed towards the stairway in a hurry when the crack of a firearm arrested her movement. She saw Archibald standing behind the chair of the man with his right arm extended holding a revolver. The man was slumped over, only restrained from falling forward by his bonds.

Theresa could see that the back of the man's hair began to mat as the blood welled where the projectile had entered. The man made a low gurgling sound as blood filled his windpipe. Archibald coolly delivered the coup de grâce by putting another charge into the dying man's head. He then walked off to an opening in the rear of the room, where he stayed for several minutes. Theresa was curious to know what he was up to, but the shock of the situation left her feeling numb. She couldn't move.

After he stepped back into the room out of Theresa's view, he was clad in a leather butcher's apron with a matching cap. After he had stripped the man naked, he then proceeded to slide the man into the open sewer grate by feeding in his body, feet first. Being a large man, Archibald had to stamp on the man's shoulders a few times to get the body to slide down past his mid-section. The body was wedged firmly into the grate and got stuck right under the arm.

"Oh dear," Archibald said disappointedly, as he rubbed his hand against his chin in contemplation. He walked off into the shadows, which apparently housed a storage closet, and returned with a broad axe.

"Oh, hell no," Theresa said. She started yelling, *Pickle! Pickle!* frantically at the top of her lungs.

Charlotte immediately appeared in front of her with an annoyed expression on her face. But when she saw Theresa's horror, she admittedly turned around and yelled a choice word as Archibald was about to bring the broad axe blade down upon the dead man's shoulder. Theresa did not see this, but she heard it just as they returned back to the mausoleum sitting in their respective seats with bewilderment all over their faces.

But it was Charlotte who broached the silence first by speaking. "I'm sorry, Theresa," she said earnestly. "I didn't know that was going to happen. The first time I saw it, I left before he shot the man because I figured that was his intent. I am not a big fan of violence, you know, unless I'm delivering it. Then it's different. Violence is never the answer, except when it is the only answer."

Theresa stood up. "I need to get some fresh air."

Charlotte went with her, and the two were standing on the steps looking up at the beautiful night sky. The air was filled with the earthy scent of rain, mixed with the aroma of the sea of roses intertwined in the wrought iron fence. The moon was high, shining through the branches of the trees with its illuminating pale glow.

The two stood there talking about their trip together when Archibald appeared a few feet from them. It was Charlotte who saw him first, and she immediately stopped talking, which prompted Theresa to look to the direction she was staring. She saw Archibald and immediately folded her arms. Charlotte modified her stance to match that of her companion.

"Oh, I get it," he said, speaking casually to them. "You two were talking about me, and became so chummy in such a short period of time, too. But, then again, I do have that wonderful effervescent effect of bringing others together."

"He's so full of himself," Theresa whispered to Charlotte, who nodded her head in agreement. "You are a criminal and a regular hoodlum at that," Theresa said to him sharply. "I saw you kill a man, and don't you dare deny it."

Archibald then turned his attention to Charlotte, whom he regarded with a look of disapprobation. "I take it that this is your witch-magic at work here?" He sighed as he shook his head slightly. "If your mother only knew that you were in the business of telling other people's business, she would be full of shame and disappointment. More shame and disappointment than you feel when you look down at your own chest."

Charlotte's cheeks turned crimson as she grumbled something that no one else heard.

"Now, as for you, Theresa, could you please be more specific?"

"Huh, what do you mean *specific*? How specific can killing someone be?" asked Theresa in angry confusion.

"I mean, can you give me any pertinent details on the person or location? Your remarks are very vague."

Theresa sighed. "It was in the dingy basement of some old building, and there was a sewer grate in the floor in the center of the room."

Charlotte added that he was a fairly large individual that needed to be cut down to fit into the drain grate.

Archibald snapped his fingers. "Ah-ha, yes, the dodgy old storage house near the Crossness pumping station. And I think I know of whom you are speaking."

Theresa scrutinized his face. "What do you mean you 'think' you know? How many people have you murdered, you fiend?"

He looked amused by the question. "I have never murdered anyone, Theresa. But I have killed a few people here and there, and that is not the same thing, especially if one is dealing with street ruffians and other persistently asinine fellows. And seriously, I don't know why either of you are acting surprised about me handling rubbish. Especially since my volunteer work was good for the Earth and the community."

He then took out a cigarette from his silver case and began smoking casually as they looked at him in amazement.

"The long and short of it is really not that interesting, as it was a very clichéd situation. That bloke you saw in the chair made his living by enforcing a tax upon the women of the lower order in certain vicinities of Bermondsey and Clerkenwell every fortnight. This so-called tax was to pay a protection fee to ensure their safety. I learned of this arrangement from a young woman that I was acquainted with who sold sweetmeats at Moorgate. I noticed that she had some bruising about her face and arms, and I persisted in my inquiries. After making several poor excuses, she acquiesced after I told her I would purchase a sum of sugarplums to be delivered to her home the following day. She came the next day with her pushcart, assisted by a small boy of maybe six years of age whom she cared for as her own. He also showed signs of misuse.

I learned that both of them were beaten because of her failure to pay the imposed tax. So, after gathering information about this gang and its leader, I sent them on an extended holiday to St. Austell to one of my cottages, while I looked into the situation. And you two voyeurs saw the conclusion of that."

Archibald turned and began walking toward the path that he and Theresa came down earlier. He walked about ten paces and stopped; he turned his head over his shoulder and spoke. "Oh yes, be mindful that in the future that just because you interject yourself into the affairs of another does not mean you are entitled to get an answer. All right, ladies, please exchange your adieus. It is getting very late, and Theresa is pretty blind at night, even with her reading glasses."

Charlotte turned to Theresa, telling her that she would escort them back to their car. Archibald walked ahead of them as the women followed behind.

"Do you think he is mad at us for prying into his affairs?" Theresa whispered to Charlotte.

"I wouldn't care if he was. But no, he's fine. He is just lost in his thoughts about something else—I'd guess the matter that he attended to while we were together."

Theresa abruptly stopped when she heard the sound of children laughing. She looked in the direction of the sound and saw the dollhouse grave bathed in the pale of light from the moon. She looked down and saw a small girl in a blue gingham dress who spoke with a Charleston accent. She asked Charlotte if she would she like to play with them for a bit later. Whatever

Charlotte said in response, Theresa did not catch because her attention was drawn to something that was moving behind the girl. A small boy in a blue sailor's suit that clung to the back of the girl's dress was eyeing Theresa curiously. Immediately, she felt enamored with him. His chubby dimpled cheeks made Theresa smile as he peeked at her grinning.

"I think she can see us," he whispered to his playmate.

"Of course she can," the girl whispered likewise back to her companion.

"Go along and play, you two," said Charlotte.

"Yes, Miss Charlotte!" The children said in unison before scurrying away in the direction of the dollhouse.

Theresa, looking back at the children, asked Charlotte if that was her brother.

"No, Theresa," she answered. "That's Benny. He got lost in the woods many years ago and drowned in a pond two miles northeast near a forgotten orchard. I brought him here to play with Fanny and the other children after I saw him one night while I was chasing some mortal through the woods."

Considering she's Archie's friend, chasing someone through the woods at night doesn't surprise me, Theresa thought as Charlotte continued.

"In the years past, in the memory of some of the oldest members of the surrounding communities, he was known simply as *The Wailing*. On occasion, his mournful sobs carried on the wind in the evenings. I was told that it was particularly noticeable during the winter months because sound drifts better without the foliage dampening it. To be quite honest with you, at first, I did not believe the story when I heard it, considering most of these rural people are as superstitious as an old woman. Things that cannot be attributed to anything else are always chalked up to an extra mundane experience, which surprisingly, in this case, was merited."

"You seem to be fond of Benny. He is just so adorable," Theresa admitted with a slight smile.

They soon reached Theresa's parked car to see Archibald, who had arrived there earlier, waiting for them. Theresa got in, followed by Archibald, who resumed his place in the front seat.

"Thank you for the unique experiences you have shown me tonight, Charlotte." She turned towards Archibald. "Plus, the interesting insights you gave me on this one, too. If you ever come to Savannah, you should stop by and visit us."

Archibald scoffed at this notion.

"Thank you, Theresa," Charlotte said cheerfully at the invitation. "I think I will come and pay a visit. It's not like I'm doing anything besides the occasionally requested hauntings, one of which I'm getting involved in tonight. Goodnight, Theresa."

Charlotte then floated parallel to the hood of the car, looking into the windshield at Archibald, who was pretending that he did not see her. She waved at him to get his attention. "Goodnight to you too, you sad bastard."

And then Charlotte floated backwards into the forest and was gone.

They arrived home before 10 p.m. after driving for nearly an hour.

"It's not like *you've* never thought about killing anyone, Theresa," Archibald eventually said, breaking the silence.

"I have under circumstances I can't recollect. Usually, when I'm at work and my supervisor is seriously annoying me. But that doesn't mean I actually wanted to do it."

"See, that's your problem, Theresa. You lack the resolve to see your plans through."

Theresa looked at him for a moment with a straight face before her attention was drawn to her porch.

"Geez, my porch looks dark. I thought I left the light on this morning." She got out of the car, followed by Archibald, and walked up the stairs. She fumbled through her purse for her keys when she heard him clear his voice in such a manner so as to draw her attention.

"What is it?"

He said nothing but only glanced at her, and then his attention returned to something behind her. Theresa turned abruptly to notice a silhouetted shape at the far end of her porch against the iron railing. She was startled and took a step back as the figure shifted on the porch. An ill-timed gust of cold wind rustling through the leaves added to her anxiety.

"Who are you?" Theresa asked nervously.

The shadowy figure knelt and picked up something from the floor of the porch. Theresa also noticed a shimmer of something as the shadowy figure moved. Theresa became even more alarmed when the figure advanced towards her.

Theresa reached into her purse, holding her hand there and blurted out, "I have a pistol, don't you come any closer." She began inadvertently taking small steps backwards. She looked around for Archibald, but he was nowhere to be seen. When she turned around, the figure was standing two feet in front of her.

"I guess you cannot find it, or you would have had it out by now." The figure said, in a soft voice with a hint of mocking.

CHAPTER 15

The light came on abruptly, illuminating the porch along with the stranger. It was a distinguished woman who awed Theresa with her style and fashion. She had her hair in a sleek chignon that made it easier to see that her ears were studded with blue diamonds that twinkled in the light. She wore a black cape that extended to her knees, covering her dress. The hood and sleeves of her cape were trimmed in shiny black fur. Her hands were covered in fine satin evening gloves, her handbag was of the finest quality, and her black brogue lace-up ankle boots with Cuban heels were made of fine leather.

One thing is for certain; she's definitely not a Jehovah's Witness, she thought.

"Wait a minute—I know you," Theresa said as she scrutinized the stranger's face.

"Yes, it's nice to see you too, Theresa," the woman said with a slight smirk on her face.

"Louisa Camille, of all people. Now this really has been a night full of surprises."

The old friends warmly embraced as Louisa Camille kissed Theresa's cheeks in the *faire la bise* fashion.

"Wow, it has been so long since I've seen you. You really have changed, including your accent," Theresa paused, realizing what she had said, recalling the lucid dream she'd had weeks prior. "I mean, you look so alluring, and that amazing scent you're wearing smells wonderful."

Louisa Camille curtsied with an air of approbation at the compliment.

"It's not a perfume, but rather a very aromatic soap made with ginger and mint I acquired when I was in Sierra Leone. Now you, on the other hand, have the hint of a pine forest with a touch of rose blossoms. That is unusual."

"Well, I went for a walk in the forest during an impromptu excursion to South Carolina. Something annoying kept telling me in my right ear that I needed a change of pace in the countryside."

Louisa Camille smiled softly at this. "Oh, so you went to the Afghanistan of North America. I must admit that I am surprised at you, Theresa. I have always pegged you as a more of a homebody, rather than a person who takes late-night walks in the forest of all places. But the results are amazing, you're so toned up."

"Look who's talking," Theresa retorted as she withdrew her keys to unlock the door.

"Theresa, dear," Louisa Camille said. "Everything we see is not often for practicality but for show.

Furthermore, looks are just there to help hide what the mind contemplates."

Theresa unlocked the door, and the two entered the quiet house as a chilled breeze swept through the porch, ushering in a new drop in the temperature. After a quick tour of the house, the two friends caught up on old times in the parlour, eating coffee cakes as the fire danced around crackling logs in the fireplace.

While they were talking, she learned that Louisa Camille actually went to the Philharmonic Orchestra that evening, and for some reason, she'd decided to walk to Theresa's house. This made Theresa wonder how Louisa Camille knew her address, considering they hadn't spoken for so many years. She also wondered what happened to Archibald since she had not seen him since they arrived home. She knew he'd turned on the porch light, but for some reason, he'd been curiously absent. During her conversation with Louisa Camille, she found herself looking towards the hallway, expecting him to appear.

"I have associates, Theresa, who are in the position to find the people I need, such as you, dearie." Louisa Camille winked at Theresa while retrieving her hot chocolate from the coaster. "There is also another reason I am this far north. I want to introduce an acquaintance to a gentleman that can give him some pointers on a career path he's gotten into his head to follow."

Louisa Camille stood up, leaning over to pick up her handbag in the process of returning her mug to the table. "Your attention is elsewhere, Theresa. You seem to be looking for someone the way you keep turning your head. I assume it's that debonair Englishman housemate of yours: Mr. Turner."

Theresa looked at Louisa Camille with a searching gaze.

"You've seen him?" Theresa asked as she stood up hastily.

"Of course I have. Not long ago, while you were upstairs. You act as if I wasn't supposed to see him or something. But anyway, he stuck his head in the room and greeted me while I was reading a magazine I picked up from your end table. We exchanged a few charming words, then he left." Louisa Camille then touched her finger to her chin.

"Now you're the one thinking about something," said Theresa. "And I know it's something out of the ordinary."

"You're very perceptive, Theresa. I was just thinking. Your friend, Mr. Turner, didn't make a sound walking along the hardwood floor, despite wearing dress shoes. I also didn't hear him go out the front door, yet he wasn't in the hallway when I got up to see. It's almost like he's a ninja or something."

As they walked towards the front door, Louisa Camille turned to Theresa. "I will be in town to the end of this month, handling my affairs here. I hope that we shall have a chance to meet up again soon. I do apologize for surprising you like this, but I will make it up to you."

Theresa stood on her porch after they hugged and said their farewells. There was a sleek black sedan awaiting her. As she got closer to the car, the driver got out and opened the rear door for her and closed it after she was seated. They drove off into the night, and Theresa went back into her house, heading upstairs where she wrote in her journal.

***

Nearly a week had passed since Theresa had last seen Archibald. She was mildly intrigued about the matter at first, but soon forgot about it as the events of the following days shifted that thought to the very back of her mind. Up until the present, Archibald had occasionally wandered off for a day or two, but he always returned with regularity. In the meantime, Theresa's workweek was very productive as she closed several important lingering deals and completed all of her reports early.

Louisa Camille, who was true to her word, took Theresa out to eat and for generous shopping twice within three days, refusing to allow Theresa to pay for anything. In fact, she had just met up with Louisa Camille that morning to join her for breakfast on the waterfront, and had just gotten home. She had a small bag of groceries that she picked up along the way and took them into the kitchen. She set the bag on the kitchen table, where she unloaded the contents before placing them in their respective places. She was leaning over, placing the last item on the lower shelf of the refrigerator when she felt a slight sensation from the ring of imperial porphyry she wore.

"How come every time I bend over you are right there behind me? And where the hell have you been?" she asked as she turned around.

Seated at the kitchen table, Archibald smiled. "Theresa, I may be dead, but I am not *that* dead. Besides, I take it that you must have missed me?"

"Wait a minute. What?" She eyed him as she walked to the table. "Anyway, you could have at least told me that you were going away for a couple days?"

The way he was looking at her made her feel suddenly bashful, so she pretended to be looking for something in her handbag.

"Alas and alack, Theresa, I told you that I had to set off for the federal capital that night. But you obviously did not hear me as the running water in the shower drowned out my voice. So, I wrote it in your planner for the corresponding dates I was absent, so you would know of my whereabouts. In fact, you have it right there."

Theresa removed the planner from her handbag and found the entry that he spoke of written in ornate penmanship.

Dearest Theresa, I have an affair of the utmost importance that I have to attend to in Washington. I will return within a fortnight. Do not bring any obese people, Jehovah's Witnesses, or any other sanctimonious persons into the house. Good luck and goodbye.

Theresa quickly returned the planner to her handbag and changed the conversation.

"So, let me bring you up to speed on what you missed while you were out of town." And she continued to recall the previous day's events much to the dismay of Archibald, who sighed despondently as she continued.

"Theresa, does it really look like I care about the events of your life?"

"*Yes*, so stop being a sad sack." She got up and walked over to his side of the table with her phone in hand to show him a picture, but he turned his head away.

"What crawled up your butt and died?"

He sighed heavily at that remark. "Once again, you and your deep-fried south of the Mason–Dixon colloquialism. Look, Theresa, it seems that you have mistaken me for a good listener."

"Dead dude, you are. So stop acting like you're not interested in the events of my life. Besides, I was just going to give you highlights anyway."

"To the contrary, most of the time, I am indifferent to your ramblings, and yet that vast expanse that is your head construes me as being attentive." And, at that, he shrugged his shoulders.

Theresa took a swipe at him expecting to hit the back of the chair, but something unexpected happened. Instead of her hand making contact with the back of the chair, her hand made contact with his actual shoulder. Almost simultaneously, the room darkened, and this was accompanied by the faint melody of far distant wind chimes, which they both heard. Then, the sound of rushing wind seemed to emanate from all directions. It came howling into the kitchen as if they were on some windswept precipitous peak. But it was only Archibald that was affected by it. Nothing else was disturbed. His clothes and hair were all in disarray by the swirling of this whirlwind flowing around him. Theresa, startled by the unexpected nature of it all, took several steps back as his chair teetered and fell over with a thud.

The sound of this unfelt wind died down quickly as it came, and there was a strange stillness throughout the whole house. The whole ordeal began and ended within a matter of seconds, but to Theresa, experiencing the moment, it seemed to last forever. After a few moments of hesitation, she looked over to see that Archibald was lying askew on the floor. As the chair landed on its side away from her, the only thing she could see of him was his legs and part of his shoulder. Both were bare as the day he was born for the suit was missing in its entirety. She thought about leaving and was in the process of doing so, when she realized that her handbag and cell phone were still on the table.

"Goddammit," she said under her breath as she turned around. She crept slowly over towards the table, keeping her eyes on Archibald's motionless body. She grabbed her things off the table, placing her phone inside her handbag, then paused a moment a few feet from Archibald and asked him if he was dead.

After several entreaties and no response, she gathered her courage and stepped a little bit closer. He was indeed very naked and very much in a mortal form as she verified this by trying to rouse him with the tip of her foot but to no avail. The situation very much perplexed Theresa, and she could see no signs of life from the body on the floor, which was just a few moments ago a lively spirit.

What the hell just happened here? How did he go from a ghost to a meat person? I mean, a physical naked man at that too?

After taking a few pictures for later reference, she said, "I know what you doing; you're pulling some type of prank. The joke's over. You were already dead to begin with and can't be any deader now. So knock it off and re-ghost yourself at once, or else!"

But once again, there was no reply from the body on the floor.

"Fine then, I'm going to teach you a lesson, you fool." Somewhat irked, she knelt down and picked up the chair he'd been sitting in, setting it to the side.

"This will have to be disinfected." She walked over to the counter and placed her handbag on it. Next, she retrieved a corn broom and headed back over to Archibald. She held the broom over her head. "It's your last chance, or you're going to be sorry."

There was still no response as she swatted him across his head with the bristles of the broom. Besides jarring his head with the blow, she repeated the process several times across different parts of his body before dropping the corn broom to the floor, overcome with a sense of despair. The reality that Archibald might be perma-nently gone numbed her body from top to bottom.

Disheartened, she stood there accessing the sit-uation. *Ok, get ahold of yourself. You can handle this. I need an old blanket from the basement to roll his body in.*

As she turned to leave the kitchen within an instant, she found herself amidst a foggy trail flanked by birch trees. She rubbed her eyes and took another look around her into the still silence. As she did, she felt something whisk past as her back was turned.

Theresa let out a deep groan as she turned around with a clenched fist.

"I know all of this is your work here, you ghoul." She told the shrouded apparition in a contemptuous tone. "You killed my frie—that ghost in my house you made mortal again and killed him."

She continued her angry discourse, but became even more infuriated when she got no response. Realizing that unlike her first encounter, she could move. She got in the apparition's face boldly.

"So, you still can't hear me? You must still have maggots in your head," she shouted loud enough that there was an unnatural echo that carried off into the distance. Theresa backed up cautiously as the specter sighed.

Uh-oh, flashed across Theresa's mind as she backed up out of striking distance, perceiving that she struck a nerve with the shrouded entity.

The apparition brought its wrapped hand up to its head and the winding sheets that covered it unraveled and fell to its feet. As it did so, long black wavy hair unraveled and cascaded down past her waist. A wreath on her head began to bloom, filling the air with perfume. The golden eyes contrasted with her swarthy skin, which gave a hauntingly beautiful image. Theresa was so enthralled that she forgot her anger completely, until her gazing eyes made contact with the apparition's own.

"So, umm, what did you use to get such flawless skin?" Theresa asked.

A raised eyebrow accompanied by a chilled smile flitted across the specter's face. It drifted towards her and brought an index finger up to its lips.

Theresa was puzzled for a moment at this unexpected gesture. But it became apparent why when she heard a sound behind her.

It was a long gasp of labored breathing that prompted her to turn around. She found herself back in her own kitchen at the entrance, feeling a bit giddy. Uneasy on her own legs, she grabbed the doorjamb to support herself before proceeding. Realizing that the sound of breathing had ceased, her eyes searched the confines of the kitchen for the body, which to her added surprise, was now gone. She stared at the empty spot where the body had been and then took a cautious step forward to verify that her eyes were not playing tricks on her. Theresa's gaze quickly searched the kitchen from wall to wall to ascertain the whereabouts of Archibald's body.

Nerves unraveling, she rubbed each of her eyes. She took several steps back in surprise. Her heart was racing. She gasped and placed her hand over her mouth. There was Archibald standing in the kitchen entrance, naked as the day of his nativity, akin to a statue with his stillness.

He looked at her with his unmoving features for a moment before breaking his silence.

"Theresa dear, a broom falling on the floor is nothing to cry about. I admit it is clumsy woman's work, but nevertheless, you'll get better with practice," he said to her straightforwardly.

Theresa turned her head away from him, wiping the tears with the back of her hand. "I'm not crying; it's just my allergies causing my eyes to sweat."

He gave her an impassive look, but she continued. "Why are you alive and why are you naked?" she asked as she gingerly prodded his abs. Theresa continued to badger him with question after question on what had transpired but to no avail.

Archibald closed his eyes and shook his head. "All I know, Theresa, is that this is *your* tomfoolery afoot here. Though, I do believe your part in the matter unwittingly. Nevertheless, I do hold you culpable as you are here and someone must be blamed for this level of sorcery."

"What are you talking about? I didn't do anything!"

"No woman ever does. But I will get into that later. As of right now, I need some clothes. I am cold in places other than my heart. Plus, I am weary of your salacious leering."

"You definitely don't look cold," she murmured as she turned her back to him.

"I beg your pardon, Theresa?"

"I said, it's not *my* fault you decided to be naked," she retorted as she glanced over her shoulder.

"Au contraire, I didn't decide on anything. As a transcendent being, such as a specter on this side of the veil, clothes are a creation of one's own fancy. They are nothing more than memories we carry over from the previous mortal existence." He then turned and proceeded to walk down the hallway. "But that's fine, Theresa; I will just sit on the porch greeting the passersby on the footway until you find me something that I can wear." He stopped midway. "Oh, by the way, if you are planning to put me in one of those beastly looking summer dresses in those boxes you have stacked in the basement, you are sadly mistaken."

CHAPTER 16

A short time later, the two were sitting in the parlour. Archibald was still examining, in silence, the articles of clothing that Theresa had provided him from one of the boxes in the basement.

"Theresa, this is a quite ingenious invention. Who would have ever thought to put sleeves and a hood on a fleece blanket? All that wasted time you spent warming up the bedsheets, and you never thought of this?"

But Theresa said nothing in response. She only continued to sit on the couch with her legs crossed, looking at him intently as she marveled. She had not said anything after she overtook him as he was attempting to open the front door of the house. Even when she led him down to the basement, she accomplished the task without even the utterance of a single syllable.

"I know I am as refreshingly pleasant to the eyes as all things great, that is something that I will humbly concede, but you can stop looking at me as if I am some genie of the Orient about to grant you one of your three wishes."

Theresa once again said nothing in response but got up and walked over to him, with her eyes fixed on him in complete amazement. She sat down adjacent to him. After studying him further, she finally spoke. "Explain to me this *sorcery* you spoke of earlier. How are you alive?"

"Well, I surmised that this corporeal existence I am currently suffering from is the work of some entity working through you as a proxy. Since I met you, I have been curious about your background, and despite all my best efforts to ascertain information about you and your family tree, I found nothing of pertinent value outside an interesting indiscretion involving your great-grandmother and a man other than her husband."

Theresa scoffed at this before speaking. "My grandmother has a lovely picture of her parents sitting in a silver frame at my mother's house and they were honest folks. My great-grandmother was the perfect picture of respectability. Nice try, though."

"I am not disputing that, Theresa. Not even in the slightest. Yet, one of the five children she sired out of that union is a product of the rendezvous in Cincinnati. But as the trite proverb goes, *mama's baby, daddy's maybe,* and unbeknownst to him, he raised the child of another man as his own. But don't fret, it is a time-honored impropriety in all of Christendom. Amen."

Theresa looked at him for a moment, seething, and stood up abruptly. "Wait a damn minute. I can't believe you! You've been digging around in my family's history!"

"Of course I have," he said to her cheerfully as her face flamed. "I perceive that you are about to say something tart, Theresa. Now normally, I would let you carry on like you are an innocent victim for the mild amusement I find in it. But since time is pressing in this affair, I am going to help you save face by nullifying your hypocritical indignation."

Theresa grew still as he turned towards her, raising her hand by the wrist that held the porphyry ring.

His tone became more formal as he looked at her ring. "I know that you have visited someone about me, Theresa. But that is an inconsequential matter. This ring here on your finger is very unusual, not in aesthetics but its properties. Even now, I can sense it teeming with an undercurrent of power of which you yourself should be acutely cognizant with your own sibylline abilities." He looked closer at the ring. "A power strong enough to make a soul mortal again." He was thoughtfully silent as she stood there with her hand still extended in his.

Theresa spoke to him softly as if trying not to break his concentration. "Are you mad at me, or are you just plotting something?"

He looked up at her, smiling as he gently released her hand. He then stood up so unexpectedly in front of her that she was startled and stumbled backward. She would have fallen if he did not catch her. He pulled her into his arms.

"Your hair smells great, and you are so soft and supple that it almost makes up for your awkwardness and excitability."

"I am not excitable or awkward," she said as she almost tripped on her own foot, stumbling back down on the couch.

"To answer your question, I am not mad at you. And yes, I am working on some intrigues."

Theresa pulled herself further to her end of the couch.

"Don't be silly, Theresa. It has nothing to do with you. But I am curious. Take off the ring for I cannot touch it while it rests on your finger."

Theresa was about to take the ring off her finger when she hesitated. "Wait a minute, why should I?"

"I just want to see if I will revert to my previous state before you placed the ring on your finger."

Theresa did as she was told, and he vanished before her eyes, leaving a pile of clothes on the couch. She looked around the room, but saw no traces of him. *He has to be somewhere nearby.* She returned the ring to her finger. Then she remembered in that instant the wind and the sound of chimes that took place earlier in the kitchen, anticipating it. But nothing like that happened. She was suddenly startled when a finger tapped her on the shoulder. She immediately turned around to see Archibald standing there with a smirk on his face.

"Oh, dear, I hope I didn't startle you. I just stepped out of the house when the removal of the ring reverted me back to my spectral disembodiment." Once again naked, he walked over to the garment that he was wearing and put it back on. As he was dressing, he said to her, "You know, Theresa, you stare at me dressing with such an intensity it almost feels like your fingers are touching my skin."

She turned her head slightly as if she wasn't looking at him, but continued to peek out of the corner of her eye.

"I don't blame you, Theresa. You can't help but be charmed by all this Adonis physique that is the Archibald."

She let her head fall back and sighed. "This fool is speaking of himself in third person. And you said I had a big head," she mumbled under her breath.

"Yes, you do. Your head suffers from excessive bigness."

"Shut up and sit down. You are done preening and flattering yourself," she said to him curtly. "Besides, I have some more questions to ask you before I forget."

He gestured with his hand for her to continue.

"So, I am curious to know why you didn't ask me where I got my ring from."

He looked at her for a few moments before answering her. "It is simple really, because I didn't care enough to ask. But for what it's worth, I consider your ring to be a vicarious gift to me, which is, in turn, a gift to you."

A confused flush crossed Theresa's face. "What are you talking about? What is a gift to me?"

"You have the luxury of my being here in the flesh, of course."

"More like the luxury of being able to know where you are physically without your supernatural shenanigans. But since you're a mortal again, I also need your help fixing things around here as well. It would be so nice to have a helping hand instead of a lecturing mouth. For instance, I was thinking about rearranging some furniture earlier, and now you can help me with your muscles." And she patted his biceps smiling at having some help around the house.

Theresa was continuing her list of chores when Archibald interrupted her saying, "Woman, you are talking to me like we are in a committed relationship or even worse, married. It is a very vulgar thing to speak to a man as if you already own his life, Theresa."

She held her ring hand up, waving it in his face. "Kinda seems like I own it now, doesn't it? Anyway, you know more than you are letting on about this situation, so let's have it all out."

He sighed. "Yes, her name was Julia Katrina Campbell."

Now we're getting somewhere, Theresa thought to herself.

"She was a bold, cultured woman who hailed from a family that had made their wealth in a sugarcane monopoly in the then-American colony of Cuba. It was this wealth that not only allowed her to cross the Atlantic, but also to become an alumna of Saint Anne's College with the illusion of independence. While in Britannia, she also became an inconspicuous suffragette who used her travels across the pond to transport finances and literature to her sisters within the movement. In fact, shortly before I even met Miss Campbell, she had participated in Pankhurst's riot in Westminster while incognito, and barely escaped arrest."

"So, was Julia another one of your playthings? Oh, now that totally came out wrong, I meant to say *friends*." Theresa grinned, expecting to be validated. But the next thing she noticed was Archibald standing up facing her with his arms akimbo under his blanket, which made it look like a cape, and that left her momentarily unsettled, and then somewhat amused.

"That is quite to the contrary, Theresa. That woman was just an imposed acquaintanceship. It was not requested." He said this with words that held a flavor of derision.

"Tell me more," Theresa said while he walked past her over to the mirror to admire himself.

"You see, Miss Campbell is the reason I am back in this world—that is—through her dabbling in the occult, a subject matter with which she'd had a fascination since her days at boarding school. By and by, one night in early March of 1912, she used an incantation to bring me back to the realm of mortals. After the shock of my apparition appearing in her bedchamber subsided, she collected herself and posed several questions to me from a small list she had composed previously, which were more suited to a clairvoyant."

Theresa, who was intrigued, got up and walked over to him as he was still standing gazing into the mirror. It was apparent to her that he wasn't looking at himself at that moment, but rather, his mind had drifted.

But as she wished to capitalize on the moment, she pressed him.

"So, what were the questions she asked of you?"

"I do not recall exactly, but I do know it was along the lines of something trifling." He brought his hand up to his chin and rubbed it for a moment. "Oh yes, it was something to do with some suitors and their financial outlook. I also have a vague recollection that one of the questions had something to do with the suffragette cause. Nevertheless, I could not answer her questions, which caused her to throw a bit of a tantrum. After she calmed down, she tried to send me back but lacked the ability to do so for you see, the incantation was incomplete. And the reason why soon became apparent for the book that she was using was not only in a poor state of affairs, but it was also missing some pages and suffered water damage. It appeared to have been someone's journal as most of the incantations were handwritten in Latin, with occasional notations written in the Shelton system of shorthand. I deduced from the water damage, which ran the ink in many places and the slight scent of smoke that the book had been stored in a place that caught fire. It still amazes me to this day that she had paid two Florins to an old crone from Bettiscombe for that book. That is the long and short of it."

He then walked over to the couch, retrieving a piece of candy from the candy dish. Theresa stood there, unsatisfied.

"That is not the long and short of it, Archibald. It's more like the short of it with omissions."

He looked at her with one eyebrow raised as she sat back down next to him, but this time a little closer. "So tell me, where did you wander off to since she couldn't send you back?"

"Theresa," he said to her in a somewhat serious tone. "I could not wander off anywhere if I wanted to. The spell that brought me back was not only very powerful, it was also a binding spell. By the power of the incantation, I was her chattel, compelled to do as she commanded. When she realized this, she had a propensity to send me on errands to spy on people she had intrigues with. I naturally detested these actions, but in spite of my feelings, I was obliged to carry out what I was commanded to do. One of these such instances involved me gathering information to deprive a young man of his father's inheritance—something he had already taken possession of in the form of a manor house—by collecting enough information to have him legally declared a bastard, thereby depriving him of both his endowment and his patrimony."

And all of this time I thought this fool was still in the world of the living for being an arrogant dick during his own natural life. Well, so much for me hoping that he'll correct that disability. Well, I guess I'll play along.

"That sounds absolutely awful," said Theresa. She stroked the back of Archibald's hand. "But especially— what she did to you, Archibald. I wouldn't blame you if you still held a grudge against her."

He sneered at this. "A grudge is only useful when it is serving as a motivating factor for revenge. Outside of that, one is just using one's enmity very poorly. Besides, I was only in her service for about a month's time before the contract that bounded me to her was terminated, so to speak."

"Well, I'm glad she figured out something to release you from part of the spell," Theresa said. "I'm actually surprised you kept in contact with her all these years. I guess you smoothed over your previous unpleasantness."

"You've guessed wrong again, Theresa, dear. The last time I saw Miss Campbell was in the spring of 1921 by pure happenstance while I was searching for a remedy for my situation. I was quite surprised to see her alive and well. Especially considering the last time we were together, I was accompanying her home when the ship we were traveling on, the ill-fated RMS Titanic, went down." He smiled at if he was pleased with himself. He turned to her with a grin. "Is there something the matter, Theresa? I see you are doing that thing with your face again."

"Shut up, and yes, there's something the matter. You find it amusing that a ship went down."

"I was reminiscing solely on the drowning of Miss Campbell. I was just recalling her flailing and subsequent slipping beneath the icy waves into the dark abyss, gazing up into the night sky with eyes that no longer see."

"You are so terrible to laugh while she drowned, Archibald. And yet, knowing you, it doesn't shock me." Theresa shook her head in disapproval.

"Rubbish, Theresa, as it is impossible for me to be terrible to anyone I dislike. Besides, it wasn't that bad. Hypothermia shut her down pretty quickly as she tried to swim to the side of the lifeboat a few yards away."

"Wait a minute—you—" Theresa struggled for words. "I mean, I know why you disliked this woman, but you could have saved her life if you wanted to. You still had the ability to intervene."

With raised eyebrows, Archibald looked at her curiously. "If you really understood, you would have not made such an absurd suggestion. I did not let her drown because I disliked her. It just wasn't my job to rescue Miss Campbell. Especially considering that it was a conflict of interest."

Archibald explained to her that the reincarnated woman had no recollection of her life prior to waking up wet and naked near the seashore a year before. She had taken up residence with some old, threadbare cottagers who had found her in that state, believing that she had either fell overboard from a ship or worse, tried to take her own life, and washed ashore. She had even taken on their surname of Ashford, and they called her Maris. Archibald had attached himself to the remote household for several days as a guest under the illusion of a traveling country gentleman. But this venture brought him no useful information.

So, the only thing she was cognizant of for the eight years of absence was being alone in the cold darkness for a long time. Something those kind old people that took her in must have assumed was metaphorical. Anyway, that certainly didn't shed any light on this situation and we're still right back at square one. But still, I do wonder why she was brought back to life and by whom? And why did Archibald show them the location of a hidden trove of silver coins buried on their property before leaving them? Did that mean he forgave her for the previous life's transgressions against him?

Theresa's thoughts were interrupted by a knock at the front door; it prompted Archibald to leave the parlour. "I can't believe he is going to really answer the door," Theresa mumbled as she got up and hurried after him. He was just closing the front door as he turned around, holding an etched crystal vase with a large bouquet of yellow tulips in his hand.

"Great," Theresa said in a tone of annoyance, looking at the flowers. "Now I have to carry these piss-yellow flowers to my neighbor because *someone* couldn't tell the delivery man to come back when they were home." She took the flowers from him and placed it on the console table nearby. Then, she noticed that the envelope had her name on it, and she snatched it, and hastily tore it open.

"Aww, he is a really nice gentleman to send me such lovely flowers. They are absolutely beautiful, and this glass vase is exquisite." She returned the card to the envelope, forgetting herself until she remembered Archibald, who was still standing at the door observing her. Swiftly producing her phone, she asked him to take a picture of her standing next to the floral arrangement on the console to throw off her own embarrassment.

She was, after all, flattered by Mr. Barnaby sending her the flowers.

After he snapped the photo, he said to her, "Well, I see that you are done with your prattering for the moment. Since I am a mortal again, I have to dress the part. I have decided that I need to acquire new clothes for my wardrobe as this will not do. Especially with a social event fast approaching that I can now attend. Well, I will leave you to continue your humoring of yourself." He smiled and then turned to open the front door.

"Just you wait a damn minute!" Theresa shouted, which caused him to arrest his movement. "I mean, Archibald," she said softly, mindful of her tone. "If you go outside wearing that fleece blanket, people are going to think you are crazy."

He turned to her, saying, "I hate to state the obvious, Theresa, but Savannah is already Bedlam without the walls. Especially with all these patients without asylums roaming freely through the streets, dumped here graciously by neighboring municipalities. I shall fit right in. Besides, a walk would do me good, especially with my new body aching as if I have rheumatism."

"Well, I guess. It appears your mind is already there. I suppose it won't be long before you have a straitjacket to go along with it."

Archibald walked out the door without even looking back, saying on his way out, "Stop being such a Negative Nancy, Theresa, it is very unbecoming."

CHAPTER 17

"Oh, everything is going fine," Theresa said to Abigail while they enjoyed their brunch on the porch of her house after their morning jog to Whitefield Square. "I have actually spent the last three days working from home in peace and absolute quiet. I was planning on going in tomorrow or Friday to turn in some paperwork that needed the old woman's signatures, but apparently Linda has abruptly left town."

"What do you mean she abruptly left town?" Abigail asked as she flung a piece of French toast down to a pigeon watching them from the sidewalk.

"I mean exactly what I said. Apparently, she left last Friday from work, shortly before 12 after she received a phone call. That is what Marcus told me, but I asked him to put someone else on the phone that wasn't as touched in the head as him, and my colleague, Leilani, verified it. As you already know, I normally try to avoid

Linda for sanity purposes, which is one of the reasons I am working from home."

Abigail mulled over the situation as the pigeon looked at her for second helpings. "Did anyone call the police to report her disappearance?"

"Not that I'm aware of," said Theresa. "It's not like this is the first time she's done something like this. It's just the first time in a long time. By the way, I almost forgot to tell you that Marcus is worried that he is possibly in trouble with his girlfriend again. I say *possibly* because she may not know of his latest infidelity, and it is his conscience getting to him."

Abigail just shook her head. "My hairdresser told me the last time he cheated on his girlfriend, she took his ass to a funeral home to show him a casket that she picked out for him if he ever decided to cheat on her again. She even made him lay in it, so he could get a feel of it while he was still alive."

Theresa leaned over to Abigail as something caught her attention. "What the hell is that on your neck, Abby?" Theresa pointed to a red oblong shape on the side of Abby's neck just above her shoulder. "You've been stung by something. See, I told you to put on some bug spray this morning."

Abigail rubbed the spot on her neck, and started laughing. "That's just a hickey that Logan gave me a few nights ago. We were supposed to go up to Limehouse to pick a package, but instead, we headed to my house. But I am surprised that you can still see it."

"The real surprise is you still having an interest in him after this long. You two are spending a lot more time together as of late," said Theresa before resuming her own meal.

"Well . . ." said Abigail, "he is a very interesting person. His mind intrigues me. It's the spiritual connection to nature that he has. I also like the way our conversations make me think about different topics that I would not normally think about. But speaking of Logan, he should be back to pick me up any minute now. He had some business with a client of his dad's to take care of in Vernonburg this morning. You know, since his dad is still on his *spiritual journey* with that stripper Harmony, sowing his wild oats. Hmm, at his age, isn't it more like sowing his granola?"

Theresa looked at her friend with a deadpan expression for a few seconds before she placed her hand on her forehead, shaking her head.

Just then, a sedan with fading paint and a bad muffler stopped in front of Theresa's house. A few seconds later, the passenger door opened, and a woman with purplish hair got out. She was dressed like an art student, trying to appear more artistic than she actually was. Then, a man dressed in a black three-piece suit exited the back seat, and talked with the woman as they walked to the trunk of the car, which had opened by itself. She attempted to carry some of his bags for him. But he graciously declined the offer, lifting the various bags with both of his hands in one quick swoop.

"Looks like you got new neighbors," said Abigail as Theresa looked up in earnest.

"No, I don't think I recognize him. But he must be the son of someone on this block. Probably came in on the red-eye this morning, which would likely explain his scruffy face, and the bags of new clothes."

The woman standing with the man closed the trunk door and reached into her own back pocket, pulling out a small piece of paper that looked like a business card. She took a pen from behind her left ear and wrote something on it before placing it into his pocket. He said something to her and then proceeded walking towards the steps of Theresa's house as the car pulled off.

Theresa stood up to observe him more closely, while trying not to be obvious by pretending to examine something on the hand railing of the porch. *That can't be Archibald*, she thought to herself as the man approaching made eye contact. *Oh geez, it is him with that cocky smile*, she concluded, sighing in disbelief.

"Where have you been?" Theresa demanded as soon as he walked onto the porch. Well, good morning to you too, Theresa. And good morning, Abigail," he said cheerfully to the two friends, but with a degree of focus on Abigail. As Archibald took his bags into the house, Abigail turned smiling to Theresa, whispering loudly, "Who is this?"

But Theresa only rolled her eyes and shook her head slightly, uttering, "No one." He came out a few minutes later, just as Abigail was trying to coax details out of Theresa.

"Abigail, I have heard so many wonderful things about you that it is really a pleasure to finally meet you in person. I feel as if we have always been friends, and it would be a great benefit to my social circle if we were." He extended his arm, and Abigail got up to clasp his hand.

No sooner had she touched his hand than he gracefully twirled her around into an embrace before returning her to her seat. He then proceeded to speak to Abigail in such a way that she was left constantly blushing much to Theresa's annoyance, as she perceived that he was up to something.

Abigail asked who he was, and he seemed so surprised. "You must forgive me for my omission; I was so charmed by you that I forgot to introduce myself."

He then told Abigail his name and what part of England his lineage hailed from. He also told her he had been in the country for some time as a gentleman of leisure who occasionally dabbled in the social sciences. Furthermore, it was Theresa who had practically begged him to share the house as her housemate, since she often works late and possibly has enemies. And as a gentleman, he could not decline a woman so adamant about having his company.

"Speaking of Theresa . . ." He turned to her and told her that the items that he borrowed were in one of the bags.

Abigail looked over to Theresa, saying, "I love your beau's accent and how he uses proper pronunciations."

Archibald quickly corrected her before Theresa could even have a chance to respond. He laughed, slapping his hand against his side. "Oh no, we're not in a romantic relationship, Abigail. Theresa and I are just sociable housemates. Besides, I would not dare encroach on the preserves of Theresa's geriatric lover."

Abigail's phone rang to the ringtone of "Incense and Peppermints" as she fumbled through her gym sack to answer it. Meanwhile, Archibald walked off the porch down to the sidewalk to converse with the letter carrier on her route. Theresa had attempted to hit him in the head with the half-eaten hash brown she'd flung at him, but his hand stopped just as the projectile narrowly passed before his face. He turned towards her and winked before continuing on with his pursuit, and was soon out of sight.

When Abigail finished her phone call, she turned to Theresa and attempted again to pick Theresa's mind about Archibald, but she could not get any more information out of her. "Well, I think it's nice that you actually let someone so cultured stay with you," Abigail said to her frankly. "You obviously don't need the money, but you do need a man around here to help with your unfinished renovations."

A devious grin appeared on Theresa's face. "I am way ahead of you. I am putting him to work in the house, since he loves it so much. Buying this house at an auction was a tremendous deal that saved me the trouble of being burdened with a mortgage. Yet, this acquisition ate a huge chunk of my savings. This is going to take me a while to recuperate, Abby."

"But it was well worth it, Theresa. I never have known you to be the type of person that would settle for anything less. Those little tacky cookie-cutter houses out in Pooler we looked at would never have made you happy. They had about as much individuality between them as sand in a bag. You wanted a house with a soul, and you got it."

Theresa shook her head and sighed. "If you only knew the half of it."

"I'll tell you what I want to know: where is your guest going to stay, and for how long? I know that you're not getting rid of your office, so it must be in the basement."

"I really don't know."

Abigail looked at her friend. "How are you going to share your house with a person and not know where they are going to sleep? That makes no sense whatsoever, Theresa. Are you a little high?"

Theresa had not thought of that, and it made her wonder. She pretended that something got in her eye to throw the attention off the question she did not know how to answer. And soon, their conversation drifted into other miscellaneous matters and went on until a quarter to noon when Logan showed up to pick up Abigail. When Theresa saw Logan, from the porch, she beckoned to speak with him, and relayed all the strange events that had happened, particularly with the ring. He seemed interested, yet not surprised. He looked at Theresa keenly and told her that the situation was beyond his expertise.

"Theresa, having the ability to see the spirit world is a special gift in and of itself. Few have it, and even fewer actually embrace it. Now, for you to have such a ring, carved from a stone that you brought back from a journey to a mysterious place, possibly in another dimension, tells me you are part of something. What that something is, I don't know, but it is a powerful form of enchantment. And I think there are more abilities connected to this ring than you know. Perhaps in time, you will learn them. I believe you are part of this mystery." He had a serious look on his face for a moment, and then it faded away into a smile.

"Look on the bright side, Theresa. It's not like you didn't get along when he was a spirit. Look at yourself now, you seem a lot more collected in your feelings than you were when we first met. And now, apparently, you have power over him, limiting his movement as he's gone from immortal to mortal. Now you have a man to deal with and not just a ghost. It seems like it's a win-win for you."

She frowned. "He is tolerable at times, but still cocky, dismissive, incorrigible, and could use a good slap to the back of his head."

"Well"—Logan seemed amused by the situation. "It seems you have options available. But unless you are moving out of this house, I think you will have plenty of time to reform him or tolerate him."

"And do you think that's funny, Logan? Even after he was flirting with Abby?"

"Abigail and I are just friends, as you know. You should also know that just because I'm from a small rural community does not mean I am the type of person inclined to jealousy. But I'm more curious about how that spirit was able to ascertain information about our first meeting."

Abigail interrupted by hitting the horn of Logan's truck to get their attention. "I'm about to take a nap, but we need to stop by the pharmacist to pick up the birth control I keep forgetting," she yelled, before letting her seat back to doze off to sleep.

"Thanks for the words of encouragement," Theresa said. "Besides, you'll make a great father."

Logan looked embarrassed. "Are you trying to jinx me?"

"Nah, I just want you to have something to think about."

Logan looked worried while he walked down the stairs to his truck, saying goodbye as he opened the door and got in.

Meanwhile, Theresa hurried into the house looking for Archibald's bags. She went upstairs and checked her own room as well as her office. She checked the closets in the bathroom before heading back down to the first floor and then the basement. She was walking up the stairs, puzzled by the peculiarity of the situation when she decided to sit down in the parlour. As she walked down the hall, she passed an empty bookshelf that was built within the wall; she stopped a few steps from it. She held her hand to the bottom of her chin mumbling to herself that "something is not right" as she looked at the bare shelves.

Then after a short examination, Theresa noticed that the recessed, built-in bookshelf was not flush with the wall and ever-so-slightly askew on one side. She knew it was not right because she had just dusted the shelves and the wainscoting the previous week. Curious, she went over to examine the bookshelf and, in the process, discovered a soft mechanical click. She pulled on it. She soon found that a little pressure caused the mechanism to release, and the bookshelf to swing slowly open on its un-lubricated hinges, groaning into a dark void.

CHAPTER 18

Theresa stood back at first, not knowing what to expect but gathered her courage and proceeded forward. In that space, she saw an old wooden door stained in a dark cherry color. It was handsomely framed and paneled and had an embossed bronze doorknob shaped like a peacock with its tail plumage extending out as a handle. The door was fitted with a similarly ornate lock plate for a lever tumbler lock complete with ward key inserted.

While she was looking around this small chamber, her right heel backed into something that fell over when she hit it. She took out a small keychain flashlight to aid her in the dim surroundings and soon discovered where Archibald had placed his shopping bags. But her attention was more fixated on what was behind this previously unknown door in her home. She stood toward the back and looked at the door for a moment, contemplating what course of action she should take next. Inhaling deeply, she opened the door. It moved silently, revealing a golden light in a room she sensed had been long shut up.

She was first drawn to the source of light in the room, which came from the ceiling, particularly from an arched window with lead-lined yellow stained glass in a motif of a white fleur-de-lis. The walls were covered in a pale anaglypta-embossed wallpaper that was complemented by slate-grey paint on the wainscoting. There was an iron frame bed that sat to the right of the door. Across from the bed was a white writing desk complete with a non-matching table chair with one cracked leg that someone had repaired by binding rope around it.

She stepped forward into the room further, curious about the unusual repair to the chair, and noticed that the nooks on the writing desk held several magazines and various writing utensils. There was a small leather-bound billfold that caught her attention as well. She walked over to it and carefully removed the dust before opening it, revealing the antique greenbacks stored inside. She put the billfold down and then proceeded to examine the magazines.

So, all this time he was residing in this room, and I wouldn't have known if it was not for this ring transforming him. I wonder, could this be the servant's quarters? She removed the stack from their nook, carefully shaking the fine dust off that had collected there for over a century.

Hmm, let's see what he has here. McClure's Magazine *February 1899*, McClure's Magazine *May 1898*, Collier's

National Weekly *for December 19, 1903, and the rest seem to be issues of* Vanity Fair *or* Ladies Home Journal.

She replaced the magazines where she'd found them and slowly opened the drawer, revealing an assortment of antique stationaries that was complete with a sealing wax kit, twenty-dollar gold pieces, an unopened packet of Bull Durham tobacco, and a unique board game in the very back called, *Around the World with Nellie Bly*.

She looked around the room and noticed that in an alcove near the door was a large wardrobe with two doors and large drawers on the bottom. Theresa moved noisily across the faded antique rug that covered the floor as she snooped through Archibald's lair. She pulled, and as the doors swung open, her nostrils met the pleasant scent of red cedar. Within this wardrobe hung several old-style black servant dresses with white aprons and various other women's dresses. The hatboxes, shoes, and other feminine effects confirmed to Theresa that this was indeed where the maid of the house used to live.

She opened the first drawer, and found a number of blankets folded neatly into the space. When she opened the bottom drawer, she found work clothes belonging to a man, brogans, a revolver, several boxes of ammunition, a crowbar, gloves, and brass knuckles.

This damn criminal here.

Theresa pushed the drawer shut. She was about to close the doors on the wardrobe when she noticed something shiny in the back. She reached forward and pulled out a silver picture frame. As she held it up, she realized that it was a picture of Archibald seated in a finely carved wooden chair facing a left angle with a very attractive maid standing behind him, resting her arm on the back of the chair.

"Well, I guess that answers a lot of my questions," she said and returned the picture to its location.

"Good," said a voice from close behind her. "That means I don't have to go through the agony of answering your questions."

Although the voice startled her, she was not too surprised that it was Archibald's.

"I wouldn't count on that, Archibald," Theresa said, closing the wardrobe doors. She turned around to see that she was still alone in the room.

Damn, I wish he would stop doing that!

She soon found him sitting on the couch in the parlour, holding his left hand up, looking at his fingernails. She sat down next to him, facing him when he spoke. "So, I see you are done with your self-guided tour of someone else's personal space."

"First of all, you could have told me there was another room in this house. Secondly, I am really curious to know how in the hell did you manage to buy all of that stuff? Oh, and thirdly that little stunt you pulled earlier on the porch with Abigail wasn't funny."

He sighed and responded to her while gesturing with his hand. "I hate to miss out on your nagging, but I have dedicated this time to thinking about that ravishing Louisa Camille who visited you. In fact, I shall marinate on her image right now." He lay back with hands behind his head and closed his eyes.

He wasn't even in that position for ten seconds before Theresa laid her own legs across his in silent protest. He sat up with her feet still on him as she scoured at him with a look that didn't seem to have any effect on him.

He said calmly, "You know, Theresa, you really do have nice feet that are very well taken care of."

Theresa wiggled her toes. "Ha, I guess that's your way of telling me you're a foot man."

"No, Theresa," he responded frankly. "I was just pointing out what is apparent. I noticed the maintenance of your feet some time ago. I just never had the opportunity to comment on them, as I have been so often distracted with your many foibles and eccentricities. Besides, if you did have bad feet, we would not even be having this conversation today, for I should have long ago at my convenience pushed you down the stairs headlong."

Theresa retracted her feet quickly and nudged him with her hand. "By the way, I saw how you were looking at the letter carrier. You were flirting with her no less—"

"To be sure, but you are wrong in the way to think I would want such a pleasant lady for a one-night stand. For that thought, shame on you." And he shook his finger at her in disappointment. "You must understand that some women are like new leather shoes; you have to wear them a few times to really break them in and enjoy yourself. And she is one of them. But I was just charming her to gather information. It is just a byproduct of her profession. Besides that, I have no immediate interest in someone who visits the house several days a week, whether I like her or not. That is very bothersome."

"You have an interesting, yet faulty thought process there," Theresa responded as she looked at him disapprovingly. "I suppose that is why you enjoyed the company of your house servant so much that you would take a picture with her and buy her expensive dresses and coats."

He only smiled and got up off the couch. "I have to change into something more appropriate and air out my room." He began walking towards the entrance of the parlour, stating, "You should know that I am expecting a delivery this afternoon, and I want to make room for it."

Theresa got up hurriedly and followed him into his room, inquiring about the item being delivered. He told her it was a small grand piano to complement the aesthetics of the parlour. This again led Theresa to inquire about the means he had to pay for his expenditures. He was taking off his shirt when he turned towards her and pointed to a large paper bag with handles for her to pick up. "Would you be so kind as to set that down on the bed and take out your shirt blanket?"

She did as she was told and was surprised upon removing the blanket with sleeves that she had given him previously to find the bag contained, from midway to bottom, stacks of cash with rubber bands around them. She picked up one of them and held it in utter amazement.

"That is \$10,000 United States currency, Theresa. That bundle of bills right there is yours to keep and to do with as you please."

She looked at the roll of money long and hard before giving it back to him in silence.

"I can't accept this. I don't know how you acquired it, and it may be dirty money. I'm sorry, but I don't mean to offend you."

"Have it your own way. I'm not going to haggle with you over ready money." He tossed the money back into the bag nonchalantly and continued to dress.

Theresa sat on the side of the bed, looking into the bag. She grabbed the roll of money that was tossed back into the bag. "On second thought, I think I will accept that gift."

"Oh, it's not a gift. It is a payment in advance for services I expect you to render."

She glared at him. "And exactly what services will that entail?" she asked as she tapped her foot on the floor.

He noticed her implications and said quite frankly, "Theresa dear, if that were the type of proposition I had in mind, I would have just got you something off the value menu."

Theresa held her hand out and presented one finger to him.

"Well," Archibald went on, "I need your assistance to set me up with a trading account, so I may buy and sell securities. This would be under your name, of course, for the obvious reason."

"I hope that's not how you're planning on laundering money, especially under my name."

"Theresa, your faith in me is slightly disappointing. But to give you some reassurance, I will have you know that account is for your benefit, not mine. That is for you to create another source of income. The majority of the money staying here at the house is hidden. And since you are wondering where I got it from, as you are continuously staring into the bag. As a specter, who has traveled the ins-and-outs of the city longer than you have been alive, I know where people keep things. I am not talking about decent people either, but rather about people who have or had something to hide from the light of day."

"So, you mean to tell me this *is* dirty money?" She fingered one of the stacks.

He looked at her and laughed. "Money is just an inanimate object that has value placed on it by the state. Whether something is *dirty* or *clean* is predicated on the projected morality of the end-user. Thankfully, I obviously do not have that issue, as I do not place blame on inanimate objects. And to satisfy your pestering curiosity, when I left you a few days ago, I went down the street a few blocks to a public house frequented mostly by college students and tourists."

"I strolled into this establishment dressed in such a curious but comfortable fashion, knowing that it would naturally arouse the curiosity of the patrons there. I find people who are enjoying spirited drinks in a relaxed atmosphere are more inclined to be straightforward. So I cheerfully greeted everyone cordially upon entering, and I was immediately assailed by people laughing and asking questions to fulfill their curiosity. There was a consensus that I had lost a bet and had to wear my curious outfit. But I told them with all sincerity that was not the case, but that my outfit was rather the effect of getting inebriated with some gentlemen of a fraternity who took all of my clothes, leaving me in my current state, with their tomfoolery at my expense."

"This gained me much sympathy, especially among the women who admired my wonderful accent, which I maximized by talking to them personally, while even shaking their hands. Some of them actually tried to offer me money, but I would not accept such outright offers. I told them that my misfortune was that of my own for being less prudent with the quality society I called my friends. I told them I was only there for the social experience and not to be incommodious to anyone. And so, as the conversations continued and the drinks flowed, a few of them took up singing. And after a few glasses of whiskey and soda, I even sang a song I knew."

Theresa shook her head while fanning herself gently with her money.

"So, I sang them "The Man on The Flying Trapeze," which surprisingly, upon completion, they requested an encore, but this time with help from the audience. But for the sake of brevity, let me just say, I met up with two interesting students from the college who were flatmates. One of which, you saw exit the motorcar with me earlier, while the fop stayed in the driver's seat. I was invited home with them, where I obtained the dungarees and shirt you see me wearing here. These Wellington boots also."

He sat on the metal bed frame by Theresa and clicked the heels of his shiny boots.

"They were some really nice people. Not only did they give me clothing and take me into their home, but they also shared their cannabis, which was of a particularly good variety. Her flatmate, Austin, went to bed shortly before midnight, and I stayed up talking with Somerset until a quarter after 1. She welcomed me to spend the night with her, which I accepted, but I told her that I was going for a walk beforehand and that I would return within two hours' time. My task was accomplished within an hour, so I returned back to the flat with that bag of greenbacks now sitting next to you. I spent the remainder of my time with them until you saw me today. The clothes you see in these bags are from side excursions in Jacksonville from yesterday's road trip to Fort George Island for academic research, as Somerset is an architectural historian."

Their exchange continued until the sound of a large truck stopped outside of their house. And a short time later, a beautiful baby grand piano rested in a space near the windows.

Theresa caressed the black and white keys with her fingers. "This is very beautiful, and it really complements the parlour," she said to Archibald, who was wiping his hand with a rag.

"Indeed," he responded. "It really fills up this space and brings out the architectural elements of the room. It's amazing what a couple hundred pounds of mahogany and sugar maple can do."

"Archie, when will they have the bench here? I can't wait to hear you play."

"I ordered a bench specifically with a moleskin velvet cushion to match the room in color, so it will take a couple of days for that to arrive as it is a custom job. They were supposed to deliver a substitute for the meantime with the delivery, but the workman said he would have to go back and get it. I think that will probably be tomorrow, since it is getting late into the day."

He eventually began performing for Theresa after substituting a table chair for a piano bench. Theresa reclined on the couch, listening attentively as Archibald performed selections from his memory. When he had finished, she got up and walked over to him, complimenting him on his performance.

"I honestly would have never thought you were such an excellent pianist, Archie. I should get you some sheets of music to play."

"If you do, it will only be to decorate the piano. I cannot read sheet music, Theresa. That was something that I never got the hang of. I can play music by ear if I hear it. I suppose it is one of those backhanded gifts of dyslexia."

Theresa looked at him for a moment thoughtfully.

"I think it's amazing how you can play by ear. I was wondering about the name of that last melody. It has a sweet, relaxed, and yet somewhat melancholy tone."

"It was composed by Chopin—Frédéric Chopin—and it is called "Nocturne in F minor, Op. 55, No. 1." There is a second part of this, and I do agree with your assessment. It was dedicated to an exceptionally close pupil, Miss Jane Willamina Sterling in 1844." He stood up and presented his seat to Theresa. "Would you like to play, Theresa? I can be your teacher."

"You know I would really like that, but just for a little bit. I have a date tonight, and I have to prepare for it shortly." She sat down and Archibald began to show her how to position her hands when there was the light knock at the door. "I wonder who that could be at this time; it's almost 7:30."

"Who knows? Perhaps it is the substitute piano bench," he said as he walked out towards the door with Theresa trailing behind. She was going to tell him to look through the peephole first, but he opened the door. He looked and said briskly, "Little boy, go home." And he shut the door just as quickly as he opened it. "It was just some ginger ragamuffin."

"Seriously, Archibald, don't you think that was kind of rude? You could have at least asked to see what he wanted, even if the answer was going to be *no*," she said with disdain as she moved past him to open the door.

Theresa stood there, looking at the individual on the porch for a moment. It was evidently a female at first glance. She had on a large dark blue floppy sun hat, a white long-sleeve blouse, drapey crocheted shorts of the same blue as the hat held up by a thin brown belt that matched her sandals. She also toted a large two-tone white and navy-blue Cape-Codder handbag on her left shoulder that appeared to be well-stuffed.

Theresa studied her face before saying, "I will need to try some samples first before I decide to buy anything. Which products are you selling, Mary Kay or Avon?"

"Huh? I'm not peddling anything, Theresa!" the guest at the door responded.

How does she know my name? she wondered as the woman took her hat off.

"It can't be." She took a step forward. "It can't be Charlotte. Charlotte of the Rose, is that really you?"

Before a response could be delivered, Archibald, who was observing the situation said with some resentment, "Who else do you know who has such a disrespectful amount of red hair and freckles?"

But Theresa and Charlotte were too ecstatic showering each other with compliments and questions to pay him any attention.

"Hey, it doesn't smell like old people," Charlotte said cheerfully as she entered the house. She paused for a moment to look at Archibald with a degree of intrigue. She took her handbag and struck him in his chest with it. "Oh, so this bastard is not an illusion. Theresa, you never told me that you were practicing magic?"

Theresa just shook her head, trying to contain a laugh at Archibald's expense and led Charlotte into the parlour to be seated before responding. "It's somewhat of a long story, but first, what I want to know is how you also came to be mortal?"

"I can tell you that, Theresa," Archibald interjected from his seat at the piano. "Since Gingersnaps likes to tell people's business, I will tell hers. She is what is called in the Germanies, *der Hexegeist*—a witch spirit. She is a singular type of spirit that has peculiar abilities, hence the form we see here this evening. But it is quite apparent that her metamorphosis is limited to how she was actually in life; thus, all meat and no potatoes."

Theresa held her head down as she rubbed her brow in an attempt to conceal the expression on it.

"I'm gonna stab you until it really hurts," Charlotte snapped at Archibald.

"Settle down, Gingersnaps, there is enough bothersome crimson coming from your head already without your flustered face adding to it."

Charlotte made a stabbing motion at him before she told to them the circumstances of her being in the city, how she was brought into town after visiting Charleston the previous day with the aid of the young man who frequently visits the Montague mausoleum asking of assistance.

"A great deal of time has passed since I last masqueraded myself as a mortal. Not since Sinjin was still alive," Charlotte told them. "When I am in this form, I have to acquire clothes to cover my mortal nakedness. I flew straightway to the room of the young man that very night, which greatly startled him when I alighted on his bed, changing into this current state. After he stopped wigging out like a wuss, he gave me a new black-and-white striped romper to cover myself. It was something that he had actually bought as a gift for someone else, but the relationship had fallen through."

She reached into her bag and showed Theresa the romper. "We talked for most of the night, and the very next day we went to Charleston to shop. Which is what you see here, and what you don't see is half in the bag. I made it to the city this morning and met up with some people who took me to the beach with them."

"How long are you planning on staying in the city?" Theresa asked.

"I'm not even sure, Theresa. Everything that has happened so far has occurred without planning. I might even travel around the world."

Archibald scoffed. "Okay, Phileas Fogg."

Theresa heard her alarm going off in another part of the house. "Oh, I have to get ready for a dinner date I'm going on tonight."

"With whom, Theresa?" Archibald inquired as he played a melancholy melody on the new piano.

"You remember the delivery guy from my job—Palmer."

He only looked at her with an indiscernible expression on his face as he continued playing.

"The one you said I got dressed up for," she said to him.

"Yes, I remember him, Theresa. But I just cannot help but think about that fellow, Mr. Barnaby."

"I know exactly where you're going with that," she said to him. "So knock it off."

Charlotte went with Theresa upstairs as she prepared for her evening, filling her in with the sequence of events between herself and Archibald up until the present. An hour and a half had passed when they finally came down the stairs.

Archibald was still at the piano; his soft music filling the house, which made the atmosphere pleasant. He had changed clothes and was in his new smoking jacket with matching slippers. He paid Theresa compliments and escorted her, along with Charlotte, to her car, seeing her off.

"I really hope he shows up tonight," Charlotte said to Archibald as they walked back into the house. "He had some kind of emergency the last time he was supposed to meet up with her and left her sitting in the restaurant for an hour and a half waiting for nothing. Personally, if he did me like that, I would've written his ass off."

He looked at her somewhat seriously as they sat down on the couch, and said, "You are thinking exactly what I am thinking, but it is a matter that she has to realize for herself. Besides, I figured something went awry when she didn't mention it when I got back from Washington." He smiled and said, "But that is neither here nor there at the moment. So what are you still doing here? Don't you have someplace special to go tonight, my adventure-seeking friend?"

Charlotte grinned. "You are not getting rid of me so easily, you rude, rusty bastard. You should know that Theresa said that I may stay as long as I like while I'm in town. I started to tell her *no*, but then I remembered how particular you are about your personal space. So I accepted the offer, and I decided to stay in for the night."

"Gingersnaps, I didn't ask you all that, and you being here is not hurting my feelings. So you can wipe that silly smirk off your freckled face."

Charlotte laughed while she shook her head. "I am going down to the market to get some of that cheesecake Theresa told me about. Do you want me to get you something?

"Yes," he said as he produced a 20-dollar bill. "Pick up a couple pints of French vanilla ice cream for Theresa. If this engagement falls through again, she's going to need it."

CHAPTER 19

Shortly after mid-morning the very next day, Theresa arrived home with a dejected expression plastered all over her face. When she saw Charlotte standing in the hallway to greet her, she tried to modify her appearance.

"Theresa, is there something the matter?" Charlotte inquired with genuine concern.

"I'm really tired, Charlotte, that's all. I just need to lay down in my own bed for a bit." And Theresa slowly slinked up the stairs to her room.

Charlotte, who had observed her from the bottom of the stairway, was thoughtful. She went outside to the shed in the backyard, where Archibald was doing repairs. She spoke with him shortly and then left the yard through the side gate.

It was about mid-afternoon when Theresa woke up, still feeling a little disenchanted. She walked into the kitchen to get something to drink. When she turned around, she nearly dropped her cup when she saw Archibald and Charlotte standing within arm's reach of her. Theresa's eyes shifted back and forth between them, trying to ascertain what they were up to. Archibald's indifferent expression completely contrasted with Charlotte's rosy smile. Theresa then noticed that Charlotte was holding a glass bowl with small folded pieces of paper in it.

"Umm, what is going on here?" Theresa finally asked with a raised eyebrow.

Archibald's eyes shifted towards Charlotte. "It's this Gingerfied runt's idea, Theresa."

"Well, I noticed that you were sad this morning," Charlotte said to Theresa. "And we decided to cheer you up by doing something nice for you. Pick one of the papers out of this bowl."

Theresa reached into the bowl and pulled out a piece of paper that was sitting on the bottom. She unfolded it and read the word, *Amsterdam*.

"Well, what about Amsterdam?" Theresa asked with a confused look on her face.

"Now that's where we are going for a picnic," Charlotte said as Archibald presented a large cooler with a blue checkered blanket folded on top.

Theresa shrugged her shoulders, and they were soon sitting on a blanket near a field of picturesque yellow tulips a short distance from the fortified city walls of seventeenth-century Amsterdam. She overlooked the beautiful landscape, complemented with windmills in complete awe as the faint aromatic scent of tulips carried on the breeze filled her nostrils.

She soon was partaking in the club sandwiches while conversing with Charlotte—who had several glasses of wine—about the beauty of the surroundings. Archibald did not participate, but instead, walked over to a grassy knoll and reclined with his hands behind his head as if he was in deep meditation.

Soon, Charlotte learned that Theresa's date had not shown up again and did not answer her phone calls after she waited some time for him. Theresa had spent her evening at the theater alone and then went to the beach to watch the sun come up.

"I'm sorry your night didn't turn out as you expected, Theresa. And to think he had the audacity not to call you."

"Well," said Theresa, "he did call, but that was this afternoon. I woke up when my phone rang. He said he had a family emergency to take care of and wasn't able to call. He actually wants to set up another day to go out, but I haven't decided yet if I should go. I mean, it is possible for a person to have a family issue, you know."

Charlotte only looked at Theresa and smiled, but when Theresa lowered her head to get another slice of cheesecake, her smile fell flat.

Just then, Archibald sat up as something from his vantage point caught his attention. There was a large procession of people going into the gates of the city.

"What do you think is going on?" Theresa asked Charlotte, who seemed just as curious. Charlotte didn't have the opportunity to answer; Archibald answered for her.

"There appears to be some type of festivity going on today. Notice how people are making merry and are dressed in what constitutes their best clothing. Now that you two are done with your chit-chat, suppose we head into the city for a look-see?" And without bothering to wait for an answer, he started off, leaving them looking at each other.

"Wait a minute, Charlotte! I'm *definitely* not trying to end up in a Dutch dungeon for looking out of place or something."

"It's the same as last time; people cannot see us." They soon caught up with Archibald entering through the city gate with the throngs of people after hastily packing up their picnic and carrying the cooler between them. The city was full of many colors and charming buildings with ornamented façades. The streets were bustling with people from all classes of society going about their business. There were artisans, beggars, street musicians, buskers hawking their goods, and even two young members of the nobility entertaining women of the road. Then, a procession headed up by an ox cart that had a small body of six musketeers split fore-and-aft made its way through the streets. A fresh-faced girl in her late teens rode in the cart as flowers were tossed in as it passed. In addition to that, the cart was followed by throngs of jubilant people as it made its way through the busy streets.

"I think they're going to give her an award," Theresa said to Charlotte.

"Well, if they are, she doesn't seem too enthusiastic about it. But then again, she might be doing that modesty thing I hear old people talk about."

They continued following Archibald for two hours or so, exploring some of the various shops and residences along the way. After being entertained by some street acrobatics, the trio crossed over a canal and stopped on the other side as Archibald paused. He was looking in the direction of a church steeple rising high above the quaint baroque rooftops.

He turned to his companions. "There's some type of event going on in the town square today, from what I can ascertain from the prattling of the crowd."

"What do you think it is?" Theresa asked him.

"Well, there are a lot of Dutch East India Company ships in the harbor, as you can see the masts from here. So it's possible some returning ships are selling their rare acquired goods from the East Indies, which is enough to attract people from the surrounding areas. By the way, you know you don't have to carry that cooler," he said as he walked towards them.

Charlotte and Theresa set the cooler down on the ground, simultaneously perceiving that he wanted to carry the cooler. But he proceeded past them, stating in the process that the cooler had wheels on the bottom and the handle extended to pull it.

After muttering to each other as they crossed back over a bridge, they realized that Archibald was now following a man who wore a faded brown cloak with a matching beret. They followed him down to the edge of the canal, where the man seemed to be look-ing for something earnestly when a long narrow punt appeared gliding across the water. It pulled alongside in front of him, and he boarded after putting a few coins into the boatman's hand while engaging in a short conversation. Archibald got into the boat, gesturing towards Theresa and Charlotte to follow him. The three situated themselves in the front of it just as it launched off down the canal.

"Is there any particular reason we are in this boat with him?" Theresa inquired of Archibald, who was sitting there in front of them, quietly observing the man's features.

"Does he not look like someone familiar to you?" he asked while his attention remained fixated on the man.

"I suppose his face does have a familiarity to it, but I can't place it." Theresa observed the pensive passen-ger's face in detail from the wrinkles to his ashen mus-tache and goatee. But she became distracted by the impressive surroundings as the punt glided out of the city into an open body of water.

"We are now on the Volewijck River," Archibald said, turning towards them. "And we are heading to that piece of land over there where you see other boats have landed."

"What is that place, and what are all those posts sticking out of the ground with something hanging off of them?" Theresa said aloud.

"It is a place of repugnance, Theresa," Archibald said. "A place where executed malefactors corpses are brought and hung up on those poles as a reminder to all. And that is why that island is called the Volewijck, which in the Dutch tongue means *the bird area*, for the birds feast upon the corpses of the condemned."

The boat slid up on the shore.

They got out of the punt, along with the gentleman, and made their way up to a group of people standing a few yards away from the macabre display. That is, with Theresa lagging behind after taking a cursory glance at the spectacles.

Charlotte walked off on her own, pulling the cooler behind her as she examined the remains of individuals still hanging up from the various poles. The man that fascinated Archibald, now seated on a wooden folding chair, produced from his cloak a large leather-bound sketchbook.

"Our friend here is drawing that young girl over there. A servant girl of one and eight years named Elsje Christiaens. From what I overheard from those sightseers over there, she was a Dane who had come to Amsterdam for work two weeks ago, but was unsuccessful in that endeavor. Unable to pay her rent, she got into an argument with her landlord, whom she murdered with an axe in a fit of passion. Sometime this morning, as we were sightseeing, Miss Christiaens was publicly strangled in Dam Square, and her corpse brought here to be exposed to the Four Winds and carrion birds. The swollen crowds we saw earlier about the city were mostly of people who came from neighboring communities to see the first woman executed in 21 years."

Theresa stepped forward and peered over the artist's shoulder, examining his progress. The face in the sketch stood out to her for some reason, and she looked up at the corpse.

It can't be. That was the girl Charlotte and I saw in the cart earlier. And to think, I actually thought she was going to get an award.

As she stared into the pale, lifeless face of the girl, Charlotte, with the cooler still in tow, came into view. She looked up at the body of the young malefactor and shook her head as she moved along.

"I wonder if Rembrandt would have painted this woman if he had the finances to do so?" Archibald said, looking at the artist's work.

"Rembrandt," Theresa said in astonishment. "As in, the *Old Master* Rembrandt the painter?"

"Rembrandt van Rijn, himself in the flesh. The master of observation, chiaroscuro, and perhaps most importantly, realism." He tilted his head to the left as he examined the aged artist's face intently. "But life has taken its toll on him profoundly as it is marred by sorrow. The man has suffered a bankruptcy and has been reduced to near poverty. He has outlived his wife, his mistress, and three of his five children by this stage of his life. And at the time of his death, five years from now, he will lose one more."

Theresa looked at the old artist somberly. "I'm amazed how people can still push forward with their passion despite so much loss."

"Perhaps, because you should never let tragedy dictate your reality," Archie responded, and he ambled off in the direction of the shoreline with Theresa following.

She stood there for a few moments in silence with him, watching the various watercrafts moving about when a thought came into her head.

"You know, I just was thinking. Could you tell me what to check for when looking for a potential mate? I mean, you know, from a man's perspective." Theresa nervously looked out at the water.

"No," he said, without even turning his attention towards her.

An awkward silence ensued, and Theresa turned to check for Charlotte's whereabouts. She had last seen her following a crowd when she heard him say, "I brought you a satin cocktail dress today while you were asleep. I left it hanging up in your office, and I wish for you to wear it later this evening when we go out to dinner."

She was in the process of formulating a response to him when he held his finger to his lips and gestured for her to continue what she initially was going to do.

Later that evening, Archibald, whom she hadn't seen since they returned home hours earlier, greeted her and escorted her to a waiting car. He held the door open for her, and they soon arrived at a cozy restaurant tucked away on the upper end of Jefferson Street where Archibald had made a reservation. The decor was chic, and the cuisine was superb. He had ordered in fluent French, which only added to Theresa's fascination with him. After they finished eating, they walked to the neighboring Pulaski Square where they had a pleasant conversation under the clear skies as fireflies flittered around them.

When they got home, Archibald headed up the steps to open the front door for Theresa. But before she could cross the threshold, he placed his arm across the doorway, blocking her entrance.

"Theresa, we went out tonight because I wanted you to see firsthand how you *should* be treated. Rather than how you *get* to be treated. Now, how you choose to be treated by someone is going to be up to you."

CHAPTER 20

The very next evening, following the excursion to Amsterdam during the Dutch Golden Age, Theresa was again sitting at a small restaurant in Port Royal. Her date for the evening, Palmer, had arrived on time to meet her there.

"I never heard of this place before," Theresa said as the waiter took their menus. "How do you find these charming restaurants?"

"I go by the word of mouth from the locals to find these gems. When I am on my routes, I always try to find a better alternative than fast food. Besides, I'm a bit of a foodie, you know." He took a sip of his drink and smiled. "Theresa, you've been surveying me since I got here. It's almost like you're trying to see into my thoughts, like a detective." He ended his statement with a nervous chuckle.

"Well, don't worry. I am not here to put you in jail. I was just thinking to myself that I'm just glad that you are actually here. Plus, you've got your haircut and you really look nice tonight. I like the mustache, it suits you well."

"Well, the third time's the charm, they say."

They continued their conversation until the waiter returned with the orders and set their plates on the table. Just as they were about to dine, Palmer's phone rang repeatedly. He stepped away from the table and took the call in private. She observed him in the parking lot speaking *nineteen to the dozen* earnestly before returning to the table. The expression of his face said all she needed to know.

"Theresa, I'm sor—"

"Save it, Palmer," she told him in an abrupt, but calm tone. "The last thing I want to hear out of your gullet right now is another one of your insincere apologies. You have wasted enough of my time toying with me already. And that is something that I shall not forget. Now, get out of my face completely and work your *charm* on your family emergency."

Palmer left Theresa sitting there after leaving a large bill on the table. She had their uneaten dinner placed in to-go boxes and then sat there for a while, thoughtful. She was reminiscing about the thoughtfulness of her ghostly friends and the dinner with Archibald. This lasted until she overheard a man talking loudly to a woman at the table next to her.

Distracted and annoyed, Theresa's attention now shifted to the coarse man. She observed that he was a barber by profession, as he still wore his hair-cutting smock. When their eyes met, he insinuated to the woman with him that Theresa was eavesdropping on their conversation. He then addressed Theresa with profanities, leaving her astounded as he departed with his company. Livid, Theresa wanted to leave immediately and tell the man off in the parking lot. But she decided to wait a few minutes, not knowing if the man was just drunk, high, or crazy. As she did so, she mechanically rotated the porphyry ring with her thumb as she fumed over the audacity of a complete stranger.

Later, on her way home from the restaurant, clouds obscured the full moon, and a fog began to creep in from the marshes. She drove across the nearly two-mile-long Broad River Bridge onto the meandering causeway. Theresa slowed down on the deserted road because she thought she saw something flit across the night sky and into the distance in the direction that she was heading. It was something so peculiar that she slowed her car to a crawl as it passed. Theresa could have sworn that she saw the shape of a dog-like creature. She reasoned with herself that it was probably a bird of prey carrying a four-legged animal or tangled in a cloth, distorted by the clouds and the span she saw it at.

Just as the moon began to peek out from the clouds, Theresa noticed that there was another car on the road. She could faintly make out the taillights in the distance. She tried to keep pace with the car, but could not because of the road conditions and soon lost sight of it. Shortly thereafter, Theresa discovered that the car had lost control and crashed into one of the utility

poles near the woods, just beyond the lonesome traffic signal at the end of the causeway. Theresa slowed
down to a halt to see if someone was still in the car.
She started to reach for her phone to call emergency
services, but the vehicle's doors opened as a man and
woman slowly emerged from their wrecked vehicle in
a state of bewilderment.

He's seething in a lot of pain, she said to herself as
the man staggered, trying to keep his bearings with the
help of his companion.

Theresa rolled down her window to let the man
know she would call for help, but stopped. She realized
it was the same barber who had insulted her back at the
restaurant. She promptly rolled her window back up.

"Talk about Karma," she said softly to herself.
"Serves that fool right. Anyway, I wouldn't want to be
minding someone else's business again."

She was about to leave when she saw a pale orb rise
from the back seat of the car. It rose through the roof,
and up into the air. There it paused about ten feet above
the wrecked automobile before slowly fading away into
nothing. The victims of the accident did not notice the
orb as they were several feet from the car sitting on the
ground, tending to their wounds.

She then had an uneasy feeling and searched
the floorboard for the phone she had inadvertently
dropped. Theresa picked up her phone and realized
that she now had no signal.

The wreck began to smoke, and Theresa got out of
her car to warn the people of the danger. They seemed
unaware of the risk they had placed themselves in

near the wrecked vehicle. She noticed an eerily pale glow from within the woods as if something had fallen from the night sky. This strange light moved quickly towards the area of the accident. She got back into her car and locked the door just as a gaunt wolf-like creature emerged from the depths of the forest. The eyes glowed like white-hot embers that left trails of smoke from them like burning incense. This menacing beast sat on its haunches as if it was waiting for something.

That *something* soon revealed itself when Theresa saw the orb reappear next to it. The orb expanded to the size of a manhole cover. And from within it, an arm extended from it, pointing towards the couple. Within the flash, the beast pounced on the two, throwing the woman against the trunk of a tree with the swipe of its paw. It then turned its attention to the man, and mauled him. His cries of agony were drowned out by the screeching of Theresa's tires as she raced away.

That is way too much Karma! Her heart raced as she made her way home.

CHAPTER 21

The workweek was coming to a close, and several days had passed since Theresa witnessed the strange events on the road home from Port Royal. She initially had a slight suspicion in the back of her mind that Charlotte or Archibald, or perhaps both, might have been behind the grisly attack on the spiteful barber and his companion. But when she got home, Charlotte was binge-watching *Sailor Moon* in the parlour, while Archibald was at his writing desk making notations of the ebb and flow of the stock market for that week. Then she remembered she still had the porphyry ring on that bound him to his mortal form. That canceled him from the equation, and her attention returned to Charlotte. But she recalled that Charlotte had gotten her hair done earlier that day at the salon. And if Charlotte had reverted back to her ghost form again, her hair wouldn't have been in the same style when she changed back. She had secretly hoped that the action she had witnessed was the work of her friends.

Not that Theresa particularly approved of it, but because she could trace the source to something she was familiar with, rather than it being the work of some unknown entity. According to a short segment on the news, excessive speed caused while driving under the influence were key factors. The driver who survived the mauling was in critical condition, and his injuries were attributed to being violently ejected from the vehicle.

"What in the world are you thinking about? You haven't said much since we got into the car?" Charlotte said as she was looking out of her window at the people walking along the sidewalk.

Caught off guard by the question because she was lost in her thoughts, Theresa smiled, and said, "I was thinking about when we went to the salon to get your hair done, and when the stylist asked where are you tender-headed, your response was 'No.' You said you enjoy having your hair pulled. Then everyone in the salon got quiet for a moment before busting out into laughter."

Charlotte twisted her lip and turned her attention toward Theresa. "While I'll admit from time to time, I am the center of embarrassment, that's not what you've been thinking about, so let's have it all out."

Theresa quickly told her everything about her date night, except for who she thought might be behind the attack.

"So, what do you think?" Theresa asked.

Charlotte just shrugged her shoulders. "Hey, shit happens. It's what some would call *Karma*. But as for your date, it's easy to miss a person's red flags when our idealistic rose-colored glasses make them indistinguishable."

"Shit just happens, eh?" Theresa responded as she looked at Charlotte out of the corner of her eye.

"Yup, sometimes it's just regular mortal shit. Sometimes it's supernatural shit. Either way, I had nothing to do with that. Now if I did, I wouldn't have a problem telling you. By the way, have you seen Palmer at your job this week?"

"He hasn't been to my job all this week. He's probably on vacation or requested a transfer. I didn't care enough to inquire from the new delivery guy. Wait—you did something to him. He's not dead, is he?"

"Come on now, Theresa. Don't be so dramatic. I only hit him in the head with a pineapple on my way back from the market. It's not my fault he wasn't wearing his seatbelt and fell out of his brown delivery truck into the street."

"Wow, umm ok. So why did you hit him in the head with a pineapple?"

"Because I wanted to show him, anonymously of course, what it's like to have an *actual* family emergency." Charlotte laughed as she continued. "He certainly had one after he was laid out on the street with a broken leg and a knot on the side of his head. I saw him with his pregnant wife earlier today when I was on my way to get a fake ID. He's hobbling along with his crutches, the side of his face still swollen, looking like a tall Quasimodo."

Theresa said nothing to this. She just had a very surprised expression.

"On the bright side, the pineapple was ok. It's the same one I made the pineapple punch with," Charlotte told her cheerfully as Theresa looked at her with a whimsical smile.

Theresa soon pulled into the front of the Casimir Lounge, where the valet gestured for her to wait a moment. "I heard that it is pretty exclusive. I think it's really nice of your friend Marcus to get us admittance into this swanky place."

"I honestly wouldn't know if it is," Theresa said. "I don't get out like that. And I wouldn't call Marcus a friend per se, he's more of an obnoxious wuss who is indebted to me for a big favor. We were supposed to go to a place overlooking River Street, but he isn't a part-time bouncer there anymore. So instead, we're here at this upscale lounge. That's Forsyth Park across the street, and that opulent hotel adjacent to this place is where he now works part-time as a majordomo."

"By the way, how come your fancy Florida friend and Abigail are not joining us for girls' night out?"

"Louisa Camille was out of town all week. She was actually at the Bromo Seltzer Arts Tower in Baltimore on business when I last spoke to her, so I didn't bother to ask her. Abby, on the other hand, already had reservations for tonight with Logan."

They got out of the car, and Theresa handed her keys over to the valet. Marcus waited for them near the valet stand. He escorted both ladies to their destination on the property, while paying a considerable amount of attention to Charlotte, that is, until Theresa swatted him in the back of the head as a friendly reminder of his precarious situation at home. He spoke to the attendant that was standing at the door, and they soon gained admittance. Marcus left to attend his duties, but not before telling them they each had $100 credit that they could use as they pleased at the bar or the kitchen.

"This place is so lovely," Charlotte said. "And these people look successful, and the air doesn't reek of attention-seeking desperation. Considering the ambiance of this place, I'm going to the powder room to see if there is someone famous in there snorting cocaine. And I want to see if they have some of those fancy fragrant toiletries on the counter I can place on my altar as souvenirs."

Charlotte walked away, meandering purposefully through a group of businessmen holding champagne glasses. In the interim, Theresa seated herself at one of the high-back stools at the bar and admired the opulence of her surroundings. The crystal three-ringed chandeliers and the beautiful artwork of Tamara de Lempicka situated around the room on walls of red damask especially drew her attention. So much so that she didn't notice the barmaid standing before her immediately. Theresa was about to say something to the barmaid when Charlotte slid into the seat next to Theresa.

"We'll take two Sangrias, please," Charlotte said. As they waited for their drinks, Charlotte started telling Theresa about her adventures in the restroom.

"So, while I was in the bathroom helping myself to the complimentary toiletries, I noticed there was this woman lying on the floor of the stall. I knelt down to check to see if she was all right, but she was snoring. I woke her up, thinking that she might have been drugged, but that wasn't the case. She told me that it was customary to sleep on restroom floors, as she was a Canadian. She had been drinking on an empty stomach and needed a nap."

"Well, what happened next, Charlotte?"

"Nothing; she crawled back under the stall door and continued her nap."

After they took a few sips of their Sangrias, Theresa noted that a man kept looking at Charlotte from across the room and told her so.

"Oh, I know, but he's just your run-of-the-mill debauchee and a profligate. Besides, that is his frumpy wife right over there, looking lost," Charlotte said as she looked in his direction and took a sip from her glass. "Let's go over there and mingle with his friends while ignoring him all the while."

"Well, now that you mentioned it," Theresa said, as she surveyed the group of individuals Charlotte was observing. "I am amazed that not a single one of them looks like a burden of the state or co-dependent on someone else."

And so, after drinking more courage, they headed off. And after socializing with various people they found interesting for some time, they returned to their seats at the end of the bar where Theresa retrieved the menu.

"I better eat something," she said to Charlotte. "All this alcohol on an empty stomach is going to have me ill or passed out on the floor of a restroom stall like that Canadian."

"Yeah right, 'all this alcohol,'" Charlotte mocked. "You barely drank one-fourth of your glass. Besides, I drank the rest of it plus my own."

"Oh, I know. I just didn't want you to feel like a lush, especially considering your extravagances during the annual Festival of the Drunks recently."

"Not a lush, just a little luscious." Charlotte pouted as she pinched Theresa's arm.

Theresa, who was trying to hold her laughter in, only smiled at first. "Charlotte," she said, as she leaned towards her. "I just realized that there are tiny gold embroidered shooting stars and crescent moons on your dress."

"Speaking of shooting stars and other twirling celestial things, look at this flaming comet."

Confused, Theresa turned toward the direction Charlotte was looking in. She saw a man in a white tailored suit with a blue-and-white striped shirt underneath, complemented by a blue and gold paisley cravat. He moved through the crowd as if he was in search of something.

"I think he's on a quest," Theresa said to Charlotte.

"He's on a quest for something alright," Charlotte said in response while keeping her eyes on him. She then nudged Theresa, speaking in a whisper to tell her that Archibald had just entered the premises.

Both of the women turned and lowered their heads to avoid being observed by him. He passed them in that tranquil and yet indifferent manner of his. He walked to the far end of the bar where he sat and ordered a drink. Archibald's entrance in the lounge had caught more than the attention of the two ladies.

Upon seeing Archibald enter, the man they'd been watching snapped his fingers and held his arms as if he was snapping castanets in a Sevillanas dance and then spun through a crowd that was taking note of his antics as he made his way towards where Archibald was seated. Theresa and Charlotte, seeing this, turned towards each other grinning, while gathering their belongings and stealthily spirited themselves to a table behind Archibald.

"Theresa," Charlotte whispered, "Put your phone on record because this may be good."

"Sir, allow me to introduce myself," the man in the suit said to Archibald in a scintillating accented voice. "I am Rodrigo Infante, and I am part of a small effervescent interpretive storytelling troupe called *Moist Nugget* out of Davao City. And in case you were wondering, I named the group after a charming nickname I was given as a young boy by the people in my village. You can call me by that nickname if you like. But that is enough about me." He sighed. "Truth be told, I could not help but notice you from afar. I must say, you are so handsome and debonair. You seem so very intriguing that I just felt compelled to come over for a chat with you."

"Mr. Infante," Archibald said to him with a slight smile after introducing himself in return. "Those compliments you just bestowed upon me are indeed absolute truths. But I perceive where this is going, and I must say that you obviously read my disposition wrong. In another respect, which I believe is due solely on your part to wishful thinking. And I totally understand that, considering my naturally charming and alluring qualities could influence one's hopes. But nevertheless, if I am ever in the mood for some buggery, it will be on the backs of womankind, such as these two semi-attractive ladies here," he stated as he turned towards the direction of Theresa and Charlotte, making eye contact with them to their momentary surprise with a wink.

"I'm gonna castrate him and use his sack as a coin purse," Charlotte grumbled with a flustered face. "You can stop recording now; he's just talking nonsense. Besides, I am going outside to see if I can find a qualified sugar daddy." And she got up and left.

"Really now, Charlotte," Theresa said in surprise as she watched her friend make her way through the crowd with her drink held high in one hand.

Theresa turned her attention back to Archibald and Rodrigo.

"Well, you certainly cut straight to the point," Rodrigo said, in a now dispirited tone.

"But don't despair, Mr. Infante, for while you were enamored with me, someone else here was also regarding you." A look of astonishment came across the face of Rodrigo.

"And how do you know this with your back turned?" Rodrigo said inquisitively, "Especially since I had my eyes on you the whole time you have been here."

Archibald smiled with delight at this. "Well, friend, it's because I am more observant than you could possibly imagine," he said, as he held up his glass to his own face and gently swirled the contents around before consuming it.

He then said without even turning around from the bar, "Theresa, would you be a dear and lean your big head back just a tad? Thank you in advance, and if you would look behind me discreetly, just beyond Theresa's bulbous head, you will see a gentleman reminiscent of a Prussian Aristocrat sitting alone in the far end booth. He has been sitting there for a quarter of an hour or so, pretending to be writing something in his planner. But if you head over there, you will find out he was doodling. He has been glancing at you occasionally. I think it's about time that you introduce yourself. So head over there; I will have the bartender send up two glasses of the house's finest Sherry shortly with my compliments. It will help break the ice, and it is a great apéritif. I might add that the house's filet mignon with mushroom sauce is quite excellent."

Rodrigo looked at him in wonder as Archibald gave him a reassuring pat to his shoulder, promoting him to proceed on his way. Now during the time since Rodrigo's departure from Archibald's side, Archibald remained seated at the bar, enjoying his glass of artillery punch. He completely ignored Theresa behind him as if she were never there.

Theresa was about to dine on her dish of coconut shrimp, just brought to her by the server, when a man with excessive swagger approached her and introduced himself as *Vance*. She was immediately thrown off by his coarse approach and somewhat cautious of how his response may be to hers. His eyes displayed a brightness that had Theresa thinking that he was hopped up on drugs. Theresa told him that Archibald, still seated at the bar, was her man. She said this in a voice not loud enough to draw attention, but loud enough for Archibald to hear that he, *himself*, was her date. But it was all to no avail as Vance apparently did not get the hint. The situation made Theresa look awkward as she tried for a second and third time to rally Archibald's assistance, and yet he apparently did not hear, despite the close proximity. Meanwhile, this uninvited guest was bold enough to sit down in Charlotte's chair, where he began speaking as if he had a chance of persuading her to enjoy his company.

"You'll look good hanging off my arms and you know it, Tiffany . . . Theresa. You are sitting over there playing coy looking like a tasty snack. And you know you want to give me a bite," said Vance with a wink as Theresa shuddered at the prospect.

"Cocaine is one hell of a drug," she muttered.

"I didn't catch that, babe," Vance said as he leaned forward grinning.

"I said there are coconut shavings on the rug. The servers should really be more careful with the food they're carrying. It would be nice if it would just *go away* out of my face."

"Don't worry, babe, they'll get to it when they get a chance." And he continued to have a one-sided conversation with an exasperated Theresa.

Goddamn, this dude can't take any hints? If Vance doesn't leave, I'm going to start shouting 'Stranger danger.'

Theresa turned her attention to Archibald's unresponsive back and looked at him coldly. Irritated at Archie's rebuff and thoroughly annoyed at Vance's persistence, Theresa was halfway through yelling "Stranger" when she heard Archibald's cheery voice stating, "Oh, Theresa dear, did you call me?"

"Hell yeah," she responded sharply to him, "like three or four times. Have you suddenly gone deaf?"

Archibald smiled. "Oh no, Theresa. I guess I am so good at blocking out your voice for my sanity's sake, I just relegated your voice to background noise even though you were less than a fathom from me. And Theresa, don't get so carried away with your henpecking. Aren't you going to introduce me to your new friend?"

Theresa said nothing but just stared at him with her right eye twitching as he seated himself next to her.

Archibald sighed as he caressed her back. "I suppose with that scowl of yours, me sweating on your lovely back is out of the question tonight—and what a shame, your lovely dress has me feeling quite randy too."

Vance, who had been observing the exchange, got up and walked away.

"What a conceited weirdo. Plus, he's musty and has on clean clothes." Theresa said before turning her attention back to Archibald. "You and your antics, I should be mad at you." Theresa shook her fork at him.

"You really have a curious way of thanking me for coming to your aide. Furthermore, are you really one to be preaching to me about 'antics' after eavesdropping or making me a party to your deception?"

"This coconut shrimp is pretty good." Theresa evaded his question. "Besides, how did you know I was here tonight? I didn't tell you about girls' night out because you're not a girl. Did you follow me?" She shoveled another piece of coconut shrimp into her mouth.

"I come here quite often, unlike yourself, homebody. The fact that you are seeing me here is completely by happenstance. And since I have seen enough of you and that ginger strumpet already in the last 24 hours, I was completely contented with ignoring the both of you tonight. But lo and behold, I was interjected into your shenanigans, despite minding my own business." He turned his attention towards a group of people gathered on the floor nearby. "You don't have enough going for you in your life of any real interest for me to follow you. Now your crafty friend, Louisa Camille, on the other hand, she is someone worthy of a further investigation, inside and out."

"So, you still think she's up to no good?" Theresa asked as she wiped her mouth with her napkin.

"I couldn't care less if she is up to no good," Archibald said bluntly. "I just want to know what she is up to. Hence, that is part of the reason why I am here this particular night, the other being the house's excellent Sazerac."

"So, you have been shadowing her all this time," Theresa said as she mimicked his disposition.

"Not in the slightest. It was just for half of an hour this afternoon after my croquet match since she was nearby. You can also stop pretending like you don't want to know what I found out. Also, I have taken the liberty to order you the chocolate apple cobbler to take home," he said as the waitress exchanged Theresa's empty plate for the take-home box. "I can see that look of sugar-cravings on your face. And don't pretend that you don't want to take a bite," he said to her with a sense of amusement, as she eyed the contents of her dessert.

"So, tell me what you found out about Louisa Camille," Theresa said, as she tasted her first spoonful. But before he could respond, she shut her eyes. Needing a moment, she held her hand up to signal him to wait; she wanted to savor this bite.

Meanwhile, Charlotte, who had been twirling unabashedly in her offbeat interpretation of the latest dance in the center of a group of wassailers, swung over to tell Theresa that it was going to be an all-nighter for her. And in fact, the people she had met were exchange students comprised of Istrian Italians who had rented a party bus to go down to Cocoa Beach for the weekend and invited her to come along. She apologized to Theresa for bailing, but Theresa assured her with hand gestures as she was still eating; all was fine.

Archibald, who had been surveying the people that were there that night with marked interest, turned his attention to Charlotte and said snidely, "What are you still standing there for? Go trot off and enjoy yourself!"

"I need to borrow $20. I didn't bring my purse, as you can plainly see," Charlotte responded.

No sooner had she uttered those words than Theresa began to reach inside of her handbag.

But Charlotte stopped her, and said slyly, "Nah, I want to borrow $20 from *him*," gesturing towards Archibald with her eyebrows.

There was a brief moment of silence as Charlotte and Archibald both surveyed each other suspiciously. The silence was broken by the sound of Theresa scraping the bottom of her take-out container for remnants of her dessert. And when she finished cleaning her fork, she said to Archibald, "Why don't you just give her the $20? You know she's good for it."

While his eyes were still locked with Charlotte's, he said to Theresa, "I know what Charlotte is good for, and it's not money."

A hint of crimson formed on Charlotte's cheeks. She then responded with poise after shaking her head slightly. "A precocious child will always become a precocious man. I'm sure that led to an interesting long life for you."

Theresa coughed in an attempt to cover her laughter as Archibald unenthusiastically pulled out his billfold, which Charlotte effortlessly took from his hand and handed back to him with lightning rapidity after relieving him of two Franklins.

Archibald seemed indifferent to the amount she took from his billfold. "I swear, the innumerable evils that come along with being flat-chested."

Charlotte's face flamed and her jaw worked. But before she could say anything, her new friends told her that the party bus was about to leave. So she left with them, occasionally looking back as she made her way to the door with her friends.

Theresa wiped her mouth with a napkin. "She is such a people person. She's going down to Florida to enjoy herself with complete strangers she just met." Theresa sighed, as she was thoughtful about Charlotte's care-free personality. "Honestly, I think I envy that vivacious trait about her. Though, I don't think I could go on a jaunt on short notice with people I just met. After all, I would be too afraid of becoming a ghost."

"Really now," Archibald said to her with interest. "So you are afraid of becoming a ghost? You must think you are better than us, you racist."

Dumbfounded, Theresa was caught off guard by his statement and could only stare back at his serious demeanor.

A few seconds passed before he winked to let her in on the farce. "Well," he said, "Charlotte has been trying to figure out what I am about for a long time. One of her methods, that you are already acquainted with, is visiting the shadows of the past. She does this in attempts to get an edge over me. She can find one clue and guess at twenty, which leads her to ramble on as if she is an expert at solving the great mystery of my existence."

"You know, I wonder about you two at times," Theresa interjected. "You two seem like *frenemies* to me."

"That's a cute conjecture, Theresa. By the way, did I ever tell you how Charlotte's mortal demise came about?" he asked, as the waitress came over to remove Theresa's empty take-home container.

"I am curious to know how you would even be informed of that when Charlotte can't remember past the point when that warlock brought her back."

"Theresa, there is always more than one way to burgle a house. And just because Charlotte has a novel, and at times, an annoying skill, which indeed along my spectrum is a rarity, does not mean she's alone with it."

"But at any rate," he said casually, "our good friend Charlotte died in a house fire."

By his countenance, Theresa noted that he found it too mirthful. "I don't know why you act as if you are amused by that," she said to him in a tone of disapproval.

"Oh, there is no need for an act, as I am genuinely amused with the scintillating particulars surrounding Charlotte's demise. Now what I tell you remains between us. Charlotte, as we both know, likes to drink copious amounts of wine since she has been back in her mortal envelope. And that is not a new trend either, as it was a contributing factor in her own death. She died in a house fire after a raucous night of drinking and *entertaining* the neighborhood twins in her third-floor sleeping chamber. She could have saved herself and jumped out of the window with her two guests to safety on the ground below. But she decided that the distance was just too far down and, with courage from a bottle, she decided to sit in the chair near the window, completely unmoved by the conflagration burning through the floors below. She just sat there calmly, motivating the plebeians trying in earnest to put out the fire while she consumed her wine with the occasional bite of cheese covered in honey. This continued on for several minutes until she drifted off into the black after caressing her lunula amulet as she uttered an invocation."

"There was absolutely nothing funny about that, you jackal." Theresa rattled off sharply as Archibald gave her a blank stare.

"A jackal? Theresa, seriously, that is not a proper way to talk to someone that tolerates you."

"Whatever. It was the second thing that came to mind that had four legs. A sick cat was the first. But it didn't have the same ring to it," she said proudly to him. "And besides, you are certainly not 'tolerating' anything." Theresa sighed. "So tell me about what you found out about Louisa Camille?

"She met with a federal official earlier this afternoon. If I am not mistaken, he was a senator."

"A senator? Are you sure? Which one?"

"Of course I am," he said to her phlegmatically. "I'm not sure of his name as she addressed him with a sobriquet, but he had grey hair and resembled a walking corpse that hasn't yet dropped.

Theresa sighed, as she rolled her eyes at his answer. "They all look like that, Archie. But what do you suppose she was talking to a senator about, detective?"

"She was engaged in chicanery with such dexterity and panache, it would have warmed my heart if I had one." He placed his hand over his chest. "And it was not for monetary gains, mind you, but rather for political favors. I must admit, your friend is a really alluring scoundrel. She even has a small spider web of hand-picked wily informants in her employ."

"You speak as if you were proud of her," Theresa said with a tone of mild irritation. But to this he only smiled slyly. "Stop smiling like an ambulance-chasing shyster."

Another carry-out container of dessert was placed before her of a larger size. Theresa's attention was then turned towards Rodrigo in the company of his new acquaintance. He nodded his head graciously towards Archibald before the two walked out of the lounge together.

"I see that your amorous friend has found success tonight," Theresa remarked.

"I see no reason why he shouldn't," he said to her. "After all, *fortis fortuna adiuvat*—fortune favors the bold. Every day, we are afforded opportunities that may impact our lives. But often we miss them because we are not prepared to take advantage of the chance. Take our new acquaintance, the flamboyant Mr. Rodrigo, for example. He was bold enough to take a gamble on this card game of fortune. And though he wasn't successful in his first hand, just by playing, he learned information that got him in the right direction, albeit with a little prodding."

Theresa glanced over at Rodrigo and his new companion just outside of the glass doors of the lounge. "They look like they've been friends for years."

"Indeed."

"Archie," Theresa said suddenly, as she tapped his hand. "Have you noticed how that old man keeps following just a few steps behind the woman with a cross around her neck? He never interacts with her or anyone? And his eyes seem to be closed the whole time." She examined the old man's worn features. "Or is he squinting?"

Instead of looking in the direction Theresa was facing, Archibald focused his attention on her. "For a moment, your unique and yet unwarranted ability almost slipped my mind. That old codger over there is an entity who has become attached to the woman in question."

"But why is he there?"

"He is there for the sole purpose of subverting her and has been doing so for several years now. You see, nothing means more to that woman than being esteemed as religious and a good parent in the eyes of others. And it is the latter attribute that attracted that entity to her, for she is not only verbally but physically abusive to her son. This is done with the intention of breaking his spirit as she harbors malice towards the lad. The child is a proxy for his father as well as her own inefficiencies. And so the entity has been a stumbling block in her own life, stepping in until she moderates her temperament. I suppose if she doesn't change, that unassuming codger will probably snatch the life out of her," he said with cold indifference as he played with his cigarette case. Archibald retrieved his watch and examined the time. To Theresa's surprise, he told her that he must go as it was almost the dead of night, and he had an appointment to keep.

He then got up and was about to leave when he paused, as if he just remembered something. He retrieved from his pocket something made of satin and lavender in color. He reached out to hand it to her.

"Theresa, I almost forgot. This belongs to you. The evident change in temperature is telling and you might wish to put this back on."

Theresa received the item, and then looked down at her chest. "How in the hell did you get my bra?"

He smiled as she stuffed the item into her handbag. "When you invited me over while you were playing coy with Mr. Vance. I caressed your back and like magic, your brassiere was in my hand. I guess that would explain that gentleman's abrupt departure; he saw it as I retracted my hand."

Theresa's eyes narrowed as she looked at him. "Well, I guess it's a good thing you didn't *caress* my butt too or you'd be handing me my panties."

"I cannot take what you never had on to begin with. Besides, what makes you think I would have given you that back if you did?" He laughed as he walked away, leaving Theresa at the table.

CHAPTER 22

The following week, Theresa was in the kitchen fixing herself an afternoon snack when she noticed, through her window, how overcast the sky had become. Then, her attention shifted to the open gate in the rear of her yard that she always left locked. That is when a disheveled man wearing a dirty hat and a trench coat ambled into the yard.

He was carrying a canvas duffel bag, while dragging his left foot in a slightly handicapped gait. Theresa headed out the back door, picked up a shovel along the way, and held it in her hands.

"I don't know who you are or what you want. But if you don't get off my property, a gimpy leg will be the least of your concerns."

But he only continued toward her. Theresa threatened him with a blow from the shovel by raising it above her head when he stopped at the foot of her stairs.

His face was very dirty, and so were his clothes. There was a large open bottle of liquor situated in his coat pocket. He let out a hacking cough that caused her to recoil in disgust.

"What are you doing with that shovel?" he asked in a raspy voice. "Shouldn't you be in the house fixing sandwiches?"

Theresa frowned and raised her shovel. She was prepared to strike when the man shook his gnarled finger at her.

"Theresa, you mustn't be so predisposed to commit acts of violence like some cockney crone."

"It's you," Theresa said. She moved closer to examine Archibald more thoroughly. "You look like shit and smell like piss."

"Yes, Theresa that is the point of this disguise: authenticity." Archibald attempted to walk past her into the house, but she blocked his admittance until he placed his clothes into a garbage bag. When Archibald had finished cleaning himself up, he explained to her the reasoning behind his latest disappearance.

"I got a wild hare the other day, and I decided to infiltrate the vagrant community in order to ascertain the source of their endless supply of markers. After gaining their confidence through my dusty persona, I was taken to the leaders of the cartel who granted me my personal supply of new markers after completing my test."

"Leaders of the cartel? A test? Really now, Archibald."

"Yes, of course. It is a very complicated system; they have rules and regulations that participants must abide by since ensured territory is oversaturated. But most importantly, workshops so that everyone is up to date on the latest techniques, which are best suited for particular areas of town."

Theresa just looked at him curiously as he told his story.

"After perusing through several leaflets there, I masqueraded as a blind beggar and seated myself near the patio of a cafe. The experience was interesting in and of itself. But what was even more intriguing was that your ever-so-comely friend, Louisa Camille, was meeting up with a bloke there. He was a particularly stern-looking man whom she referred to as *Mr. Cake*. He, in turn, addressed her as *Mrs. Éclair*. They proceeded in a short conversation around which the gist concerned a particular package en route to its destination. During their exchange, she gave him an envelope concealed within a menu that appeared to be full of money."

"So, what's so special about that? He obviously delivered a package for her, and she paid him."

Archibald held his hands together and stared at her intently for a moment. "My myopic friend," he said to her slowly, "I can assure you that Mr. Cake does not work for the parcel service. Furthermore, the package that was delivered had the beating pulse of a missing person."

A missing person; what the hell is he talking about? Whoa, I can't believe Linda's disappearance actually slipped my mind. I wonder if that makes me a bad person.

"Yeah, so I totally forgot about that. After all, she could just be on a personal vacation or in rehab.

Honestly, I don't recall any real concern from anyone outside of being slightly curious. And even that may have been an overstatement. Wait—don't tell me you seriously believe that Louisa Camille had something to do with the absence of Mrs. Byrk?"

"Oh, so now we're *slightly curious*?"

"Spill it!"

He told her in short that the owner of her company had been abducted, drugged, and smuggled out of the country. That she was in Havana, Cuba, confined to asylum as a lunatic. Archibald then praised the efficiency of the plot, telling her that the whole scheme from start to finish was conducted in less than 48 hours.

Theresa pressed him for more to find out how or if Louisa Camille was tied into the caper when they heard the melody of the doorbell. Soon, Theresa was escorting Louisa Camille into the parlour where she was about to tell her friend that she was just talking with Archibald. But she noticed he wasn't there as he had been when she left him moments ago. Nevertheless, the two friends seated themselves and conversed. Nearly ten minutes had passed before Archibald presented himself into the room.

"Oh, now Theresa, I did not realize we had a guest," he said apologetically as he kept his eye on Louisa Camille. "I thought you were just talking to yourself again with the usual palaver when I heard an attractive response from the kitchen. Forgive me for my oversight, Mademoiselle DuPont." He walked over and kissed her hand with the graces of the aristocracy.

As her hand remained in his, he said to Theresa without even looking at her, "Theresa, would you be a dear and fix our guest some refreshments?"

A look of indignation appeared across Theresa's face.

But before she could respond, he said to Louisa Camille, "No, I should serve you with my own hands."

Quickly, he left and returned holding a silver salver that contained a beautiful frosted pitcher with three matching goblets. Theresa eyed everything intently since she had never seen those items before that moment. Archibald set the tray down on the coffee table, revealing it was full of many dainties from Maria cookies to small sandwiches. He filled the three goblets before seating himself right next to Theresa's friend.

Louisa Camille took a sip of her iced tea gracefully as Theresa drank hers unceremoniously with one gulp as she watched them.

Both of them are way too friendly and I don't like it.

From that point on, Archibald and Louisa Camille carried on as if Theresa was not even in the room. She felt even more excluded as they conversed seamlessly in various languages. Theresa also did not approve of Louisa Camille's coquettish demeanor towards Archibald and was glad when she departed.

"Good, she finally left. Now you can pull your head out of her ass." Theresa walked back to the parlour from the front door, rolling her eyes and losing her smile in the process.

"Theresa, don't be silly. Louisa Camille is not the type of woman you pull out of," he said with a wink as they sat back down on the couch. "But on a side note, you should work a bit more on hiding your envy. It is very noticeable, and your friend, without doubt, could perceive that with her knack for reading people."

"Whatever. Now you're the one who is trying to boost your own ego," Theresa said aloud, turning her nose up at him.

"Wonderful theatrics with you as always, Theresa," he said as he clapped his hands slowly in a mocking manner. "Now, I should tell you that your friend, excuse me, *our* polyglot friend has an uncanny level of sagacity and yet, a subtle crafty quality. I deduced that it is this latter entertaining attribute that brings her here to this city. She is indeed here on business, shady business as I mentioned earlier, but that is only half of the story. That woman has something else ambitious up the sleeves of that blouse."

"And how do you know all of this in such a short time of talking to her?" Theresa inquired. "I was right here, and I caught none of that when you two were conversing in English."

"Most conversations also involve the ability to pick up on the nonverbal cues, Theresa. Nevertheless, when she speaks, it is cleverly with dulcet words, as she artfully knows how to exert charisma. It is a stratagem to lower another's defenses so she may wield her influence. This lady of leisure, with all her impeccable social graces and other favorable nuances, is just a cover. He rubbed his chin as he was pondering something. "That type of skill cannot be learned in books, but rather it is taught to one who has the ability to receive the information. I should say that she was a disciple of a master at some point."

Theresa smiled at Archibald and then started laughing abruptly. After she gained control of her humor, she apologized. "It just occurred to me that Louisa Camille was devising a scheme against you."

"Oh, is that so?" stated Archibald, who seemed amused by the explanation. "You should know that your own humorous assessment is quite to the contrary, Theresa. She was trying to pick my mind to determine my place within the gentry in a roundabout way. Now you, on the other hand, are just serving as an alibi."

"What the hell is that supposed to mean?"

"Strange," he said to Theresa while feigning surprise at her response. "It's strange how you did not find that amusing. It is curious indeed that scheming charade never occurred to you in regard to Louisa Camille and yourself. I mean, is it not odd that this friend, who has been out of your life completely for years, shows up out of the blue just to take you to fancy restaurants and shower you with expensive gifts from top-end retailers who have the best surveillance? Meanwhile, this all takes place conveniently within the timeframe of the disappearance of your gaffer.

"But the kidnapping aside because that was just child's play. Louisa Camille's cloak and dagger exploits also extend to the death of Senator Fairfax a short while back, as my sources revealed to me. Officially, his death was listed as a heart attack; without delving into the details, that is only partially true. The old senator had help to cross over while he was in a shoddy motel. His body was found alone in his bed, still in a state of arousal after an anonymous tip.

"The investigation concluded that he had carnal relations with a woman other than his wife. But given his past extramarital indiscretions, that was of no surprise. The blue pills that he had for his lack of rigidity were also deemed a contributing factor, coupled with the strenuous exertion, were literally the nails in his coffin. Naturally, the woman he was with, an incognito Louisa Camille, could not be located. For the sake of his widow and his political associations, it was prudent to sweep this situation under the rug."

Theresa only looked at him with a blank expression.

"You certainly don't seem surprised at what I just told you," he said to her, wishing to elicit a response.

"Seriously, after all the strange supernatural shenanigans that have transpired over these last few months, nothing really surprises me anymore. And in fact, a run-of-the-mill murder would seem normal. Even though the senator would have still been alive if he wasn't such a philandering hoe, I still don't see the point of Louisa Camille getting it on with a nasty old man in the first place?"

"It was nothing personal, just a stealth usurpation of power, Theresa. The purpose of Fairfax's death was to create a vacancy seat in the senate. A vacancy that has since been occupied by a young man named J. Faraday, appointed by the governor to complete the late senator's term. You see, Mr. Faraday is Louisa Camille's personal puppet. But for what purpose he has been elevated to that position is yet to be seen."

Theresa's mind immediately recalled the prior supernatural visitation to Louisa Camille's house, where she had overheard some of this plan.

Amazing, she really got Faraday appointed to office. But I still can't get over the fact she slept with that decrepit man with a weak heart to bring that ambition into reality. She shuddered at the thought of the old senator's naked body.

Archibald, who was still observing her, said with a grin. "I suppose you will give back all those gifts she showered upon you now that you know what she is?"

Theresa looked at him with a raised eyebrow. "I don't know what in the hell you're talking about. I am not giving anything back. These gifts are too lavish and expensive for me to be worrying about something that has nothing to do with me. Besides, it's no different than your shady activities—both of you are just refined criminals."

He stood up suddenly and cracked his knuckles. "Well, it's time for *this* refined criminal to prepare for his evening of fine dining overlooking the river."

"Sure, I'd love to go! I can wear that dress that the other refined criminal brought me," she interjected while scrambling to her feet and was out of sight within an instant, to his surprise.

CHAPTER 23

Late that morning on the following day, Theresa rummaged through the kitchen cupboards when she paused after finding what she was searching for.

"Oh, you're dressed already. I didn't realize that you'd left the house this morning," said Theresa, as she observed Archibald's reflection in the surface of a new stainless skillet she was admiring. He was already seated at the table with a newspaper in hand.

"I left early, just before daybreak for a pleasant morning stroll through the Old City before the panhandlers and the tourists had a chance to inundate and fester. You'll be surprised how pleasant this city is under the first rays of sunlight. By the way, Theresa, I noticed you've been shuffling about with those skillets and pots. I take it that you planned on cooking something special tonight." He looked at her with an amused expression. "Perhaps you wish to follow in

311

Louisa Camille's footsteps and knock off that geriatric colonel Barnaby for personal gain?"

"Nope, not even close, you fiend. I'm still deliberating on what to make for my family get-together," she said with her hand on her chin, contemplating the matter. "Honestly, I don't know what to prepare that's easy and cheap. I don't want to go over there empty-handed either; I'll never hear the end of it."

"Ah, so I take it that this gathering of kinsfolk is today? And I'm glad that you made up your mind about going."

She nodded her head as she sat down at the kitchen table and began to look through an unopened stack of envelopes, sorting them into two separate piles. "To be honest with you, I feel somewhat obligated to go. My sister, Traci, told me that everyone in the family thinks I am rich now since I bought this house. Plus, to give life to this myth, my grandmother's hella nosey neighbor saw me a few weeks ago looking spiffy in an outfit Louisa Camille bought me."

As Theresa went through her mail, a large Manila envelope, in particular, caught her attention. She pondered the unopened piece of mail with concern before opening it.

"Theresa," Archibald said, noticing the dour change in her facial expression, "I gather from your expression that those contain the results of a really important medical test from the way you are looking at the envelope. Maybe the results would explain why you've been looking a bit haggard as of late."

Theresa glanced at him over the top of the envelope with a cold stare before she proceeded to open it. She retrieved several documents and technical drawings that she surveyed intently. One, in particular, had a seal that caught her attention. After returning the contents to the folder, she went over to Archibald, who was sitting at the other side and looked at him for a moment with tears welling up while he was reading his newspaper. She wrapped her arms around him affectionately for a few moments, showering him with appreciative praises, squeezing him. All of which totally caught him off guard.

"Archie," Theresa said, her eyes still welling up and spilling over. "I cannot believe you covered the expense of submitting my patents to the Patent Office. You really have such a big heart! It's almost unbelievable."

"To the contrary, Ms. King, my so-called big heart is a lot smaller than you would imagine. Though, I would admit what I did for you seemed rather eleemosynary on the surface. You see, my dear, I decided to give you a pick-me-up in funding the patent process of your inventions, which in turn, if fortune is on your side, would increase your revenue substantially in the fullness of time."

"How is that exactly a bad thing?"

"It's not; it's actually a good thing. With more money in your coffers, you will be more inclined to move out."

Theresa scoffed and then laughed. "You've really got a twisted mind, you know that?"

"No more twisted than the shirt I'm wearing, thanks to you." After emitting a long, deep breath, he spoke with a tone of disappointment. "Yes indeed, it appears you have thoroughly rained on and rumpled my shirt. And to make matters worse, I have decided as of now that this is my favorite shirt."

Theresa, who was a bit taken aback by his crass behavior, decided to annoy him further by hugging him again tightly. But to her surprise, something unexpected happened. She wrapped her arms around him and nearly fell forward as she realized she was holding nothing but his empty clothes in her hands. Startled, she let the clothes fall down to the floor and took several steps back from her chair when she noticed Archibald standing at the entrance of the kitchen newly attired. A look of confusion appeared on her face as she observed him. She gazed down at her left hand and rubbed the porphyry ring with her thumb.

"How in the hell were you able to vanish and reappear while I have this ring on? That is not how it is supposed to work!"

This response amused him as he walked into the kitchen, retrieving his clothes and folding them neatly before setting them aside. "Theresa, dear, you should not look so disappointed. As you can clearly see, that enchanted ring of yours, hewn from a piece of porphyry, is still working charms as I am still here in the flesh. I just learned how to circumvent its power of binding. But don't fret, as I do enjoy masquerading as a mortal. I just like having some latitude in the situation for my own welfare," he said as he resumed surveying his paper with a grin.

By this time, Theresa had seated herself back at the table. But now, she was just a few inches from him. "And how did you come by *this* knowledge?" Theresa inquired of him in earnest.

Sighing and shaking his head as he folded his paper, he said, "No. I only found out as secondary information latterly for the aforementioned reason. But I will share with you the scanty details I have ascertained on the matter. The arcane island where you acquired that wonderful charm of yours once held a remote temple headed up by a high priestess. Where it is located is unknown, but there is a clue from antiquity: *East of the Mausoleum at Halicarnassus in the shadows of Nisibis.*"

She thought for a moment on what he just told her before responding. "What is the name of that island?"

"I find it very uncanny that you should ask that, Theresa," he said as he mused on her query. "The name of that place from a dead language is literally translated into *The Forest of Chimes.* Those are the exact words that I have heard you utter some time back on separate occasions as you slept in the parlour.

"And that is the entirety of my knowledge on the matter as it was relayed to me en passant. By the way, if you are even thinking about asking Charlotte or that Logan fellow on a crapshoot, senior or junior, that inquiry would be dead in the water."

"So how am I going to find out who brought me there, and for what reason I am so special?"

"I would say that *special* is a tad bit of an overstatement. After all, you were not the first or the second choice; you're the third-place option. But when it is time for you to know the reasoning behind this, I am sure you'll be the first to know."

Obviously, this crafty bastard knows a lot more than he's telling me.

"Anyway," she continued in an acerbic tone, "since you know it all, please tell me why my boss was placed in a crazy house in Cuba?

"Theresa, I really know nothing on that account. All the same, I can only conjecture that she is kept alive there for the purpose of making her suffer or to remove her out of the picture for a while for whatever reason. I say that because Louisa Camille is more than capable of killing someone at her leisure. Perhaps you should pose that question to Louisa Camille for a direct answer?"

Yeah, right. He has to be facetious to even suggest that. I do want to know, but not at the cost of damaging our friendship. Or, to end up in the trunk of a car on my last ride. Besides I'm not trying to judge her, I'm just curious about the matter, not concerned. Maybe one day, I'll make Marcus ask her in a roundabout way, so that if she does take swift vengeance, it won't be against me.

Archibald interrupted her train of thought. "You are taking an excessively long time to sort this out in your head. Besides grinning like a Cheshire cat with a scheme, you really need to start cooking."

"Never mind that," Theresa said. "I have to wash up, find something to wear, and pick up some cheese-cakes for tonight's event." She got up and scurried out of the kitchen, but not before she realized Archibald was looking at her with a mischievous expression. And that alone prompted Theresa to stop dead in her tracks.

"I almost forgot to remind you of something; you can't come with me to my family gathering. Sorry, but not sorry, dear. Besides, I don't plan on being there long anyway. I plan to fake an illness. So, I'll see you back here soon."

CHAPTER 24

"Sorry I'm late, everyone," Theresa said in a raspy voice, feigning illness, to the already assembled family members. She walked into the dining room of her grandmother's house, carrying a tray of cheesecake.

After placing the cheesecake in the refrigerator, her niece, Tater Tot, showed her to her seat, which was next to her own. Tater Tot promptly handed Theresa, much to her surprise, a disposable surgical face mask with a hole near the size of a quarter cut out where the mouth would be.

"I'm sorry to do this to you, Auntie," Tater Tot said to a dumbfounded Theresa. "But I have a presentation coming up within a few days at school on why a German candy company sells hard gummy bears in America that hurt your teeth. So, I don't want to catch whatever it is you got going on over there."

Theresa looked at the blue surgical mask with a frown and remarked on how small the opening was.

"I know you don't expect me to really pass my food through this small hole," Theresa said.

"Of course I do," Tater Tot responded enthusiastically. "You're sick, so I suspect you don't have much of an appetite. But it's still big enough to get your utensils in your mouth."

"Oh, you're so cute at this age," Theresa said as she stuffed the mask into her purse in a sleight of hand that was unnoticed by her niece.

"Not to toot my own horn, Auntie, but I am under the impression that I would be cute at any age."

"Really now," she said while patting her niece's head. "With all of these older women in this house, your imagination is giving you some amazing optimism."

Theresa looked around the table for an empty seat, while her kin were either engaged in conversation or staring at their phones. The only exception to their activity was her father, who had fallen asleep. She didn't have to look far as there was an empty seat directly in front of her. She was about to move to this seat when her niece informed her that she could not.

"And why is that?" Theresa wanted to know.

She was promptly informed, "Because that seat is already assigned, and this is where Nana wanted you to be seated."

Theresa shuddered at the prospect and inquired from her sister. "Assigned to whom, when everyone is already here?" she asked, gesturing towards the empty chair across from them.

Traci looked at Theresa curiously for a moment. "Just so you know, Theresa," Traci said to her sister. "The seating arrangements have been changed unexpectedly due to a recent addition to our gathering. Now we are *so* fortunate to sit closer to our *beloved* grandmother on this side of the table. So be on your guard about the coming inquisition into the affairs of our personal lives, especially since you are fortunate enough as to be sick *so* often around these family events that you cannot attend regularly. I truly envy your selectively frail immune system."

A smirk appeared across Therese's face. "By the way, is Dad ok?" she asked her sister as she observed her father nodding his head to stay awake.

Traci smiled. "He's just pouting; Mom told me he hasn't been saying much to her these last few weeks."

"Well, why not? Did they have an argument?"

"You can kind of say that it was more like a disagreement of sorts. Dad wanted a maid around the house, and he hired one after Mom told him that was a great idea, since she's always traveling. But the maid he hired was someone she certainly didn't approve of. She told him his hypertension and bad back would not allow him to take on a mistress at his age."

Theresa held her head down and shook it softly as her sister continued.

"He has been tart ever since then."

"Where is Grandma Bailey, by the way?"

"She's probably showing off that old photo album of herself when everything on her body was perky. There is a suave man here who is apparently an aficionado of still-life paintings that she has been entertaining ever since he got here. And I use the word 'entertaining' loosely because she was outright flirting with him when I checked in on them shortly before you walked in, suffering gravely from your illness. Anyways, I heard him going into detail about grandmother's father's landscape painting over the fireplace, which is a good thing, if you think about it, because it keeps her preoccupied from prying into our personal lives before we have something to eat.

"Ah, speak of the Devil . . ." Traci said with a nudge of her elbow to her sister's rib as the old matriarch proudly entered the room, making her way to the head of the table as the various conversations settled down to a murmur.

The matriarch observed those in attendance for a moment before she finally spoke, thanking everyone for their attendance with cordiality and grace. She said a brief prayer for the table, and they began passing around the assortment of dishes to load up their plates as they desired.

As Theresa was passing a dish of macaroni to her sister, she now noticed to her surprise that Archibald was sitting down directly across from her. He was casually conversing with her mother and aunt in a very friendly manner, paying special attention to her mother. Her mother was lumping praises on him for his taste in fashion. The others soon joined in. He even stood up momentarily to display with alacrity his white trousers, white cricket vest, Winchester shirt with black tie, and a navy-blue blazer. Her surprise at his presence soon morphed into a seething resentment that caused her right eye to twitch.

"You," she said to him in a low but peevish tone. "I thought I told you expressively that you could not come with me."

"Pardon me one moment," Archibald said to the two women he was conversing with, "Theresa is obviously feverish, and so I must mend reality for her."

He turned his attention to Theresa and smiled. Archibald then proceeded to tell her that he had abided by her wishes, as he did not travel with her. He also pointed out that he didn't need her permission to go anywhere, especially since he was an invited guest.

"Really now," said Theresa, who doubted his claim, "And who invited you?"

"I did," interjected Mrs. Bailey calmly. "Mr. Turner occasionally stops by the Golden Age Center as a volunteer and plays the piano most excellently for us seniors. He is my guest and I invited him as a nice cultured addition to our table. Theresa, I am surprised that you would be as curt as you are to such a kind man, but I suppose it's because you are not feeling well that you are unreasonably irritable."

Mrs. Bailey then turned her attention to Archibald who had a smirk of approval at Theresa's chastisement. "Mr. Turner, you never told me that you were familiar with my granddaughter, Theresa. I had intended on introducing you two at some juncture as she is the one

I told you about." She leaned forward as if to whisper, but the whole table heard her anyway. "The one that is chronically single. How did you two become so familiar with each other?"

"I hope it is something unique or romantic like out of a storybook," Tater Tot said. "It would be so fitting since he is so handsome." Tater Tot shrunk to the other side of her seat after Theresa pinched her right thigh especially hard.

"Not even in the slightest, my dear child," Archibald said cheerfully. "I actually was walking down the footpath for good health, minding my own business while enjoying the tranquility of the night, when I was verbally accosted by our Theresa here. She was yelling out of her bedroom window with her hair disheveled like some wind-tossed banshee. But despite the scour you see now on her face, we are the best of friends."

With the exception of Theresa, Archibald enthralled all who were at the table into arousing admiration with his stories and his charismatic personality. Between amazing them with his knowledge of places and peoples, he had Theresa's family firmly captivated by his presence. He even exchanged friendly repartee with Theresa's niece that left her exclaiming in admiration and someone whispered that he was a savant. He also made it a point of how similar—and yet dissimilar, in a roundabout way—Theresa was from Traci.

His presence there annoyed Theresa for two reasons: the first being that because he was so unusually affable with her family, she surmised that he was up to something. The second reason was that she could not leave the function early as she had planned because she felt compelled to watch his antics.

When he excused himself to go outside and make a phone call, Theresa breathed a sigh of relief as she shoveled some sweet corn into her mouth. But that relief was short-lived as the attention that was previously focused on Archibald was now focused on her. Theresa did not notice at first because she was now too busy enjoying her meal when it occurred to her that no one was talking. She looked up, and everyone was staring at her with pleasant expressions on their faces.

Her grandmother ventured to speak first. "Even though you were always a bit on the homely side, Theresa, I always figured that you would bring home a nice, unassuming man. Then as the years carried on, one after the other and that never happened, I reckoned I was waiting for you to come out of the closet. And considering how much you liked sports growing up, that analysis seemed to be plausible. But that never came to fruition, and you don't even like cats, so you had me totally confused. Then you surprise us all with this pleasant, well-spoken, and charming Englishman, who despite all your foibles, dared and cared to be associated with you."

You know what, I think it would be really cool if this old biddy choked on her food today, Theresa thought as her grandmother rambled on.

Archibald returned to the dining room, and the matriarch promptly addressed him. "If you don't mind me asking, young man, what is it about our Theresa that attracted you to her?" Theresa cleared her throat as Grandma Bailey added, "I mean as a friend, of course."

"Ah, Grandma Bailey," he said cheerfully, "Theresa has so many illustrious facets that I would be at a loss for words trying to do so extempore. But when I look at Theresa, the color pink comes to mind, as well as seeing so much of myself in her." He paused, thoughtfully. "Pink like the blood of Jesus that is in us all."

"But blood is not pink, you English twit," Theresa snapped, seeing through his subtle allusion.

Archibald's countenance changed to present a more solemn expression as he said calmly, "Theresa, you mustn't be so insensitive in your judgment of others. There are varying degrees of color blindness prevalent in my family to which I am not immune, so I often call colors mistakenly. However, my handicap allows me to interpret them. I don't mind your occasional witticisms at my expense, but please refrain from remarking about something I cannot help."

After he said this, Theresa's grandmother and mother chided her. Even Tater Tot, who had exchanged seats to sit next to Archibald, got up from her seat at the table with her plate in hand and walked over to where Theresa was sitting. She looked at Theresa disapprovingly and took one of Theresa's biggest pork chops off of her plate and placed it on her own.

Before she returned to her seat, she said to Theresa, "Bullies do not deserve two pieces of pork chop. Be thankful that I left you with one." And she turned her back on Theresa and returned to her place at the table before Theresa had a chance to respond.

I wish I was really sick, Theresa said to herself. *I couldn't think of a better group of people to share Ebola with.*

Theresa decided that it would be more prudent to keep her thoughts to herself and play along. Even when she passed out slices of her cheesecake for dessert, she did so with a smile, albeit when she gave Archibald his slice, she stuck a large knife in the center of it—with a pleasant smile of course.

Later that afternoon, when Archibald finally got home, a disagreement in the parlour over the previous events metastasized into a heated discussion that affected Theresa more than Archibald. In fact, he was not affected by it at all, but rather displayed a cool indifference that only drew her ire more keenly. Besides that, he was always able to counter her points with his practical logic.

Finally, after Theresa completed a long tirade, Archibald sighed heavily. "You know, I really thought your clucking would never be over. It was starting to become mildly annoying."

Archibald then got up from his seat and stretched out his arms as if he was tired, which prompted Theresa to get up as well. She blocked his way and told him that he couldn't leave until she had her say.

"But you are saying nothing, Theresa," he said. "Perhaps, one day you will in the reign of Queen Dick. But as for the present, you are just rambling with overbearing chatter that is really making it hard for me to ignore you."

Before he even had a chance to say another word, Theresa, in a fit of passion, struck him with the palm of her right hand across his cheek, and a resounding *smack* seemed to echo through the house.

She immediately stepped back in surprise as she realized what she had done. But Archibald only stared at her, unfazed by the assault. His cheek was crimson where she had struck him, and blood began to gather at the corner of his mouth. Still calm and collected, he retrieved a handkerchief from his blazer pocket and wiped his mouth. He then unbuttoned his shirt and removed it carefully so as not to get blood on it, laying it neatly next to his jacket on the arm of the couch.

"So we're frisky, I see," he said to her as he felt the side of his face. "That was a bloody good hit, my capricious friend. Why I actually saw a flash of white, and my face is still tingling from the blow."

His serenity in the situation worried Theresa. From his demeanor, she knew there was going to be a reprisal and she contemplated how to play for time.

He advanced forward, casually pushing her to the side with his forearm, while stating in the process, "Move, woman, you are in my way."

Theresa proceeded to shove him back when he turned around, suddenly grabbed her arm and whirled her around with such rapidity that she momentarily lost her balance. She righted herself and struggled valiantly to get free of his grasp, managing to bite down on his arm. Archibald, in turn, grabbed her by the back of her shorts and lifted her up off the floor before flinging her effortlessly onto the couch several feet away.

Before she even had time to recover from her flight, he pinned her down on the couch and was delivering several blows across her backside. "If you want to act like a petulant child, I shall treat you like one. You can modify all of that incessant whining too. It's only your pride that's hurt."

Theresa protested and continued to whine and tussle until there was a loud, distinct knock at the front door.

Archibald released his grasp as Theresa whispered, "It's the police!"

She quickly headed towards the foyer with Archibald in pursuit. They jostled one another to see who could open the door first, but they both arrived at the same time. As the door swung open, they realized their visitors were only two teenagers in matching green and yellow uniforms peddling cookies.

The two young girls stared at both of them and then at each other before laughing. As Theresa was trying to hold up her shorts with one hand, wiping perspiration from her brow with the other, while nudging Archibald with her elbow.

"Hey asshole, I want some cookies," Theresa whispered to him as he buttoned up his shirt calmly.

"As you can see, she obviously can't keep her hands off me," he said to the girls while exchanging a bill for two boxes of cookies.

Theresa closed the door and was about to open a box of cookies right there in the foyer when she overheard the two girls outside, referring to them as freaks.

"Can't keep my hands off of you, eh? You are one imaginative bastard," she said as she walked toward the staircase with the box of cookies tucked under one arm while holding up her shorts and caressing her sore backside.

"And just so you know," Theresa said, as she stopped on the stairs, "I would not sleep with you if you were the last person on earth and I was out of batteries!" She took a few steps up the stairs before pausing briefly to flip him off.

***

The very next morning, Theresa awoke lazily to the first rays of cresting sunlight in her room. She sat up in bed and realized that Archibald was sitting by the window already dressed for the new day. He was looking at something outside with his head making irregular movements. She curiously watched him for a moment. "Archie, what are you looking at, and what are you talking to yourself about?"

"Oh, good morning, Theresa. I did not mean to wake you. I was over here just counting."

"Counting? For what? Are you trying to go back to sleep?"

"Oh, heavens no," he said with a chuckle. "I was just counting to see how many people were left in the world besides us. It may surprise you, but I have counted 38 so far within the last 15 minutes. Hold on, make that 43. A group of people just got into a car to carpool."

Theresa, now fully awake, tossed her pillow in his direction. "Wait, I smell food! Did you really cook me breakfast?"

"Don't be silly, Theresa. It's takeout. You know I don't do women's work." He said as he sat down on the bed next to her.

Theresa cut her eyes at him as she pushed him aside and made her way out of the bed. She was reaching for her robe in the closet when she noticed a large pink travel backpack sitting on the floor near the door. Her attention turned to Archibald, who was still sitting on the bed looking at his pocket watch.

"I figured that going on a holiday in the West Indies was in order considering everything here is *all Sir Garnet*. You have accrued plenty of vacation time, and a change of scenery would do us both good. We shan't be gone any more than a few weeks, Theresa. I have a chartered plane at my disposal, and we can leave tonight."

"A few weeks is a lot of time together on vacation. It's like something on the spur of the moment that couples would do. You know, people who are actually dating because *someone* actually asked the other to be in a meaningful relationship with them." She tilted her head as she stared at him.

"So you are really going to make me say this?"

"You're damn right," she affirmed as she nodded her head.

He sighed, and spoke to Theresa in such a way that she smiled. But she did not give him any answer. Instead, Theresa joined him at the window, staring out as the warm rays of sunlight that illuminated her face made her pupils resemble jewels of amber. As she gazed out on to the new day, she observed two jays chirping in the branches of a red mulberry. They appeared to be fussing, then preening before heading southwards together into the great blue skies.